W9-CHZ-477

BLUE
FIRE

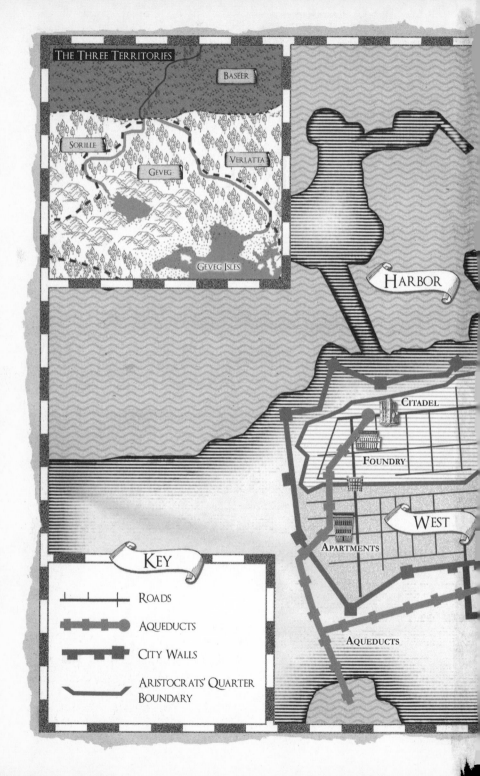

THE THREE TERRITORIES

BASEER

SORILLE

GEVEG

VERLATTA

GEVEG ISLES

HARBOR

CITADEL

FOUNDRY

WEST

APARTMENTS

AQUEDUCTS

KEY

├──┼──┼──┤ ROADS

AQUEDUCTS

CITY WALLS

ARISTOCRATS' QUARTER
BOUNDARY

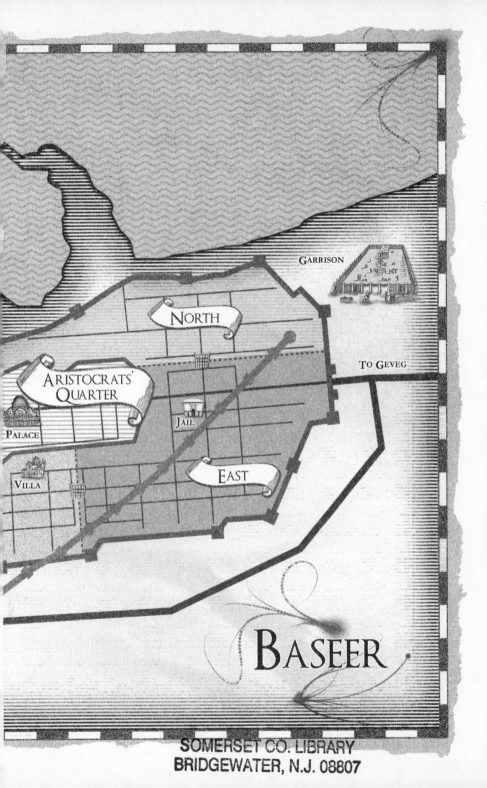

GARRISON

NORTH

TO GEVEG

ARISTOCRATS' QUARTER

JAIL

PALACE

EAST

VILLA

BASEER

Also by Janice Hardy:

THE HEALING WARS: BOOK I
The Shifter

THE HEALING WARS: BOOK II

BLUE
FIRE

JANICE HARDY

Balzer + Bray

An Imprint of HarperCollins*Publishers*

Balzer + Bray is an imprint of HarperCollins Publishers.

The Healing Wars, Book II: Blue Fire
Copyright © 2010 by Janice Hardy
All rights reserved. Printed in the United States of America.
No part of this book may be used or reproduced in any manner whatsoever
without written permission except in the case of brief quotations embodied
in critical articles and reviews. For information address HarperCollins
Children's Books, a division of HarperCollins Publishers,
10 East 53rd Street, New York, NY 10022.
www.harpercollinschildrens.com

Library of Congress Cataloging-in-Publication Data
Hardy, Janice.
Blue fire / Janice Hardy. — 1st ed.
p. cm. — (The healing wars ; bk. 2)
Summary: While trying to lead the Takers out of Geveg, fifteen-year-old
Nya is captured by bounty hunters and taken to Baseer, where she escapes and
soon finds herself helping the Baseeri.
ISBN 978-0-06-174741-0 (trade bdg. : alk. paper)
[1. Fantasy. 2. Healers—Fiction. 3. Fugitives from justice—Fiction.
4. Sisters—Fiction. 5. Orphans—Fiction. 6. War—Fiction.] I. Title.
PZ7.H22142Blu 2009   2009053446
[Fic]—dc22   CIP
                                                             AC

Typography by Carla Weise
10 11 12 13 14   LP/RRDB   10 9 8 7 6 5 4 3 2 1
❖
First Edition

For Kristin and Donna,
because they said yes.

BLUE
FIRE

ONE

Responsibility was overrated. Sure, it sounded good—take control of your own life, make your own choices—but that also meant you had to pay for your own mistakes. And if your life and choices hadn't gone the way you'd planned, well, then your mistakes might reach deeper than your pockets could afford.

I hoped mine were deep enough for the mess I'd caused.

I watered the lake violets in the front sunroom. Just busy work, but I had to do *something* other than sit in the town house worrying while my friends were out risking their lives. I should have been out there with them, but I'd been recognized on our

1

last rescue mission, and it wasn't safe outside for me anymore. Not that Geveg had been all that safe in the five years since the Baseeri invaded; but being hunted by the Duke, his soldiers, Geveg's Governor-General, and who knew how many trackers added a whole new level of danger.

"Is Aylin back yet?" asked Tali, lurking in the doorway. Some girls hovered behind her, a few Takers we'd rescued last week but hadn't managed to smuggle off the isles yet.

"No," I said, "she's still out looking." So was Danello, but Tali always worried more about Aylin, which was silly. Aylin could take care of herself—Danello was the one with the street smarts of a hen.

"Is it bad that it's taking so long?"

I hesitated. "I don't know. It depends if the recruiters are snatching people off the street again."

The Takers behind Tali paled and backed away. None had been grabbed by the Healers' League's new "recruiters," but we all knew people who had been: pulled from their homes, dragged to the League, forced to heal—even if it killed us.

It was nine shades of wrong. The League used to invite only Takers with strong healing talents to become apprentices, those who had real futures as Healers. But now? You didn't have a choice. The

Duke demanded that any Taker with even a trace of healing ability had to serve at the League. The lucky ones were trained. The unlucky—they wound up in a small, windowless room somewhere, being experimented on.

The Duke of Baseer had his war to win, whatever the cost to us.

"I'm sure they're fine. There's nothing to worry about."

I glanced at the Takers behind Tali, slipping away one by one to go cower in their rooms. It shouldn't be this way. The Healers' League was supposed to train Takers to heal and help. Becoming a Healer used to be something every Taker dreamed of, like Tali had. Like I had.

Now it was just a nightmare.

Tali hadn't moved, and she had that little-sister-stubbornness look about her again. "Should we go look for her?"

If only I could. They *had* been gone an awfully long time. "You know we can't leave the town house."

"*You* can't, but I can."

"You can't either. It was hard enough rescuing you from the League once. I'm not letting them get you again."

She pouted, her brow wrinkling the way it always

3

did when she was trying to decide if it was worth an argument or not.

"You can help Soek with lunch," I offered. "You know how much he needs it."

"He's making that fish stew again," she said. "Took me three days to get the smell out of my hair last time."

"Maybe you can—"

"Nya, I can help with the Takers, you know I can." She stared at me, defiance in her brown eyes, and tucked a curl behind an ear. She'd dyed her blond hair red, like Aylin's used to be, and it had put some fire into her as well.

"It's just too dangerous right now," I said, more gently this time. "Can you please check on the others and make sure they're okay? You know how scared they are. I'm fine here, really."

Tali didn't say anything, but the defiance was gone, replaced by concern. "Are you sure?"

"Yes."

"Really? Because you don't seem fine."

"That's 'cause someone keeps pestering me while I'm planning how to smuggle people off Geveg." I meant it as a tease, but Tali folded her arms and frowned.

"You're not planning—you're watering lake

4

violets and looking miserable."

"I can do both." I grinned, but she clearly wasn't buying it.

"Nya, you don't *have* to be miserable."

My grin vanished. I'd earned my misery, but I'd paid the price for Tali's life willingly, a life for a life. It *shouldn't* be easy to toss that guilt overboard. Besides, everything here in Zertanik's town house was a constant reminder of what I'd done, who I'd killed. It didn't matter that he didn't need it anymore, or that it made the perfect hiding place. There was some justice to selling off his stolen loot to help the very Takers he'd tried to hurt, but not enough to make it right.

I set down the watering can and sighed.

Tali came over and rested her head on my shoulder. She used to do the same thing when we were little and Mama had scolded me.

"Well, you're worrying over nothing," she said, filling the silence when I didn't say anything. "Barnikoff will hide them in his boat, same as always."

"Someone saw me with him the last time. The Governor-General might be watching now." Which meant there was one more person who might get into trouble because of me. I shoved my hands into my pockets.

Not nearly deep enough.

"They saw you?" she asked, worried now. "Who did? The League?"

"I'm not sure—"

The front door of the town house rattled. I jumped up and hurried into the foyer, my heart pounding. *Please, please, please let them be okay.* Tali followed, for once staying away from the door without me telling her to.

Aylin stepped inside and my chest loosened. A boy about twelve trailed behind her. He was pretty grimy, so he'd probably been hiding for a while. Skinny, too, and his face lit up at the smell of fish stew. My heart clenched again, but then Danello walked in, watching the street a little too cautiously as he shut the door.

"What happened?" I said, not as relived as I should be now that they were back. "I was getting worried."

"We were just extra careful on the way back," Aylin said. She glanced at Tali, then looked at me in a way that clearly said she didn't want to tell me what was wrong in front of Tali. So many things *could* be wrong, I didn't even want to guess what it was this time. "But we found him." She nudged the boy forward.

"Winvik," Tali gasped, running over. He looked equally glad to see her. "I thought you'd left Geveg."

"I tried, but I couldn't get a boat to the marsh farms."

"You know each other?" Aylin said.

Tali nodded. "Winvik was in my apprentice classes at the Healers' League."

"And the spire room?" I asked softly.

"Yes." A flicker of fear crossed her face. So Winvik had also been forced by the League to heal until he'd carried so much pain he couldn't move. No wonder he'd risked starvation to stay free.

"Welcome, then," I said, smiling. Neither Aylin nor Danello smiled with me. Saints, it must really be bad then.

Footsteps thumped down the stairs and Takers peeked over the railings at us. We had four other Takers in the town house right now, people we'd saved who wouldn't be experimented on by the Duke to see if they developed special "abilities" he could use for his own purpose. I hadn't yet figured out what that purpose was, but that was part of our plan.

Step One: Rescue as many Takers as we could and keep them away from the Duke.

Step Two: Find out what the Duke wanted with them.

Step Three: Stop it.

Of course, steps two and three were turning out to be a lot harder than anticipated, but we were doing okay so far with step one. And truth be told, that was the one that mattered the most.

Danello cleared his throat.

"Tali," I said, "why don't you take Winvik to the kitchen for some of that stew and then show him to a room?"

She frowned for a heartbeat, like she knew I was trying to get rid of her. "Come on—it's this way."

Aylin watched them leave, then stepped closer. Danello did the same.

"What happened?" I asked.

"This." Danello handed me a folded paper.

I unfolded it and my breath caught.

A poster, with *my* face on it and a five-thousand-oppa reward underneath.

Five thousand oppas?

Saints! For that much money I'd turn *myself* in.

THE SHIFTER, MERLAINA OSKOV,
WANTED FOR MURDER

I bristled. It wasn't murder. It had been an accident. . . . *Zertanik, rubbing his hands eagerly; the Luminary, watching with untrusting eyes. Both offering me the lives of Tali and the others if I flashed the League's pynvium Slab, released the pain it held so they could steal it and sell it to those in need.*

I took a deep breath. No, that was a lie. It wasn't an accident. I'd made the choice. Geveg had needed that Slab, the only pynvium left in the whole city. Without it, we wouldn't have been able to heal anyone. Healers couldn't deposit their pain in the metal, where it couldn't hurt them. Zertanik had never cared about that—he'd been eager to take advantage of those who couldn't afford real healing. The Luminary should have cared, though. He ran Geveg's Healers' League, so it was his responsibility to protect our Healers, not use them.

They were terrible men. I shouldn't feel guilty about killing them.

I pictured red mist on the walls of the Luminary's office, all that was left of him and Zertanik after the flash, disintegrated by the pain I'd released from the Slab. My guilt remained. I'd *known* it would kill us, and I'd done it anyway, to save Tali and the other apprentices.

I'd just honestly thought it would kill *me*, too.

"At least they don't know your real name," Aylin said, but her voice trembled.

Danello nodded and cupped my cheek in his hand. "And you look different now, too."

Like Tali, I'd cut my blond curls short, but I'd dyed them brown. Aylin had dyed her hair Baseeri black, something I didn't have the stomach to do.

Danello had kept his blond hair, since fewer people had seen him. They weren't the best disguises, but not many at the League had gotten a good look at our faces. *At least, not the ones still alive.*

"Maybe no one will recognize you," Aylin said.

"Maybe." I cursed myself for saying it. I was supposed to be done with maybes. But maybe you were never done with maybes.

"The posters are all over the city," Aylin said, tossing her hat on a front table of carved wood with onyx inlays. Worth a fortune, perhaps enough to pay the bribes we'd need for passage to the mainland if we ran. Running would be harder now with the reward out there.

"Soldiers are putting them up," added Danello. "A lot of people aren't happy about it. We saw one of the shopkeeps tear it down right in front of the soldiers. He called you a hero."

Hero *and* murderer, all in the same day.

"They nailed the poster up again and he ripped it down again." Danello shook his head. "You should have seen him."

"That's when they beat him up," Aylin said. "We got out of there fast after that."

People I didn't even know were getting hurt defending me. Some hero. No matter what I did, someone suffered.

"You okay?" Danello asked, taking my hand and rubbing his thumb across my knuckles.

"I didn't expect this."

"You knew the Duke was looking for you."

"No, not that. The shopkeep. People sticking up for me."

Aylin huffed. "You saved the lives of thirty Healers, stopped the Luminary from stealing Geveg's pynvium, and basically spat in the Duke's eye. Of *course* they're going to stick up for you."

"I'd be happier if they didn't." I had more responsibility than pockets already. I'd gotten everyone into this, so I had to protect them. Grannyma used to say, a life saved was a debt owed.

"Well, you're a hero now, so get used to it."

Or a murderer, depending on who you asked.

A heavy knock shook the front door.

"Are you expecting anyone?" Danello said in a low voice.

"Soldiers trying to arrest us?" I joked, though it didn't sound at all funny. Danello motioned me to stay back. I ducked behind a doorway with Aylin while he peeked out the window.

"It's the rent collector," he whispered.

My stomach tightened. We'd paid for the whole month just last week.

"Maybe she'll go away," I said.

Another hard bang.

"Or maybe not," said Aylin.

Danello held out both hands. "What should I do?"

More insistent banging. She'd start to draw attention if she kept it up. Soek left the kitchen, a dripping wooden spoon in his hand. He held it like a weapon, and with good cause. He'd been in the spire room with Tali too.

"I know you're in there," the rent collector shouted. "Open up and talk to me."

For the love of Saint Saea, I didn't need this today.

"Open it," I said, stepping into the hall.

She didn't wait to be invited in. Just marched right past Danello and over to me. "Rent's due."

"We already paid it."

"It's due again. And it's gone up."

I folded my arms and tried not to scream my frustration. A handful of jewelry had convinced her Aylin, Tali, and I were Zertanik's daughters. She'd doubled the rent, probably planning to pocket the extra, but let us stay. She could throw us out if she wanted, and we had nowhere else to go. "How much?"

She grinned and handed me one of the reward posters. "Five thousand oppas."

TWO

I didn't know whether to scream or shiver.

Danello scowled. "How could you turn her in? She's Gevegian, same as you."

"Look, I could have gone to the Governor-General and gotten the reward money from him. I *didn't*. But I can't let five thousand oppas pass me by." She glanced around the town house, her eyes shimmering with greed. "None of this is yours anyway, so what do you care if I get some? We all win."

Not if she took so much it drew attention at the alley market. That was the only place in Geveg to sell stolen goods, and even though the soldiers were bribed to look the other way, if enough riches hit the market at once, people noticed, so they *had* to report it. We could both benefit if she didn't get too greedy. She needed us to pose as tenants for the Baseeri owner. If he discovered Zertanik was dead, he'd claim everything in the town house for himself.

I looked at Danello, red-faced and shaking his head behind her.

"Can I offer you something in Verlattian teak?" I said, waving at the sitting-room furniture. If she wanted money so badly, let *her* haul it away.

"No, I think those blue crystal decanters are more my style. And maybe these statuettes?" She brushed past me and ran her fingers over the goldstone figures of the Seven Sisters. "These will cover it."

And then some.

"Help yourself."

"A lot for one person to carry."

I gritted my teeth. "I'm sure we can find you a pack of some kind to carry them. Aylin? Could you check upstairs, please?"

Aylin slapped the banister, muttering something about finding a bag big enough to stuff her head into, and disappeared.

The rent collector pursed her lips and looked around the room. "More than just the three of you living here now."

I crossed my arms. "We have guests for dinner."

"Fine."

Danello yanked open the door and she jumped. She recovered fast and put her sneer back on her face.

"Next week works better for me anyway."

She lumbered out, and Danello slammed the door behind her.

"That's not right!" he said as I sank to the stairs. "She can't just come in here and—"

"Yes, she can." I knew how he felt, though. I'd seen the Baseeri do the same thing to my family's home. Only they took it all. Saints! It wasn't fair.

"We'd better sell off what we can now," Tali said, sounding just like Mama. We'd heard her say a lot of things like that right before the war started. *Might as well stock up on food. Jewels trade better out of the setting anyway. You're safer at the League with your grannyma.* "She's never been upstairs, so she can't take what she doesn't know about."

"We also need to look for a new place to live," Aylin muttered.

"Who's going to rent to us?" Danello said, not nearly as quiet. "And how will we find someplace large enough for everyone?"

Odds were we wouldn't. "Maybe it's time to leave Geveg."

Shocked silence, but they couldn't argue with the idea. There was a lot of money in the town house, enough to bribe a fisherman for passage off the isle, no matter how tempting the reward was.

"We could go to the marsh farms," Danello said. "Da, doesn't your friend need help?"

His father nodded. "He does. He's barely keeping his farm running. Some money and extra hands would let him hold on to it and help us out."

The Duke cared about Takers and pynvium, not sweet potatoes and sugar. I'd never done any farming before, but it sounded good. Honest work, fresh food, open fields with lots of places to run and hide if we had to. The soldiers probably wouldn't look for us in the marsh farms either. Mama used to take Healers there every few months since the farmers didn't have their own, and it always took her at least a week to visit them all.

"Should you ask him first?" I asked. "Showing up with fifteen people is a lot to put on a person on short notice." And I didn't want to abandon the town house until we knew we had somewhere to go.

"Might not be a bad idea. I haven't spoken to him since we went into hiding. He may have lost the place by now."

"How fast can you get there and back?" We'd

need time to search the town house for as many valuables as we could carry anyway.

"A day or two. He's not far from the marsh docks."

Danello's little sister, Halima, dashed over and hugged him.

"I won't be gone long, don't you worry," his father began, then looked at Danello. "You okay to watch them?" Something in his tone made me think he meant more than just the family.

Danello nodded. "I'll keep an eye on everyone."

"Hold them safe. I'll be home tomorrow night."

"Be careful, Da."

"I will." He sounded strong, but I caught the worry in his eyes.

Bahari glared at me at like I was purposely sending his father away. Jovan nodded stoically as ever, while Halima just looked scared. Danello's father hugged his family one more time, then went upstairs to pack a bag.

"What about the Takers?" Tali asked after a minute.

"They'll come with us."

She shook her head. "I mean the ones we haven't found yet. There are dozens more out there at least."

"Tali, I can't save everyone."

"I know, but—"

"If we stay here, we risk everyone else getting caught."

"Maybe we can get the word out that we're leaving so more can come find us?"

"Someone besides the Takers will find out. The soldiers are actively looking for me now."

She sighed and nodded. "I was just hoping to find a few more missing friends."

"Me too. Maybe we'll find some before we have to leave." I turned to the group gathered on the stairs. "Everyone, go to your rooms and start searching for anything of value. Smaller is better since we'll have to carry it, but if it'll sell, grab it."

"Who's gonna sell it?" asked one of the less-trusting Takers we'd found. I couldn't blame him. League guards had broken into his family's home in the middle of the night looking for him. He'd barely gotten away.

"We'll choose folks to go to the alley market first thing in the morning. If a bunch of us hit the vendors, it won't be as obvious we're selling off a lot at once and they won't lower the prices on us. After, we'll split up the oppas and make sure everyone has enough in case we get separated."

This seemed to make everyone happy.

"A friend who repairs boats has been helping us smuggle people off the isle. He usually has several at a time he's working on, so he'll have enough space to get us all to the mainland." Risky to use Barnikoff again if there was a chance he was being watched, but we could trust him. He had a good heart and no love for the Duke. "With a little luck, we'll be able to leave tomorrow night as soon as Danello's father returns."

Or a lot of luck. It wasn't nearly as easy to get off the isle as I was making it out to be, but they didn't need anything more to worry them.

"What happens if this farmer doesn't want us there?" a Taker asked.

"We'll find another farm. Let's not worry about that right now. Once we get out of the city, we'll have more time to figure out where to go without soldiers breathing down our necks."

Aylin kept sneaking me looks, and she'd have her own set of questions as soon as she got me alone. So would Tali, no doubt.

The others though? A few looked unsure about this plan, and I wouldn't be surprised if they grabbed their share of the money and ran. And Saints help me, a few less people to worry about suited me just fine.

21

But what if we weren't welcome anywhere? Refugees from the Duke's siege of Verlatta couldn't be fleeing just to Geveg. The farms might be flooded with them. We might get there only to find there was no room for us.

Or worse, we might find the Duke cared about sweet potatoes after all and there was nowhere to run *to*.

"Can we keep any of this for ourselves?" Tali asked as we searched through the drawers in Zertanik's study. She dangled a string of rose-colored beads from her fingers.

"We need to sell as much as we can. We don't know who we'll have to bribe or how long it'll take us to find work once we're settled."

"What if we can't find a place?"

"We will. Hand me that knife, would you? This drawer is locked."

Tali slipped the beads over her head and passed me the knife. "Half the drawers and cabinets in this place are locked. Zertanik didn't trust people, did he?"

I jammed the knife into the lock. "He *was* a thief."

"I guess that would do it."

The lock popped and I pulled the drawer out. Stacked on the bottom were pages written in neat glyphs, like Papa used to write.

Those are funny letters, Papa. What do they do?

They help me teach the pynvium to hold pain, Nya-Pie.

Pynvium talks to you?

No, but it listens.

"Nya?" Tali touched my arm and I dropped the pages. They fluttered to the carpet. "What's wrong?"

"Nothing. It's just . . . nothing." I grabbed for the pages before she saw them, but she snatched one first.

"Papa used to write like this."

"I know."

"Enchanter's glyphs."

It surprised me she even remembered. She'd been seven when he died, and he hadn't done much enchanting in the year before that. Like everyone else in Geveg, he'd been busy fighting a losing war.

She stared at the pages, her eyes watering, then wiped away the tears. "Are they worth anything?"

"I don't know. Depends on the enchantment, I guess."

"They're easy to carry, so we should try to sell

them." She collected the pages from the floor and smoothed them. "Are there more?"

"I didn't look."

She rooted around in the drawer and pulled out a thin pynvium plate the size of a book. Glyphs were carved into the metal with the same neat handwriting as the papers. Shiverfeet raced down my spine.

"Ooo, pretty." She ran her fingers across the glyphs. "This is worth something for the pynvium alone. Look how blue the metal is. It has to be pure." She handed it to me.

I jerked away. "That's okay."

"What's wrong?" She stared at me funny, then looked at the pynvium. "It won't bite."

"I . . ." Didn't want to touch it. Didn't even want to be in the same *room* with it, and I couldn't say why. "Put it back."

"Put it *back*? Do you know how much this is worth?"

With the pynvium shortage going on, probably more than anything else in the town house. I still didn't want it near me. "But it's . . . wrong."

She looked at me as if I'd lost my mind. The way I felt, maybe I had. "Fine, it's gone," she said. It thunked into the drawer and she shoved it closed.

I could feel it though, and I'd never been able to sense pynvium in my life. Hadn't even sensed *that* one until I saw it. It didn't feel like what Tali had described when she'd tried to teach me how to push pain into pynvium like a real Healer. No call, no hum, just a quiver at the bottom of my stomach.

It couldn't be my shifting ability, either. Moving pain from person to person had nothing to do with those glyphs. But there was sure as spit *something* wrong.

"I'm going to go check the library," I said, jumping to my feet.

"Nya!"

I ignored her, eager to get out of that room and away from the pynvium. I shut the library door and flopped into a chair big enough for me *and* Tali. The quiver faded, but my unease remained.

What was wrong with that pynvium? I'd never felt that way around the metal before.

A chest with a band of blue around the lid, carved with glyphs. Men from the Pynvium Consortium had brought it, and Papa had yelled at them. "You brought that here? To my home? You don't even know what it does!"

I'd never seen Papa afraid of the glyphs before. Had they bothered him as well? I'd hidden, scared

25

of the shouting and the way my stomach felt after looking at the chest. Grannyma had found me in the closet and put me to bed. She'd rocked and sung lullabies until I'd fallen asleep.

"Nya, you in here?" The door opened and Aylin stuck her head in.

"I'm here."

She glanced at the books lining the shelves but didn't pick up any this time. There were quite a few books missing, so she must have more than enough to read for a while. "We've got quite the pile of treasure building downstairs. I had them dump it all on the dining room table."

"Thanks."

"You okay? You look queasy."

"I'm fine." I stood and put my palms over my belly. "Don't think Soek's fish stew liked me much, but it'll pass."

She nodded and rifled through a desk drawer. "Did you want to start going through it all or do you want me to handle it?"

"You can do it. You have a better eye for what sells."

"Merchant's daughter." She grinned but then looked sad. She always did when she talked about her mother. Not that Aylin ever said much. None of us talked about our families. "Oh, I don't think everyone is turning over everything they find. I caught Kneg slipping a gold frame into his pocket."

"That's okay. We'll have more than enough, and I can't blame them for wanting a little extra. Wouldn't you swipe something?"

"Who says I haven't?" She stuck her tongue out at me and twirled toward the door. "I'll organize the goodies by value. We can bag them up and keep them in your room overnight."

"Sounds good."

Aylin shut the door as she left. I sighed and started going through the drawers and shelves, though there wasn't much besides books. A few candlesticks might earn a good price, a vase that looked like water crystal, but otherwise—

My guts quivered, same as in the study. My hand froze over the bookshelf, then dropped away. More glyph-carved pynvium? But not just locked away in a drawer. This one was hidden behind the books.

Why lock one away and hide another?

I took a steadying breath and yanked out one of the books. Then another, and a third, until the shelf emptied and a small chest appeared. No blue band, thank the Saints, but a simple iron box with a lock on the front.

My stomach quivered again.

Just open it.

My hand wouldn't move.

Take it.

I shoved the books back onto the shelf and raced from the room.

THREE

The alley market wasn't one of my favorite places, and not just because I'd never had anything to sell before. Everyone there was a thief—buying stolen goods, selling stolen goods, looking for stolen goods. You had to watch your pockets as well as your tongue, and if you slipped up at all, someone would rob you of something.

We'd decided six of us would go. Me, Danello, Aylin, Tali, Soek, and Jovan. More would likely draw attention, fewer wouldn't be able to carry or sell enough to keep us afloat very long. We'd sell in pairs to watch each other's backs.

"Everyone remember how much to try and get?" I said a block from the alley. Aylin had done a good job estimating what our bundles were worth. Odds were we wouldn't get all of it, but the closer we got, the better.

"I remember." Jovan already had on his bluffing face. He'd surprised us all last night when we tested each other to see who could lie the best. Tali wasn't nearly as good, but she had an uncanny way of making you want to give her what she asked for anyway. She called it her hungry puppy face and said she'd gotten many an extra dessert at the League with it.

I could believe it. And I'd have to remember that next time she tried to talk me into or out of anything.

"We'll go in separately. Don't look at each other, and once you've sold your goods, meet back here."

Aylin frowned and shook her head. "Not here. Anyone following after we sell might jump us." She looked around and pointed to the bakery. "That works. Buy something and linger inside."

"If you see soldiers," I added, "get out, but *walk*, don't run."

"Got it. Let's go," said Soek. He and Tali would follow Danello and me, with Aylin and Jovan last.

Danello grabbed my hand and we walked the last block to the alley market, keeping an eye out for soldiers and thieves. The market changed locations, but you could always find it in the poorest parts of Geveg. It wasn't that different from the regular market squares, except no one had their wares on display and everyone conducted business in whispers. Today it was just off the docks.

Our bag was full of silverware and metalwork, so we walked up to a stall with a hammer-and-forge sign hanging off it.

"And what can I do for you today?" the merchant asked. She smiled, but her gaze weighed the bag like she could guess its worth on sight.

"My aunt left me her silver and it's all ugly." I pulled out a few pieces. "Figured I'd sell it off and buy something nice for myself."

The merchant picked up a candlestick and turned it this way and that, a slight frown on her face like it wasn't the pure silver we both knew it was. "It *is* ugly."

"You should see the forks."

"You have the whole set? I know a woman who wants to get her mother-by-marriage an ugly gift."

I slid the Verlattian teak box out of the bag. Her eyes widened just a bit.

"The box isn't bad."

It was better than not bad. The wood gleamed, the grain patterns rich and dark.

Aylin and Jovan passed us and went to a jeweler's.

Aylin had amazed us all last night with her tale of woe, about her beloved who died in the ferry accident and left her alone, and now she had to sell off all his gifts. How her mistress had given her a few trinkets to help ease her through this tragedy. She seemed exactly like a maid who'd snitched from her mistress's jewel case.

The merchant ran her fingers along the wooden lid and lifted it. Silver sparkled in neat rows. "I'll give you two hundred for the set."

"The candlesticks alone are worth that."

The corners of her mouth tightened for a heartbeat. "I'd say more like one hundred, maybe."

I shrugged, feigned indifference. Inside, it was hard to stay calm. Two hundred oppas was more money than I'd ever seen at once.

"Does your boy there ever talk?"

"Only when someone's trying to steal the fish from our net." Danello folded his muscled arms and glared at her.

For a moment I thought I saw a smile. "Lucky girl, you. Let's see, I can probably do . . ." She inspected the pieces slowly, no doubt trying to decide how much she could cheat us.

"But it's goldstone!" yelled a familiar voice. "It has to be worth more than that."

I glanced down a few stalls and tried not to suck in a breath. The rent collector was arguing with a vendor, waving one of the statuettes in his face. I forced my gaze away and hoped she was too busy to notice any of us.

"Three hundred," the merchant finished.

"It's worth at least six."

She shrugged. "You can always sell to the silversmith." She didn't take her hands off the box though.

"Give that Baseeri rat my aunt's silver?" I turned and spat. "I don't think so."

The rent collector glanced my way, then snapped around. She looked from me to the silver on the table, her eyes narrowing as if I were selling off *her* property.

Behind her, Tali and Soek left the art vendor. Tali started grinning as soon as her back was turned, so she must have done well. Aylin and Jovan were still at the jeweler's, but the jewels were being wrapped up so they had to be close to a deal.

"How about five then?" I said.

"You'd be robbing me at that price."

The rent collector stalked over. Danello intercepted, keeping her a stride's length away.

"What are you doing?" she asked, pointing at

me. "What are you selling? Are your little friends here?" She spun around. "There's one! Where are the others?"

The merchant frowned and pulled her hands off the silverware box. "Perhaps now isn't the best time."

"Now is fine," I said quickly. "Nothing to worry about."

Danello had the rent collector by the arms, but she wouldn't stay quiet. "I could have turned you in and I didn't! You owe me!"

My guts twisted. "Shall we split the difference and say four?"

The merchant's attention was on the rent collector now, her brow furrowed as if she were thinking hard. Then she looked at me.

Please, Saint Saea, don't let her recognize me.

Aylin had fluffed my curls so my head looked bigger than the poster, and lined my eyes and cheeks with powders to make me look older.

"Do I know you?"

"No."

"Those are mine." The rent collector surged past Danello and grabbed at the silver.

"They are not!" I snatched them away just in time, but the merchant was backing off, worry on

34

her plump face. A crowd had gathered, some watching in boredom, others probably waiting to see if we'd start fighting and drop something.

"Don't try to cheat me, Shifter, or you'll be sorry!"

I gulped. The merchant gasped.

"You're the girl from the posters!"

"Deal's off." I threw the silverware box into the air as Danello shoved the rent collector into the crowd. She fell, knocking over a few people, and money and silver hit the street. Cries of alarm and joy rose, and no one seemed to care about me anymore.

I headed for the bakery, walking fast but not running. Soldiers patrolled these streets, and while the vendors paid them to walk past the alley market, they had no trouble stopping anyone who came out of it at a run. "Anyone following?"

"Don't think so. The merchant wouldn't leave her stall unattended. I don't think the others heard the rent collector call you Shifter."

I could only hope.

We ducked onto a porch and crouched down behind the railing. The bakery was across the street, but I didn't want to go inside if we were being followed.

"Wait, someone just left the alley," Danello said.

"A boy, nineteen, maybe twenty. I think he's looking for something."

I peeked above the railing. Danello was mostly right, but the boy wasn't just looking for something, he was looking *out* for something as well.

Angry shouts came from the alley market. A patrol came down the street, their steps hesitant as if they weren't yet sure if they wanted to get involved. The boy dropped and tied his sandals, even though he had no sandals to tie.

"He's hiding from the soldiers," I whispered. "If he was after me, he wouldn't do that."

"What's he looking for then?"

I held my breath as the soldiers walked closer to the kneeling boy. I recognized that tenseness, that fear, that desperate praying that they wouldn't notice you.

A woman screamed and the soldiers ran for the alley, passing the boy by a few feet. He stayed down for a second more, then jumped up. He stood in the street, turning slowly, his face pale.

"Shifter?" he whisper-yelled. "Are you out here? I need your help. Please, we're in trouble."

I started to rise and Danello pulled me down. "You can't risk it."

"What if he's a Taker?"

"What if he's a trap?"

I looked again. "He's too scared to be a trap."

"Let me approach him then. You stay here." He didn't wait for an answer, just hopped up and walked over. The boy startled and stepped back, but he steadied himself like he expected Danello to attack him. They spoke for a minute, then Danello scanned the street.

"It's okay," he called.

I came out of hiding.

"You were right," Danello said. "His sister is trapped at the docks. Trackers are after her."

"You have to save her, please," the boy said. "I was in the alley trying to buy a weapon so I could attack the trackers and I heard that woman call you Shifter. The Takers, the ones who are hiding with us, were all talking about you. Some say you can help us."

I'd never faced a tracker before. Guards and soldiers were one thing, but trackers were trained to hunt down Takers. We'd been far too lucky avoiding them so far. I should have known that luck wouldn't last.

"Where is she?" I asked against all better judgment. But turning your back on trouble only let it sneak up on you.

"On berth three. By the traps."

Rows of traps littered berth three: fish traps, crab traps, duck traps, probably some mouse and rat traps. The whole place was one stinky maze.

"Which traps?"

He pushed both hands through his brown hair. "I . . . uh . . . I'm not sure. When we saw them, we started running."

Running? No wonder she caught their attention.

"I think there were at least four of them," he said. "Maybe more."

Four trackers? Saea be merciful.

"We'll need help to get her," I said. Danello hadn't spoken, but he didn't look any happier about it than I did. "Follow us."

I headed into the bakery. The others were all there, looking worried. Tali had mango cream filling all over her mouth but didn't seem to be enjoying it. Aylin shot me her oh-Nya-what-did-you-do-now? look. "What happened?"

"The rent collector saw me and caused a fuss, but we got away. This boy's sister is trapped on the docks. Trackers are after her."

"What's the plan?" Aylin asked.

"She's on berth three. We'll split up and look for her," I said.

"We'll signal if we find her," Danello said. "Three caws, then two, like we practiced."

"Got it." Tali nodded.

"No," I said. "You're going to the town house with Soek and Jovan." All three started arguing and I waved my hands to quiet them. "Listen, the rent collector is probably going to tell the soldiers about me, so the town house isn't safe anymore. You three need to get everyone out and head right to Barnikoff's." He'd be surprised when they showed up, but we didn't have a choice. "It's go now or get caught."

Tali folded her arms. "I'm not leaving you." Her eyes teared up and she leaned in closer. "If they catch you, we'll be separated again. I'd rather be caught with you than all alone."

I pictured Tali on her own, trying to find food, avoid soldiers. Stay alive. "Okay, but you do exactly as I say and stay close."

"I will."

I turned to the others. "Let's go."

We left the bakery and hurried to the docks, the sun already beating down on our heads. Aylin and I headed into the maze while Danello and the boy followed the outside paths. A few paces ahead a lake gull squawked and took flight, its white feathers stark against the brown and green of the crab traps rising like cliffs around us. Lake gulls usually spooked at things they thought might eat them—and these days that meant people as often as crocodiles. I dropped and Aylin and Tali dropped with me, taking cover behind a drying rack.

Footsteps shuffled about thirty feet behind us. Slow, steady, cautious. Too heavy for a scared girl, but not heavy enough for a dock worker. Then another set of footsteps. Maybe these trackers were working in pairs—one flushed the prey and the other caught it.

I gestured at Aylin to sneak around and try to see who the footsteps belonged to. She nodded and crept along the stacks.

Footsteps again, then—

Polished boots and dark trousers stepped into view. A tracker! I heard a scraping sound, like a weapon being drawn.

"Come out, come out—we know you're here," a woman called, her voice cold yet teasing.

My heart raced. I looked for Aylin, but she was no longer in the tight walkway. Tali's eyes were wide, but she stayed low and silent.

I peeked between the traps for a better look at the woman. She turned a slow circle, her hand out in front of her. I tiptoed away from the tracker until

I reached the end of the row and ducked behind a dock shed. If the trackers kept moving forward, I could—

Sniff.

I turned toward the sound, my feet ready to bolt the other way. The boy's sister! She was about my age, but small as Tali. She'd wedged herself under a cleaning table at the edge of the dock about fifty feet away.

Waves sighed against the canal walls and hissed through the reeds growing along the boat-launching ramps. The tracker stood by the closest ramp, a blue-black pynvium rod in her hand. Much better than a sword. As long as she didn't use it on anyone but me.

I turned to Tali and pointed to a dinghy leaning against a post.

She nodded.

A fake gull cried out—three caws, close. Aylin was probably on the other side of the sister. I cawed back twice. The tracker turned away and I darted across the row, slipping under the dinghy. Tali slipped in behind me a breath later.

The tracker moved away from the launching ramp, narrowing the distance between her and the girl. Danello slipped behind the tracker, darting across the row. The brother had to be there, though

I didn't see him. I hoped he didn't do anything reckless to help his sister.

The tracker stiffened and turned as if she'd heard us.

I left Tali and moved closer, testing each footstep before settling my weight down on the bleached planks of the dock.

Movement under the cleaning table caught my eye. The sister leaned forward as if about to run, terror on her face. I shook my head and she sat back.

Creak.

I froze. The tracker snapped around and raised her pynvium weapon. She glanced at the traps and pulled a knife from her boot as well.

Creak.

The tracker followed the sound, her head cocked, her weapons ready.

The sister gasped, soft as a splash. I held up my hands and mouthed, *Stay*. She nodded.

The tracker was right on the other side of the traps from me. She took another cautious step in her shiny black boots and then stopped.

She narrowed her eyes. She cocked her head again and stepped closer to the wall of crab traps separating us.

Had she sensed me?

Jeatar had warned me about that before he'd left Geveg. "The Duke will hire the best trackers to come after you. The ones who can sense a Taker like a Taker senses pynvium. The good ones can sense a Taker just by walking by."

If she'd sensed us from this distance, she was *really* good.

"Come out, come out, little girl," she called louder.

I held my breath. Light drops of sweat dotted her brow and upper lip. Was she scared? If so, maybe I could catch her off guard, give the others time to move in and the sister time to move out.

"I know you're here," the tracker called. She held up one hand, inches away from the traps hiding me, as if she could feel me behind the wood. "Is that you, Shifter?"

I swallowed my gasp. She had to be guessing. She couldn't possibly know it was me.

"I'll leave the girl alone if you show yourself. You're a much better prize for the Duke than she is."

The dock creaked again. Aylin or Danello?

"You can't evade me for long, Shifter," the tracker said in that irritating singsong voice.

Maybe not, but that didn't mean I wouldn't try.

"You can't run," she continued. "We have guards

43

on every bridge off every isle. Soldiers at all the pole-boat docks. If I don't get you, one of my men will."

Men? Since when did trackers hire others to help them?

I caught another glimpse of the tracker through the holes in the traps, then she was gone.

"Got you."

FOUR

I gasped and spun. The tracker had a pynvium rod in her hand. She flicked her wrist and—

Whoomp.

Pain flashed from it, stinging my skin like blown sand. She gaped at me, shocked that I hadn't collapsed to the ground screaming in pain. I guess they hadn't figured out *everything* about me yet.

Something thumped against the traps around me. They clattered forward, spilling over the tracker like trash thrown from a window.

"Looks like I got *you*," Aylin said, heaving an armful of nets at her.

"Vyand?" a man yelled.

"Her—" she began.

I dumped more nets over her and cawed three

45

times. Two more caws answered right away. The tracker was quiet for only a moment, then started screaming and thrashing about.

"Tangle her up," I said.

Aylin helped me truss her up in the nets like a chicken on All Saints' Day. The tracker's screams turned to angry squeals and curses.

The boy ran to his sister and dragged her from the nook. Danello popped out from behind the traps. "More trackers are headed this way," he said, pointing over his shoulder.

We left, staying low and moving as fast as we dared.

I slowed as we neared North-Dock Bridge, checking the crowded street for the guards the tracker claimed were on all the bridges. Dozens of haulers and day workers shuffled between the docks and the production district on the main isle, but none of them looked like guards.

We crossed the bridge slowly, moving with refugees and workers. On the other side of the bridge, I angled to the canal side of the street so we wouldn't draw attention from some soldiers hassling a family of squatters.

"Danello, Aylin," I said, "drop behind and check for anyone following."

"Got it."

Aylin vanished into the crowd, light on her feet as the wind, Danello less so, but he was getting better at it.

A refugee jostled me. I turned, glad for the excuse to look behind us. A block away, two men walked side by side. Their clothes said poor, but they didn't glance at the soldiers or shy away when anyone walked close. Their dark hair was neatly trimmed and neither wore a beard. People that nondescript were usually the ones you had to watch out for. Danello and Aylin were about twenty feet behind them, walking on opposite sides of the street.

A burned smell drifted over the bridge as we crossed into what used to be a Baseeri-occupied neighborhood. Most of it had been burned in the riots a few months ago, right after the old Luminary had claimed Geveg's Healers were all dead. Well, that and me proving the Luminary had been lying and was *really* trying to steal the League's pynvium. No one had been happy about *that*.

They'd gone mad, attacking the League, burning down Baseeri-owned shops and homes, giving the Governor-General an excuse to send in his soldiers and a legitimate reason to hurt us.

I looked at the Healers' League rising above the

other buildings in the distance. The gaping hole where the Luminary's office had been was a sharp reminder of why the trackers were after me.

What's done is done and I can't change it none.

"Nya?" Tali said, looking at me funny. "Why are we slowing down?"

"Sorry." I picked up the pace again.

Three men rounded the corner in front of us, their gazes scanning the street. The tracker's men? I turned around, heading back the way we'd come.

The tracker woman stepped out of an alley.

I froze. So did Aylin and Danello, now in front of me and on the other side of the tracker. Having her trapped between us didn't make me feel any safer.

A plan, I need a plan.

The tracker smiled, but there was nothing friendly about her grin. She had a sword out this time and her knife in the other hand.

"Found you before lunch," she said. "Stewwig owes me ten oppas."

"You must have me confused with someone else," I said, trying to hold her attention while Aylin and Danello crept up behind her.

"I don't think so."

Danello dived at the tracker, sending her flying

forward and into a pain merchant's window. The glass cracked but didn't break. Folks turned, their hands covering worried frowns.

"Run!" I yelled. Two of the three men closing on us blocked my way. Another was coming up behind them. Huge, with thick arms, his sleeves rolled up like those of a man who was there to do a hard day's work.

I shoved Tali away from the approaching men. She stumbled a few steps then stopped, her expression waffling between fear and anger. The Taker and her brother fled for the canals.

"Tali, go," I cried.

"Not without you!" She darted over and grabbed my hand, trying to pull me away. Aylin was running at us, her hand outstretched as if she planned to grab me too.

The tracker was on her feet again. She whipped out another pynvium rod and aimed it at Tali and Aylin.

Whoomp.

A strange tingle ran down my arm. Aylin screamed and collapsed to the street. Tali didn't, but she *should* have.

We gaped at each other longer than was wise. She'd resisted the flash! She'd never done that before. I'd seen flashed pain hurt her. She wasn't immune like I was. How had she done it?

Two of the tracker's men tackled us. I dropped and landed hard on the street next to an unconscious Aylin. I grabbed her ankles and *drew*.

Tingling pain ran up my arm, not nearly as sharp as real pain would have been, and it wouldn't last long. The tracker's men grabbed me. I struggled to turn and grab their exposed flesh but couldn't reach them.

Danello leaped onto the big man from behind. He spun and punched Danello in the face. Danello snapped back and went down.

I kicked the shins of one of the men holding me. He cried out and loosened his grip on my arm. I yanked hard, sliding my wrist out enough to get my hand on his skin.

I *pushed*.

He hissed and let go, shaking his arm like something had stung him. I reached for the man holding Tali a heartbeat before thick arms wrapped around my shoulders. I reached up, barely able to get my fingers on his forearm. I *shifted* the last of what I'd taken from Aylin into him. He grunted softly but didn't let go.

Tali's arms were pinned now, and another man

was tying her hands. She tried to bite him and he slapped her.

"Hey!" I kicked out at him but missed.

A few fishermen scowled and started forward, but the tracker stepped up and held something out.

"This is a legal bounty warrant on the Duke's orders." She smiled briefly, satisfied as a cat. "Any interference in this claim is punishable by conscription."

That stopped the fishermen. They might risk prison to help me, but no one wanted to fight for the Duke. The crowd that had gathered grumbled and moved away.

"You've given us quite the chase," she said.

"Who are you?" I asked, shaking as a soldier bound my hands with rope. Danello lay on the street, softly moaning.

"Most call me Vyand." She stepped forward and held the reward poster next to my face. "Good likeness, except for the hair. That was smart." Vyand grinned at the big man. "Look at that, Stewwig, two Takers for the work of one. Not bad."

"Let her go!" I said.

Vyand stayed just out of kicking distance. "Merlaina Oskov," she said, using the name I'd given to so many who now wanted me captured. "On the order

51

of Duke Verraad, I herby bind you for the murder of Luminary Duis Steek."

She leaned in closer and whispered into my ear. "But we both know that's not why he *really* wants you."

Ropes bound my wrists together, same as Tali. Vyand had thrown us into a prisoner transport waiting in the rear courtyard of the Healers' League. High stone walls and wrought-iron gates I recognized well fenced us in even more.

The courtyard gate clanged open and Vyand entered, followed by four armed men. Tali slid closer and grabbed my hand.

"Listen up," Vyand called, walking over to us. "You have been extremely annoying. If you give me any more hassles, you'll spend your nights in a box belowdecks, where it's hot. Behave yourselves and you'll get to sleep in a cage on deck, where it's cool."

She flicked a hand in the air. "Mount up."

The cage dipped to one side as men climbed onto the driver's bench. Seconds later the transport lurched forward and rolled onto Grand Canal Street. I frowned. Vyand was going to parade us through the streets, as if proving to Geveg that I was caught.

Crowds of Baseeri gathered and watched the transport pass. I'd never been booed before. Yelled at, spat on, beaten, yes—but not booed.

"Abomination!"

"Murderer!"

"I bet I've healed some of those people," Tali muttered, dodging a rotten orange.

"Tali, about that. What did you do when Vyand flashed us?"

"Nothing."

"You had to do *something*. The flash didn't hurt you."

"It burned a little, but that was it. Think I'm immune like you?"

"You weren't before."

She shrugged. "I was trying to get you to leave. I wasn't thinking about anything but dragging you out of there."

Wait . . . *dragging*. She'd been touching me. I closed my eyes, pictured us standing there. I'd felt something just before Vyand flashed us. A tingle, like she was *pulling* something from me. What if it had been my flashing immunity? Did she *borrow* it?

"Put your hands over mine," I said. "See if you can shift into me."

"What? I can't do that."

"Just try."

She put her hands over mine and . . .

"Nothing."

"I didn't feel a tingle this time either." Maybe she hadn't done anything. I could have blocked her from the pain, or the angle of the flash had missed her. Maybe I'd drawn it away just as it hit her.

"You have a plan to get us out of here, don't you?" She looked at me, hope in her eyes. Her confidence was touching, but I wasn't so sure I could live up to such faith. I had no idea how to get out of a locked prisoner transport. I couldn't even escape in a city I knew as well as my own name.

"They can't keep us in this cage forever. When Vyand opens the door, I'll shift and we'll run."

She frowned. "That's not one of your better plans."

"It's all I have right now."

"Okay. Tell me when you think of something else."

"We're going to get out of this," I promised. She smiled, but I don't think she believed me.

The taunts and thrown items stopped when we reached a rundown neighborhood. People watched us go by, their expressions hard and cold, but for Vyand's men, not for us. I could see the hopelessness, the defeat. That's what the Duke had done to us: turned us into people who let our children be dragged through the city on display and hauled off to the very man who'd beaten us.

"Free the Takers!"

Danello? Shouts rang out all around us. Men with clubs and nets ran from the crowd. They swarmed over the main guard, catching him in a net before he could do more than turn. A half dozen more ran for the horses. Aylin, Jovan, Bahari, Enzie. Even Winvik!

A high-pitched whinny split the air. The horses reared, front legs pawing as some fishermen tried to throw blankets over them. The driver was on the ground, unconscious. I caught a glimpse of Barnikoff swinging a stick at one of the soldiers.

"See? We don't need a plan. We're being rescued!"

The horses shrieked again, and one kicked out its rear legs. The cage shuddered as hooves cracked against the front. The horse kept thrashing, trying to throw off the man clinging to its harness. The cage rocked like a boat on rough water.

"Push harder!" Danello called above the noise.

I screamed as the cage toppled and dragged the horses to the ground. Tali tumbled over me, her knee smacking painfully hard against my head. The door screeched open and a man hauled her out. Another seized my arm and yanked me to my feet. He hurried me away from the cage.

"No, my friends are that way." I tugged to return, but the man wouldn't stop. Vyand's men might have been surprised by the attack, but they hadn't stayed that way long. More had appeared, surrounding the others with swords and pynvium rods. Danello backed away, shielding Tali and Aylin.

"Wait, please!"

The man kept leading me down the street.

Away from Danello and Tali.

Away from *everyone*.

Saints and sinners! This wasn't a rescue. It was a *kidnapping*.

"Let go of me!" I couldn't break free of the man's grip. I pounded on his hand, but it was like smacking rock. I leaned over and bit his shoulder.

He gasped and let me go.

"I don't think so," said another man, coming up behind me before I could take a step. He grabbed my arms and half carried me down the street. There wasn't a soul around.

They hauled me into a rundown boardinghouse half a block farther along the street. The first man opened a door on the ground floor and shoved me inside.

"We got her," he said, shutting the door behind us.

"Good."

I snapped around. A boy about twenty stood there.

"What's going on?" I asked, though my guts knew only one reason why anyone would save me from a tracker and take me away from my friends.

"We're earning a quick five thousand oppas." He elbowed the man standing next to him. "See, Uncle? I told you this would work."

FIVE

They wanted the bounty. Wanted it so much they'd kidnapped me from a *tracker*. A good plan, actually. Insane, but good.

"What about the girl in the transport with me?" I asked as they bound my hands.

"Don't know, don't care," said Uncle, rubbing his shoulder. "She might even be free by now. Those men at the docks were pretty unhappy about a pair of Takers being arrested."

The boy nodded. "Especially that one guy, right, Fieso? Blond hair, tall. You should have heard him going on and on about you being a hero. He had the whole berth in an uproar."

Danello.

"Oh, yeah." Fieso chuckled and shook his head like he couldn't imagine anyone sticking their neck out for someone else. "Resik listened for a minute and started smiling."

"That's when I got the idea." The boy, Resik I guess, winked and tapped his temple. "Let them do the risky work, and if they pulled it off, we'd grab you right out from under their noses."

These people would see soldiers burning houses and use it as an excuse to steal what was left behind. My escape options were few. I had little pain to use, and outrunning them with my hands tied was unlikely. I couldn't count on a rescue, and I wasn't even sure the others had gotten away. Vyand might have captured them all.

"What are you going to do to me?" I asked.

"Kill you," said Uncle, casual as you please.

"Head works as proof, right?" Fieso added. "We got a box anywhere? Heads are messy."

My stomach threatened to make a mess right there. "You don't have to do this."

"You got five thousand oppas? We'll turn you loose."

"Wait! The posters don't say anything about me being dead." They paused. "The Duke wants me alive. Kill me and you'll get nothing."

Fieso frowned. "Nobody ever wants criminals alive."

"The Duke does. He needs me." For what I wasn't quite sure, and I hoped they wouldn't ask. Luckily, they didn't strike me as the smartest fish in the lake. I didn't want to be handed over to the Duke either, but it beat having my head chopped off. Hard to think up an escape plan without a head.

"I don't think so." Fieso picked up an axe I hadn't noticed on the table.

Please, Saint Saea, no.

Resik held up a hand. "Hold on, what if she's right?"

"Easier to carry a head to Baseer," muttered Fieso.

"Not if it don't get us nothing." Uncle stared at Resik as if he could divine the future from the pattern of his freckles. After a long minute he walked over and sat on the table next to Fieso. "It'll be harder to get her there, but the boy makes sense. Posters said nothing about killing, and they usually do. The carriage is big enough to take her."

"Not big enough to hide her."

"Resik," Uncle said, waving him over. "Go fetch that trunk off the carriage. She oughta fit in there."

"Wouldn't it be easier to let me walk?" I asked.

"Not if you run."

"What if I promise not to?"

"You know," Fieso said to Uncle, "heads don't talk so much."

I shut up.

Resik laughed.

"Go get the trunk so we can get out of here."

This was *so* not good. I casually studied the room, hoping something would inspire a perfect escape plan. One table, three thugs, three chairs, and four bedrolls. No windows. Just the one door. Uncle had already demonstrated his viselike grip, and Fieso was bigger and wider, with so many scars he obviously didn't mind getting a little bloody in a fight.

Uncle wasn't paying attention to me. He had his head down, studying papers spread out on the table. From the glimpses I caught, they were maps. Fieso watched me the entire time, his face blank.

He chuckled. If crocs could laugh, they'd sound exactly like that. "She's a sly one. Look at her—planning her escape."

"Was not," I said.

"Oh, sure. I saw them pretty brown eyes looking around."

"Can always blindfold her," Uncle said without looking up from the maps.

Fieso slid off the table and walked to the bed-rolls. "And gag her. Ten oppas says she'll scream all the way to the traveler's house if we don't."

Uncle nodded. "Yeah, fine."

Fieso pulled some cloth strips out of one of the packs and came to me. I had no idea what the strips used to be, but they didn't look clean or soft. The closer he got, the more I could smell them. Something sour.

"Please, don't."

"Look at that," he said, tying a heavy knot in one of the strips. "Manners *and* sneakiness. Open."

I shook my head. He grabbed my jaw, pressing his fingers into my cheeks. My mouth popped open and he shoved the knot into it, then tied the ends behind my head. I winced as he snagged some of my hair in the knot.

Fieso grinned and snapped the second cloth tight between his hands. Dust sprang out and floated around my head. I held my breath so I wouldn't sneeze.

"Might wanna close your eyes." He stepped behind me. "This one's a bit dirty."

I squeezed my eyes shut as he tied the blindfold around my head. At least it made it easier to hold back the tears.

Heavy thuds, muffled voices. The first sounds I'd heard in close to an hour. I'd been counting the minutes but lost my place at twenty-something when someone sneezed. I'd hoped it was Fieso, though it wasn't much in the way of revenge.

The door opened and the thumps grew louder.

"What took you so long?" Uncle asked.

"It's a trunk. It's heavy," Resik said, followed by a large bang. "And there's lots of people out now, all yelling and throwing stuff. The streets are swamped."

Hands seized my arm and yanked me to my feet, dragging me toward—I assumed—the trunk.

"Grab her," Fieso said, and hands lifted my feet. I writhed but they just gripped me tighter. I reached out and found flesh, maybe an arm, and *pushed* my aching head into it. A man cried out and dropped me into something that smelled of fish stink and mold.

Something smacked me in the head as I tried to get up, and they all laughed.

"Stay," Resik ordered as if I were a dog.

The lid thumped shut, and what little light came through the blindfold vanished. He'd bound my hands, but not my arms, so I pulled off the blindfold, then yanked the gag out of my mouth. My mouth felt dry as a beach, but as soon as I heard crowds, I'd yell my lungs out.

One end of the trunk lifted and I knocked against the side. The other side rose a moment later and we were moving. Faint noises reached me after a few minutes, growing louder with every jostle. I rocked as the trunk rocked, banging into the sides as we went down the front steps. I'd never been one for lake sickness, but the heat and the swaying had my stomach flipping.

I listened, straining for sounds of people who might actually help if I started shouting. I prayed the others were safe and sound and heading for Barnikoff's.

Voices yelled—commanding voices. Soldiers or guards for sure. "Settle down or you'll be arrested," said someone who *had* to be a guard.

"Help!" I kicked and pounded my fists on the sides of the trunk. "Help!"

The trunk dropped hard to the ground. I kept kicking and yelling, until a six-inch chunk of knife blade sliced through the top, cutting into my cheek. I jerked away and pressed a hand against it. After a heartbeat, the blade was yanked out.

"Next one goes through the side, where it's heavy," Fieso said through the hole. Most of me rested on that side, my back flat against the trunk. "I don't want to risk the money, but heads don't try to escape."

I stayed quiet. And still, despite the sting in my cheek and the blood trickling down my neck. Smells from the tannery oozed through the cracks in the trunk, mixing unpleasantly with the fish and mold. The smell of fish got stronger. Horses whinnied, wood creaked, and waves swished around dock pilings.

We had to be at the traveler's house on the docks, the only one with a stable. Unless you were military or very rich, horses and carriages weren't allowed on the isles. That never stopped people from ferrying them over, though. Housekeeper Gilnari made a good living stabling both.

Once I was on their carriage and off the isle, I was done for. I had to escape before they boarded the ferry.

Please, Saint Saea, do something. I'm out of ideas.

Voices drifted over, but nothing I could make out. Probably Uncle getting the carriage brought around and the horses ready.

"Let me help you with that," someone called.

"No, I got it," Fieso said, banging on the side of the trunk my back was pressed against. "You scream," he muttered through the hole in the trunk, "and anyone who tries to help you dies."

A minute later someone grunted and I was swaying. The trunk dipped sharply at one end and I crumpled onto my head. A sharp jerk and it righted again.

My heart and my hope sank. I had to be on the carriage now.

"Can she breathe in there?" The voice was muffled, but it sounded like Uncle.

"I gave her an airhole," Fieso replied.

"Gonna need more than one."

The carriage rocked, then the blade punched through the lid—two, three, four times—then again in the front. I flattened myself against the side.

"That enough?"

"Better make 'em wider."

The blade returned, twisting in each hole until grape-size shafts of light shone through. "Happy now?"

"Yeah, she won't bake to death. Won't it get messy in there?"

"Not if we don't feed her."

I shivered despite the growing heat in the trunk. It was four days, maybe five, to Baseer by road. I'd gone three days without food before, but never longer. I'd known folks who had, so I could probably manage, but how long could I survive without water?

"Ferry's boarding."

"About time," said Uncle. "Saints, my head is killing me. Wake me when we hit the mainland. I'm gonna nap."

A door squeaked and shut, and the carriage lurched forward.

The shifted pain. How long before it thickened Uncle's blood and wore out his body? It had taken only a day for Danello and his brothers to get pain sick after I'd shifted their father's pain into them, but there had been a lot more of it. How soon until Uncle got sick?

How soon until he died?

Hope and guilt merged in a very uncomfortable knot in my guts. I'd killed him sure as if I'd stabbed him, only he didn't know it. I didn't see any of them going to a Healer. Maybe a pain merchant, but I doubted there'd be any of those along the way.

I shouldn't feel guilty. He'd have killed me in a heartbeat. Cut off my head, just for money. Still, Healers didn't take lives.

The crowd's shouts echoed in my ears. *Abomination! Murderer!*

I wasn't a Healer and I never would be. I had other paths: hero or murderer.

Saints forgive me, but I felt more like one than the other.

My stomach rolled with every sway, queasy again from the heat and closeness of the trunk. I focused on breathing—in, out, in, out—trying not to be sick. I didn't think Fieso would open the trunk for any reason, no matter what noises I made or smells I emitted.

Reins cracked and the rocking got worse as the horses picked up speed. Getting to Baseer faster might help keep me alive, but it was a whole lot more uncomfortable. I banged off the sides, bruising my bruises and opening up the cut on my cheek again. Already every inch of me hurt. My arms and legs burned from being crumpled like dirty laundry, and I doubted my spine would ever straighten up again. At least I'd have some pain to shift when they *did* let me out.

And kill more people?

I swallowed the thought. They weren't people, they were criminals—*real* murderers. It should have made a difference, but the knot in my guts didn't go away. Maybe I could escape without shifting.

I always had before, though I'd never been in this much trouble.

Hours later the light vanished from the holes in the trunk. The carriage slowed and stopped.

Footsteps.

Someone fumbled with the latch and the lid lifted. Fresh air poured in and I gulped it like water. Night had fallen and stars speckled the sky over Resik's shoulder.

"You move even a little bit," he said, hovering over me with a knife, "and I'll slam this lid down hard as I can."

"I won't."

He dropped a water flask onto my lap.

"Thank you." Sweat dripped into my eyes, but I didn't wipe it away or go for the flask yet.

He shrugged. "Be a waste of money if you died on us."

"Are you really this heartless?"

He seemed taken aback at that, his expression shocked, then guilty, then angry. "It's business. Nothing personal."

"Trade places with me and see if you still think so."

"You'd do the same thing."

"No, I wouldn't."

"Yeah, you say that now, but try turning it down when it's offered. Not so easy."

I smiled, which seemed to unsettle him. "I've turned down more wealth than you'll see in your entire life."

"Then you're an idiot." He slammed the lid shut and relocked it.

I sighed, sucking down the water and treasuring the last of the fresh air before it grew stale again. Maybe I *had* been an idiot. Where would I be now if I'd really accepted Zertanik's offer, emptied the League's pynvium Slab, and helped him and the Luminary sell it? Would I be standing in Verlatta, showing them empty healing bricks of ill-gotten pynvium and demanding a fortune for them? Or living without worry in my own villa with Tali and Aylin?

Most likely I'd be dead or sharing a prison cell with both men. I had a feeling either was better than what the Duke had planned for me.

SIX

The trunk opened again, maybe two days later, but I wasn't sure. The sky was gray tinged in red this time. Sunset.

"What's wrong with him?" Resik asked, looking both mad and scared.

"Wha?" I squeaked, my mouth too dry to talk.

"Uncle won't wake up. I know you did this, so heal him."

I said nothing.

"Tell me or you won't get any more water."

"Yo—won—" I coughed and my lips cracked.

Resik ran a hand through his hair and looked around. He yanked a much bigger water flask out of his pocket and dropped it on me. "Drink, then tell me."

I sucked down the water, warm but good. My head stopped pounding, but the rest of me still hurt. I handed Resik the flask. "You won't get paid if I die."

He groaned in frustration and walked away, leaving the lid open. I reveled in the cool, fresh air. Much too soon he was back.

"Heal him and I'll let you out of the trunk. We'll keep you inside the carriage with us."

"If I heal him, it'll kill me instead and you won't get any money."

He swore. "You're lying."

"You need pynvium to heal and you don't have any." Not that it would do me any good if he did, but he didn't know that. "You can have five thousand oppas or your uncle's life. Your choice."

He banged his fist on the trunk and walked away again, muttering. Then he was back once more.

"You can shift it into someone else though, right? That's why the Duke wants you so badly?" He glanced away and brushed a hand across his upper lip. "Someone like—"

Fieso yanked him away from the trunk. "What are you doing?"

"Nothing! Just giving her some water."

"Stay away from her."

"I will."

"I mean it."

"I heard you the first time." Resik reached over and shut the lid, but not before I caught the hateful look he shot at Fieso.

The lid opened again and pale sunlight poured in. The air tasted damp and clean. The sword pointed at my face shone bright.

"You're going to get up, get out of the trunk, and heal my uncle." Resik kept his gaze on me, but it jerked, like he really wanted to look somewhere else.

"Where's Fieso?"

"Don't worry about him, just do what I said."

I sat up, muscles burning and tingling as blood rushed into them. My head spun and I gulped in air until it steadied.

"Hurry up!"

"I've been folded in a trunk for days," I said, gripping the side with my bound hands. "Moving isn't easy."

Standing would be even less so, though that worked to my advantage. I wouldn't have to fake tumbling out of the trunk. I hauled myself to my feet and pitched over the side, the trunk toppling after me. I landed hard at Resik's feet.

His *bare* feet.

I guess that's how he'd sneaked away from Fieso.

I seized his ankle with both hands and *pushed*, sending all my aches and pains into him. He cried out and dropped on the trunk, cracking the side and breaking it into pieces. His legs no longer worked, and he ripped the lid off its hinge while struggling to get up.

My legs suddenly worked just fine again. I couldn't shift hunger or thirst, so things were still a little swirly, but the pain was gone.

I grabbed the sword and braced it between my knees, blade edge up, and sawed away at my bonds.

"It hurts," Resik moaned, curled into a ball.

I didn't look at him, but it didn't stop the guilt. He wanted to kill me, same as his uncle. Why should I care if either died?

I shoved the prickly thought away as the ropes snapped free. We were stopped on the side of the road, with nothing but rolling fields as far as I could see. No canals to dive into, no alleys to cut through, not even a tree to hide behind.

"Resik?" said Fieso.

I jumped. Faint smoke curled up into the sky on

74

the other side of the carriage. A campfire. If they were camped, the carriage and driver's bench were probably empty.

"You'd better not be messing with that girl again."

I rose, sword out, and circled around the carriage. I glanced toward the driver's bench and frowned. It was empty, but the horses grazed fifteen feet away, tethered to a post in the ground. So much for stealing the carriage. How hard were horses to ride? Maybe I could steal one of them. I didn't see a bridle, though, just loose ropes around their necks.

"Resik? Answer me."

Fieso was closer now, and the only thing between me and freedom. My hands shook and the sword tip wavered. I'd get only one chance to catch him by surprise. I kept all Danello's fencing lessons firmly in my mind. Thrust, parry, lunge.

"Are you—ah, hell." Metal scraped—a sword sliding out of a scabbard. "Where'd she go?"

Resik moaned and mumbled something I couldn't catch.

I gripped the sword tighter and readied myself to lunge.

Fieso's shadow appeared first, bending around the edge of the carriage, then—

Crack!

Sharp pain flared behind my knee and I toppled forward, dropping the sword. It fell point first into the grass and wobbled.

"Good hit," Fieso said, yanking the sword out of the ground.

I rolled over. Another man stood behind me, a three-foot reed rod casually resting on his shoulder. The carriage driver?

"Tie her back up," Fieso said.

"Me? I'm not touching her."

"We can't leave her loose."

"Force her into the trunk again."

"Can't. Resik broke it, the idiot."

"Fine." The driver stomped off and rooted around in the carriage. He came out with a coiled length of rope. "If she does that shifty thing, I'm gonna make sure you feel it worse."

Fieso stepped closer and put the blade against my throat. "You won't do anything, will you?"

"No." I lay motionless while the driver retied my hands.

"We'll be in Baseer in a few hours. I'll put her in the carriage and keep an eye on her 'til then."

The driver shook himself as if the very idea gave him shiverfeet, but he opened the carriage anyway.

Uncle was slumped inside, his face pale and sweaty. Fieso climbed into the carriage and shoved Uncle out. He moaned as he tumbled to the grass. Ashen skin, sunken eyes. I'd guess he didn't have much longer.

"You should take him to a Healer."

"Why? More reward for us." Fieso turned to the driver again. "Get those horses. I'll watch our girl."

The driver frowned but did as ordered. Resik was probably still lying in the grass behind the carriage. For a heartbeat I wondered if anyone would stop and pick them up.

Fieso waved the sword at me and swung it toward the open carriage door. I climbed inside and sat. Fieso came in after, the sword never wavering.

"Now then," Fieso said, leaning against the padded seat. "Let's discuss the rules. You speak, I'll kill you. You try to escape, I'll kill you. You move at all, I'll kill you. You do what I say, or I'll kill you. Nod if you got it."

I nodded.

"Good. Rules start now."

I followed the rules all the way to Baseer. The landscape outside the window never changed, just green fields and farms stretching forever. I couldn't even imagine how many people all those fields must feed.

The afternoon sun hovered over us by the time we reached the city walls. Golden stone disappeared into the distance, higher than most buildings in Geveg, maybe thirty or forty feet. Every few hundred yards, a tower loomed.

On the right, between the city and the river, was some kind of military fort. Rectangular, with a wide ditch around it. Barracks in neat rows. Armed soldiers posted around fortified walls, and towers at all four corners.

Was that the Duke's army?

The carriage slowed at the gates, tall, with wide iron bars thick as my wrist. I saw at least five soldiers, but there were probably more.

One soldier walked up to the carriage door. She opened it, her hand on her sword. "Your business?"

"Delivering a prisoner for bounty."

She looked at me and nodded. "Bring her out."

Fieso slid down the seat and tugged on my rope. "Out."

I got out, graceful as a frog.

"This way." The soldier led us over to the guard station. Boards with reward posters nailed to them hung behind it. Faces of all kinds stared out at me, including my own.

"That's her there," Fieso said, pointing.

The soldier paused, then pulled the poster down. "Bring her to holding while I send someone for the magistrate." She called over another soldier. They spoke briefly, casting glances at Fieso; then the second soldier waved us on.

"Follow me."

"What about my carriage?" Fieso said.

"Tell your driver to ride on through. He'll see the tether posts on the left."

We stepped through the giant gate and into Baseer. My throat tightened, as if the air itself were poison.

Baseer. I'm in Baseer.

A square cage sat in the middle of a fenced pen. The soldier opened it and motioned me inside. I walked past her and plopped to the cool stone floor. Some welcome. Maybe it was a warning to all who came through the gates—obey the rules or pay the price.

"How long 'til I get my money?" Fieso asked. *My* money, not *our* money. Shame the driver didn't hear that. I bet he'd be joining Resik and Uncle along the side of the road before nightfall.

"I don't make the magistrate's schedule," the soldier said. She pointed to a bench not far from the cage. "Wait there."

Fieso sat, and not long after, the driver took a

place beside him. People, carts, and carriages walked and rolled past us, but not many looked my way. I guess with so many faces on the reward posters, prisoners in the cage weren't unusual.

I sat quietly, my head hanging down as if I were too scared or weak to do anything else. Wasn't far from the truth, but I could move my wrists a little. With luck, maybe I could slide a hand free. No clue what I'd do after that, but every mile walked started with a step.

"What's taking them so long?" Fieso said after an hour. He jumped to his feet. "How hard is it to count out some coins and put them in a chest?"

I guess he'd never tried to count to five thousand before.

The driver didn't seem as concerned. "They gotta find guards to leave with all that money. Baseeri thieves'll just rob it if they get the chance."

That was a surprise. With their dark hair, I'd assumed they *were* Baseeri.

"Hey," Fieso called to the gate soldiers. The same woman as before looked up. "When's he getting here?"

She shrugged.

"I hate these people."

The sun was halfway to the horizon when a carriage rolled up.

"About time," Fieso muttered. The driver yawned and stayed on the bench.

The carriage door opened and an armored man stepped out. Not the usual silver chain armor the soldiers in Geveg wore though. This was dark and looked heavier. Next, a woman appeared.

Vyand.

"You got my money?" Fieso called, his hands on his hips.

"Your money?" she said, a cat's grin on her face. A second man in armor left the carriage. The two men on the driver's bench climbed down as well. The woman soldier from the gate walked over, followed by the man she'd spoken to earlier.

I had a feeling nobody in that carriage worked for the magistrate, and my guts said the two soldiers at the gate were working for Vyand. Bribes paid better than bureaucrats.

Fieso dropped his arms and tensed. The driver must have realized something was up, because he got off the bench. Vyand strolled toward them, her armored bodyguards in her wake.

"I have *their* money." She pulled a pouch off her belt and tossed it to the woman soldier. She caught it in one hand and nodded once. "My thanks again."

"Always a pleasure."

Fieso's hands clenched. "You trying to cheat me?"

"You stole *my* property and accuse *me* of cheating *you*?" Vyand tsked. "I'll take my Shifter now."

"I want my money first."

"Sorry, it's my money."

Fieso dived at her, a knife suddenly in his hand. He sank it up to the hilt in her side and she cried out, fingers pressed against her stomach. Blood seeped through the cloth.

The driver drew his sword as Vyand's men drew theirs. All except . . .

One of the armored men dropped to a knee, placing one hand over Vyand's wound and the other on her forehead. His eyes narrowed, his cheek twitched, then the color returned to her cheeks. He pressed his bloody hand against his armor.

His *blue* armor. *Pynvium* blue.

SEVEN

Saints and sinners, a healer-soldier in pynvium armor! This is what the Duke was doing with his Healers? Training them to kill?

It was awful. It was . . . I shuddered. Terrifying. How could you kill soldiers who could heal their own wounds and push the injuries into their armor? They'd be unstoppable.

Fieso and the driver were clearly the better fighters, but it didn't seem to matter. Fieso's knife slipped between the armor plates, drew blood, and had to have pierced organs, but the healer-soldiers just pushed the pain into the pynvium and kept fighting. They neither dodged nor danced, weren't light on their feet like Fieso. They didn't have to be.

The other men helped Vyand to her feet. She was pale but steady. All three stood back and watched the healer-soldiers, as did a few of the gate soldiers. Why were they fighting for Vyand? She couldn't have hired them. The Duke would never give weapons like that to anyone. Was he *helping* Vyand? But why? Wasn't paying her enough?

The driver screamed and went down. The healer-soldier ran him through, then smiled like he'd enjoyed doing it.

No one could stand against the Duke with an army like this. No one.

I wiggled my wrists harder, faster, trying to get out of there before the healer-soldiers killed Fieso. Skin ripped, but the ropes stayed tight. I ground them against the stone floor, the edge of my sandal, anything that even looked like it might cut.

Fieso put up a good fight, but he wasn't going to win. He tried to run, but the soldiers caught him and shoved him down. Vyand smiled, looking impressed, and whispered to the man next to her. He made notes in a small book I hadn't seen before.

I gasped. Was this a test? Was the Duke letting Vyand borrow the soldiers to see how they'd do in a real fight? What kind of power did she have?

The healer-soldiers advanced and finished Fieso

off. He didn't scream, just grunted in pain and collapsed. Vyand nodded, seemingly very pleased with the soldiers' performance.

This was worse than the rows of pain-stuffed Takers in the Healers' League. Worse than the riots, the fighting, even the random beatings. If the Duke turned those soldiers loose on Geveg, we wouldn't survive. It wouldn't be like Sorille. We would die not in fire but by the hands of those who should have been keeping us alive.

Vyand snapped her fingers and her men dragged the bodies away, behind the carriages where I couldn't see. She walked over to me, plucking at her bloody uniform.

"Look at this. Ruined. Blood never comes out." Not as flippant as she probably intended, and I caught the strain in her voice. Getting stabbed like that took time to get over, even if you were healed right away.

"Guess you'll have to burn it."

"You're probably right." She frowned and wiped her fingers on her pants. "Now then, do we just pick up where we left off?"

"Where's my sister?"

"Thinking over the most important decision of her life. A waste of time if she's anything like you."

"Where is she?"

"Do you really expect me to tell you?" She sighed. "I thought you were smarter than that."

"Well, what about my friends? Did you capture them? Can you tell me that?"

She patted her glossy hair into place. "I really have no idea who you're friends with. If they were part of that sloppy rescue attempt, then yes, I did."

"Are they here?"

"Enough questions. Come now, out." Vyand waved at the gate soldier, who unlocked the cage. The healer-soldiers followed, keeping their hard gazes on me as if they'd welcome another fight. Saea willing, they'd be like every other Baseeri soldier I'd ever met and they'd want to intimidate me, shove me around a bit, get their pretty blue armor close enough to touch.

How much pain did it hold now? Fieso had fought hard, landed a lot of hits. The bigger one had Vyand's stomach wound as well, and those hurt something awful. I rose to my feet, swaying as the ground tipped under me. I banged into the bars but stayed upright.

"I see dinner is in order," Vyand mused. "Did they feed you at all?"

"No. They locked me in a trunk." I made a show

of taking deep breaths, gauging the distance between me and the big healer-soldier. I could probably get both him and Vyand, maybe even her drivers and one gate soldier.

Vyand huffed. "Amateurs."

I took a hesitant step, then let my knees buckle. I stumbled forward, hands outstretched as if to catch my fall. They slapped against the pynvium armor. I pictured dandelions blowing in the wind.

Whoomp!

Pain flashed. Men screamed. Vyand screeched in pain and frustration as the men around her collapsed. She fell a breath later. I ran into the crowd, legs shaking but keeping me up for now. They wouldn't for much longer, so I needed a place to hide—fast.

I didn't hear the gate soldiers coming after me yet, but they would. So would Vyand as soon as the pain faded and she could move again.

I had no idea where to go. The street was narrow, with vendor carts shoved up against tall buildings made of the same golden stone as the wall. Bright tiles of every color and pattern were pressed into the stone, making it impossible to tell where one building ended and another began. Windowsills and shutters were painted in equally bright colors, no two in a row the same hue, painful to even look at. I tugged on one, hoping to slip inside, but it was just decorative, not a real window at all. Only wood nailed to the wall.

I kept moving deeper into the noise and mess. The buildings were five—no, six—stories tall. The top floors had short balconies, but the lower floors didn't—not that I had the strength to climb onto one anyway. I saw no alleys. Buildings butted up against each other and the street seemed to go on for miles.

It felt like the entire city was crashing down on top of me.

Quick gasps and sudden movement ran through the crowd behind me—the familiar warning that soldiers were on the way.

A boy dashed by, running into the thick crowd. Three other boys chased him. They vanished in a heartbeat, swallowed by the mob.

Street kids. They always knew where to hide.

I followed them, weaving between women intricately wrapped in patterned cloth and men with beaded vests and no shirts. Past children with braided bands tied around their heads. One man had a snake thick as my leg draped across his shoulders. People shoved me and I shoved back. No one said excuse me, but they didn't yell either. Not one seemed to care about the ropes around my wrists.

The street boys darted between garish vendor stalls, ducking under piles of rugs woven in dizzying patterns. I pushed a rug aside and crawled through.

It was some kind of hidey-hole, maybe an abandoned stall. Dark and scented with cinnamon, the tiny space butted up against a building and probably wasn't even noticeable from the outside. I spotted another child-size hole in the wall a few feet ahead. The sound of faint footsteps and laughter floated out. My fear urged me to crawl into the tunnel, but who knew what I'd find on the other side.

Shouts and cries came from the street. Heavy boots on stone. Orders yelled.

"I don't care—find her now!" Vyand said, sounding angry as a wasp. "Bribe the guards to seal the gates. Hire more men and sweep every street in the quarter—just get her back."

I pressed against the wall, then turned and ran my fingers along the broken bricks around the tunnel. Not as good as a knife, but better than nothing. I rubbed the ropes up and down along the edges, sawing through the fibers until my arms ached. I was halfway through the first loop when scuffling echoed in the tunnel. I froze for a moment, then scooted away from the hole. No room to hide in the small area, but if I was quiet enough, and the boy was in enough of a hurry, maybe he'd race right by.

The scuffling grew closer and I reconsidered my plan. He couldn't miss me. A blind cat would see me huddled here. I grabbed a chunk of brick and raised my hands.

A dark head popped out. "Ahh!" He flinched away.

"I'm sorry." I dropped the brick. "I won't hurt you."

He didn't move, just lay there with one hand blocking his face, gasping.

"I needed a place to hide. I'll go soon, promise."

The hand dropped. "You scared me."

"I'm sorry. You scared me too."

"Really?" He grinned. "Nobody's got scared of me before."

"Well, you got me good."

He nodded, looking quite pleased with himself. He wasn't the street boy I'd followed—much younger, maybe eight or nine. "Who tied you?"

I hesitated. "Soldiers."

"They do that. Was you stealing?"

"No, I'm the one who was stolen."

He laughed. "Never met somebody that got stolen before. Need those cut?" A knife appeared and glinted in the shadows.

I held out my hands. "Yes, thank you."

"You talk funny," he said as he cut through the ropes.

"So do you."

He giggled at that too. The ropes fell away.

"Thank—"

"Shhh!" He thumped a finger against my lips and leaned toward the rugs, his head cocked. Steady footsteps echoed. Wood cracked and a man swore, then started yelling.

"You can't paw through my wares!"

"We can search whatever we want. Stand back."

"Put that down!"

Metal scraped against metal. "We can always add another to tomorrow's hangings."

Silence, then the ransacking noises began again.

"It's the Undying," the boy whispered.

"The soldiers in pynvium armor?"

He nodded. "Come thisaway." He headed into the tunnel, quiet as fog. I followed.

Blackness swallowed us a few feet down, and only the boy's breathing let me know he was in front of me. After a while light shimmered ahead, and the tunnel finally opened into a storeroom of some kind, one that was old and forgotten, with mildew growing on the walls.

91

"Better we go out here," he said, pulling a key from around his neck and unlocking a door in the far side. "Extra better for you."

"Where does this lead?"

"Fountain Plaza. It's past the Eket Street gates, so the hunt won't find you." He cracked the door and peeked out. "Go now, fast, before night comes."

"I don't have anywhere to go."

He frowned and shook his head. "Can't stay with us—Iesta won't like it. Moraat Street has the most unlocked windows. Crews are gone come dark."

I stepped out into the sunset. "Which way?"

"Down there. Third block to the right." He pointed at a wide street lined with warehouses. The cross street looked the same as the one we'd just left. Vendor carts, too many people, and no clear places to hide.

"Thank you."

"Saints hold and keep you." He locked the door and ran off, vanishing into the crowd within a few strides. I was afraid to move.

I'd never seen so many people in my life! It was as if all of Baseer were on this one street. And it wasn't just people. Baskets of chickens, guinea fowl, and marsh ducks clucked, chirped, and squawked alongside crates of animals. Cages of bright birds hung above boxes of colorful lizards. Women walked with dogs on leashes, cats in beaded bags, and even monkeys on their shoulders.

I couldn't see any patrols, but Saints knew how they'd squeeze between all these people anyway. Maybe they were all on the other side of the gate the boy was talking about. He couldn't have meant the main gate, but hadn't Vyand said something about quarters? Maybe the city was sectioned off by gates like the canals broke up Geveg.

My stomach fluttered, and not just from hunger. If there were gates, then soldiers probably checked who came through them. I could be trapped here.

Trapped in Baseer.

I hugged myself, chilled despite the heat. A few people glanced my way, and the longer I stood there, the more turned to stare. I stepped into the crowd. I guess here people noticed you only when you *weren't* moving.

A tall man with pictures drawn on his arms elbowed me as he passed. I ducked away, bumping into a woman with a basket balanced on her shoulder. The lid popped open and some pears dropped out. I caught them and hid them behind my back, but she didn't turn around.

I wove through the crowd to a bright red building

and sat behind some boxes. I ate, the pear crisp and sweet in my mouth. A brown and gold cat watched me from under a cart, his striped tail flicking. He was the only one who seemed interested in me. I bit off a bit and tossed it to him. He sniffed it, grabbed it in his teeth, and slipped back under the cart.

I felt instantly better after eating, though not well enough for any more escapes. I needed more food, something to drink, and a place to sleep until my strength returned. I'd try the warehouses soon as it got dark. The fountain offered water, but food I'd have to steal.

Plenty of vendors around, and none were paying much attention to their wares. All were focused on calling customers over. I crossed the street, lingering beside a smoked-meat vendor who promised his rabbit would make you younger. When he turned around to hand an old woman a basket of food, I snatched a handful of meat strips and scurried into the crowd. I did it again at the bread vendor's, plucking three small rolls off the end of his cart.

No Gevegian vendor would be so careless.

I chewed as I walked, delighted to find the bread stuffed with a cheese-and-fruit filling. Three blocks down I reached the fountain that gave the plaza its name. A stone bench circled the fountain, but the plaza was quiet. A few people were sitting on the street side, so I took a seat opposite, my legs and feet grateful for the rest.

I scooped my hand through the water and gulped it down. Bleh. At least it was wet. I drank my fill and ate the rest of my bread. The meat strips I saved for breakfast. My knees still shook, but I wouldn't fall over if I had to run.

Shadows cut across the street as the last of the sun faded. People hurried off, packages clutched to their chests. I scanned for soldiers and saw nothing but a lamplighter starting his rounds. He was the only one not rushing, and by the time night fell, soft orange glows lit the street like a string of pearls. Finally I was alone.

I didn't like it. I'd gotten used to having Tali and Aylin with me, and a town house full of others. Used to walks with Danello along the canals. I lifted my chin and stared at the empty streets and tall buildings that lined them. Tali was out there somewhere, and so were Aylin and Danello. Someone had to know where the Duke hid his Takers—and where the trackers took their prisoners.

Wait, the boy might know. If I could find my way back to the storeroom door, I could wait for him. If he didn't know, his street pack might. I'd known packs like that in Geveg. Tali and I had joined one briefly when I was ten, right after Baseeri soldiers had thrown us out of our home.

I left the fountain, my footsteps loud on the stone street. It was so quiet. No waves, no lake birds, no music from the show house. It was just . . . creepy. Every step echoed as if someone were walking next to me.

I bent and slipped off my sandals. I heard more echoey footsteps coming up behind me.

My heart raced. There was nowhere to go. Nothing but buildings and walls and fake shutters that should have been windows. The closest bushes were too low and thin to hide behind. I dashed to the fountain and scooted under the stone bench on the far side.

Someone was running my way, breathing fast. Maybe more than one. The echoes made it impossible to tell how many. Hard steps hit the ground close to me, then a splash and whooping laughter.

"You shouldn't have run, girl!"

EIGHT

All my instincts said move, run, shift, *anything*, but the warning wasn't for me. I heard a smack as flesh hit flesh and a girl cried out, then a breathless thud. Laughter followed.

"You know it's worse when you run," a boy said. Probably a street pack, and he sounded like the leader. "You could have just handed over your bag, but now we'll have to hurt you."

A grunt, a thump, and a whimper.

Stay still. Don't move.

I put my hands over my ears, but I'd suffered too many beatings not to recognize the sounds now. The girl cried, sharp sobs from fear and pain. I inched along the ground under the bench until I could see.

Three of them, two boys, one girl. All looked about sixteen. Another girl the same age was lying on the street, a bag next to her.

The pack leader bent toward the bag.

"Don't, please. I need those," the girl said, reaching for it.

"We need them more." He kicked her and she curled into a ball.

"They won't do you any good!"

"Everything sells to somebody." He stomped on her leg. She screamed as something snapped. "Maybe even you."

I rolled out from under the bench and got to my feet. They had their backs to me, kicking the sobbing girl. Killing her.

She's Baseeri. She wouldn't help you.

Probably not, but wrong was the same in any city.

I got to the first one before he even knew I was there. Kicked him behind the knee. He went down, clutching his leg and yelling. I barely heard him with so many other voices yelling in my head.

Tali: *Help the girl and run.*

Aylin: *Stay out of it and hide.*

Danello: *Roll and flank them from behind.*

I dived and rolled, knocking the attacker girl's legs out from under her. She hit the stone, hard, and screamed.

The leader was already moving as I sprang to my feet. He moved into a fighter's stance and eyed me carefully. "Brought friends, eh?"

"Leave her alone."

"Or what? You'll push me over and bruise me?"

"I'll kill you." I smiled same as I'd smiled at Resik. I hoped it was just as unnerving. "Only you won't die for days."

He laughed. "Don't see no weapon on you."

"Maybe I *am* a weapon."

The other boy was on his feet again, helping his girlfriend. She pressed a hand to her back and tears rolled down her face. The pack leader didn't even glance their way.

"I think you're lying," he said.

I shrugged. "It's your life."

"Iesta, wait." The other boy put a hand on his arm.

Iesta? This was the same pack the nice boy who'd saved me belonged to? So much for hoping they could help me find Tali and the others.

"What if she's one of *them*?"

Iesta hesitated, then laughed again, but it didn't sound as cocky as before. "She's got no armor. Can't hurt us."

I edged closer to the whimpering girl on the street. She wore sandals, the tops of her feet bare and within reach. I hoped Iesta was worried enough to leave us alone, but he didn't look like the type to leave a fight. He did, however, look like the type who got angry easily. And angry people made mistakes.

"Scared of a little girl, Iesta?" If I couldn't get Iesta to run, I'd have to hurt him. No, not hurt. Kill. No street pack I ever knew could get healing—not even the leader. *Please run.*

He stopped pacing and glared. The other boy shook his head.

"See? See? She *wants* you to fight. No girl's got guts enough for that."

Iesta harrumphed. "Or she wants me to think that."

He charged. I grabbed him by the arm, twisting like Danello had showed me, and threw him to the street. Surprise washed over his face as his breath whooshed out.

Got you.

He jumped up and lunged for me again. I missed my grab and he tackled me, knocking us both down and pining me under his knees.

"Just a tough talker after all," he said, flipping open a knife. He thrust it toward me. I grabbed his wrist, stopped it, and reached out my other hand toward the girl's foot. Skin touched skin and my leg burned as I *drew* her pain away, her leg broken just as I'd thought. Plus she had cracked ribs and deep bruises. Iesta hollered when I *pushed* all that into him.

"Help me!" Iesta dragged himself away, his eyes wide, his face white as mist. The other boy darted back and forth as if scared to come near me.

"What if she—"

"Get me out of here!"

The boy grabbed him under the arms and hauled him down the street until the leader started screaming and pounding on his arm. He got him to his feet and slipped an arm around his waist. They limped away in the same direction the girl had gone. Probably the storeroom I'd been in earlier.

He'd probably die there. My stomach flipped, but I took a deep breath to steady it. I'd had no choice. I'd warned him, told him to leave us alone. He would have killed me and the girl if I hadn't shifted. *Did that make it right?*

I shoved my guilt away. "Are you okay?"

She didn't answer, her face just as scared as Iesta's. She backed away, scraping her feet against the stone.

"I'm not going to hurt you," I said, my hands out. She stared at them and sucked in a breath. I hid them behind me. "I'm trying to help you."

"I . . . they . . ." She licked her lips, and her gaze darted to the bag and the things scattered across the street.

Blue Baseeri uniforms.

This time *I* backed away. She was military. She was with the Duke. Saints, I'd helped one of the people trying to kill *me*.

I stopped, staring at her like she stared at me, each of us terrified of the other. She couldn't be a soldier—she was far too scared. She was also afraid of the uniforms, even though they were clearly hers.

"I'm not one of the Undying," I said softly.

"You're like them though."

"Only a little. I can heal."

"You can do more than that." She glanced into the shadows where Iesta had gone. "I'm glad, but, well. Yeah." She laughed nervously and tried unsuccessfully to stand. Maybe she'd never been healed before. I'd seen folks disoriented from it the first time.

Her fear returned. "What did you do to me?"

"Nothing. I just healed you. You were badly hurt, so give your body time to get over the shock. You'll be fine in a minute."

She rubbed her leg. "Promise?"

"Promise."

She calmed a little, enough to start stuffing uniforms into her bag. I picked one up and handed it to her.

"Thanks," she said, voice trembling. "And thanks for helping me and healing me. I know better than to be out past dark, but I had to—" She glanced down at the uniforms, then shook her head.

"It's okay. I don't think they'll be back tonight." I walked over to the bushes where more uniforms had fallen. I picked them up and paused, glancing at the girl. I slipped a uniform under the branches and brought the rest to her. "I think this is the last of them."

She tucked them away in her bag. "You shouldn't be out here either, even if you are—" She stopped.

"Dangerous?"

She hesitated, then grinned. "How about 'different'? It's past curfew and it's not safe."

"I noticed." I helped her to her feet, and she stayed on them this time. "I don't have much choice though," I said. "I'm trying to find my friends. A tracker caught them."

She gasped and covered her mouth with her hand. "Don't try to find them. They're gone."

"I can't do that."

"But . . ." She took a breath and stared at the stars for a moment, then sniffled and looked back. "No one gets away from trackers."

"I did."

She didn't say anything at first, but I could tell she was impressed. She slung the bag across her shoulder. "Maybe you could get them out, then. But I wouldn't try if I were you. *Especially* if I were you."

She had a point. It didn't matter though.

"I still have to try," I said. "Do you know where the prisoners are kept?"

"There's a jail on Keldert Street, but if they've been processed, they won't be there anymore."

"Where would they be then?"

"He'd have them." She looked behind me and pointed to a building I hadn't noticed before, settled on a hill in the distance. Tall, solid, with spires and fences and walls.

The Duke's Palace. Getting in there wouldn't be so easy, but the jail I could do.

"I have to go," she said. "Thank you again, and good luck, though I really do think you should find a place to hide and forget about your friends."

Never. "Which way is Keldert Street?"

"That way. Five blocks down, turn right at the

104

plaza with the Duke's statue. Follow that street until you see the Broken Nose Taproom on your right. That's Keldert. Then it's just a few blocks to the jail."

"Thank you. Any gates in the way?"

"No. North Quarter gate is past the jail. I really have to go." She grinned an apology and fled, vanishing into the night.

I walked over to the bushes and picked up the uniform. Getting inside the jail was not going to be a problem at all.

I made one wrong turn and had to retrace a few steps, but I found the jail without too much wandering. Unlike the buildings in the rest of the city, this one sat alone in a square of trampled grass, a flat brick building that looked a lot like the ovens the potters used to harden their clay. Tether posts stuck out of the ground on one side, but there were no horses or carriages tied up.

Extra lamps lined the front along the street, and light brightened the barred windows next to the door. I spotted thin windows along the wall near the roof, but nothing I could fit through even if I managed to climb that high. No other windows but the ones by the door.

The thing that churned my guts though was the platform behind the building. Four gallows stood empty, the hangman's nooses swinging gently in the breeze. *We can always add one more to tomorrow's hangings.* I guess that's what happened to the Duke's prisoners who weren't Takers.

I had to get Aylin and Danello out of there.

I slipped into the shadows half a block down and pulled on the uniform. It floated on me, the sleeves too long, the pants bunching up on the tops of my feet. I rolled up the waist so it rested better on my hips, but I still looked like I was playing dress-up in Mama's old clothes.

I crept along the buildings, staying low and in the shadows. If I could get a peek inside, maybe I could tell if the guards were regular soldiers or Undying. As long as there weren't any trackers inside to sense me, like Vyand had on the docks. If so, it wouldn't matter what I was wearing.

I paused at the last corner before the open yard. Forty feet of space stretched between me and the jail. After that, maybe inches between me and any guards looking out or posted by the windows.

And if they saw me? I studied the dimly lit streets. Two led in opposite directions, one toward where the gates probably were, so that wasn't an escape route.

The other led toward the fountain. There had been a few walled courtyards to climb into, and some trees worth climbing. Maybe I should have put some of the streetlamps out, just in case.

Just save them already.

Now or never. Danello and Aylin were depending on me. I dashed across the yard and flattened myself against the warm brick. No one raced out of the jail, or any other building. Maybe this wouldn't be so hard. If I stayed low enough, I'd be in the shadows cast by the windowsill. You wouldn't even be *able* to see me from inside.

I slid down the brick and started sneaking toward the window. Just a few more feet and—

Arms grabbed me from behind, and a gloved hand clamped down over my mouth.

So much for easy.

NINE

I wiggled and kicked, trying to hit a shin or a knee. My fingers dug into an arm, but it was covered in thick leather, just like the glove against my mouth. I kept fighting anyway, all along the side of the jail and even when they dragged me around the corner toward the gallows.

My feet touched brick. I shoved as hard as I could, smashing into the person holding me and knocking us both backward. We toppled over and the arms came loose. The moment I hit the ground I was rolling, away and up and—

I knew that face. I stopped running, but my heart didn't stop pounding.

"Jeatar?"

I hadn't seen him since he'd left Geveg, days after he'd carried me from the shattered League and hidden me in Zertanik's town house. He'd said he was going to continue working against the Duke, but I hadn't realized he'd gone to Baseer.

He sat up and hung his arms over his knees. "It *is* you."

"What? How?" I took a deep breath to settle my mind and self. My instinct was still to run, to hide, but seeing Jeatar was a good thing. It meant I was no longer alone.

"Neeme told us what happened with the street pack," he began as he got to his feet. "When she said a girl healed her and shifted pain, I knew it had to be you. Then we found one of the uniforms missing, and Neeme said you'd asked about this jail, and well, I know only one Shifter dumb enough to walk into that kind of trouble. I came as fast as I could to stop you."

What was Jeatar involved in this time? Another secret mission for the Pynvium Consortium? "What are you doing here?"

"I live here, remember?"

"You never told me that."

"Well, I do. Now, tell me what *you're* doing here." He folded arms covered to the elbow in leather blacksmith's gloves. The rest of him was also covered. High collar, long sleeves, with very little exposed skin.

I grinned. "You thought I might shift into you?"

"I knew you'd put up a fight if I didn't have time to warn you I was there. Answer me."

"I'm pretty sure Aylin and Danello are in the jail. They were captured by a tracker while trying to rescue me." I quickly told him about the kidnapping and flashing the Undying's armor. I neglected to mention Resik or Uncle.

"I heard about that this afternoon. We have people who pay attention to what the Undying do." He frowned. "That's when I started worrying you were here."

"So is Tali."

"Was she captured, or did she follow you here?" he asked. I didn't like the look in his eyes.

"Captured. The tracker said she was making some kind of decision."

He closed his eyes a moment, then opened them. "Then we might be able to save her."

"You know where she is?"

"Maybe. Captured Takers are given a few days to make a choice. Train at the camps or *work* for

Vinnot." He frowned, uncertainty wrinkling his face.

My breath caught and my feet were ready to run again. "He's still doing the experiments."

"We think he's doing more than that."

"We have to get her out of there. Where is she being held?"

"Most likely in one of the secure buildings near the main gates. Getting in won't be easy, but if we go right now, we might get her before she's moved. If not, she'll likely be gone in the morning. Breaking her out of the camp will be impossible. We'd have better luck finding her if she chose Vinnot."

I shook my head. "She'd never choose that." Not after what Vinnot had already done to her.

"If they decide she's too young to fight, she won't have a choice."

I didn't want to think about that. "The camp. Is that what I saw on the way in?"

He nodded. "Most of the Duke's army is garrisoned there. City defense is housed at the citadel inside the inner walls near his palace."

I'd never get in there unless I *joined* the army. I looked at the gallows. "What about Aylin and Danello?"

He hesitated. "The prisoners in this jail are

scheduled to hang tomorrow."

"Then we have to rescue them tonight."

"I'm sorry, but it'll be hard enough trying to convince the others to help Tali. They won't do both."

The others again. My head swam with so many questions and fears. I couldn't leave Aylin and Danello here, not if they were going to be executed tomorrow.

"If Tali goes to the camp," I began, the words almost impossible to say, "will she be okay?"

Jeatar looked at me as if I'd just suggested handing her over to the Duke myself. "We can't get her out of the camp. It's *inside* the fort, heavily guarded to keep people in as well as out."

"But she won't be hurt or killed?" My heart broke just saying it.

"You've seen the Undying. You know what they do." He gave me a sad look. "Few want to suffer all that pain or inflict it on others. But the commanders make them. They twist minds and bend wills and create the weapons the Duke wants. How long do you think Tali can last in there?"

I had no idea. She could be stubborn when she set her mind. And she did know how to get what she wanted. She'd try to be brave, but I'd protected her most of her life, and she hadn't faced half of what I had. Saints, was I really thinking about this?

"Nya, if you want to save her, we need to go now."

Saving Tali meant letting Aylin and Danello die. Saving them meant risking Tali's mind. Her Healer's spirit. Five years of Baseeri occupation couldn't break that spirit. Neither could Vinnot. She'd be okay longer than Aylin and Danello would.

"No," I said, hardly believing it myself. "I have to save my friends first. They'll be dead by tomorrow. Tali will still be alive. They need me more right now. I can't walk away and leave them here."

He didn't say anything for a while.

"You can't just throw on a uniform and walk in there either. That uniform is twice as big as you are."

I looked at him. Tall, broad shoulders, twice as big as me. "It'll fit you."

"Absolutely not."

"You can pretend to be a tracker and bring me in. We could walk right in and straight to the cells."

"No."

I pulled off the baggy uniform and straightened my own clothes underneath. "Here, put this on."

"You're not listening to me."

I put my hands on my hips and gave him my

most serious stare. "Jeatar, you know me. What makes you think I'll let you talk me out of this?"

He stared back, his gaze far more serious than mine. I held out the uniform. He stared a second longer, swore, and snatched it from my hand.

"If you get us caught, I'll hand you over to the Duke myself." He pulled the shirt over his head.

"No, you won't."

I didn't catch his mumbled reply through the cloth, but I probably didn't want to anyway.

"It'll be fine," I said. "You drag me in there like you just arrested me. We go into the cells and look for Aylin and Danello."

"You really think it'll be that easy?"

"Yes." It had to be. Any harder than that and we probably didn't stand a chance.

"Uh-huh." He pointed to my wrists. "I arrested you and you aren't even bound?"

Hmmm. "I could hold my hands like this." I made two fists and pressed my wrists together.

He sighed and shook his head.

"Wait." I looked at the ropes hanging from the gallows. "Do you have a knife?"

He pulled one out and handed it to me.

I hurried over, my flesh crawling as I ran up the gallows steps. I tried not to imagine Aylin and

Danello swinging while Baseeri cheered, but the image wouldn't leave my mind. I cut one of the nooses down and ran back. "This will work."

"Yeah, I suppose it will." He didn't sound happy about it though. He looped the rope around my wrists, tying it with a knot that pulled free when he tugged on it. "Are you sure you want to do this?"

"Arrest me already."

He grabbed my upper arm and pulled me toward the jail's entrance. I stumbled along next to him, off balance with my arm yanked up so high. He didn't have to make it *that* realistic.

We entered the jail. Bright lamps lit the room and I squinted, blinking until my eyes adjusted. By then all four guards were on their feet and staring at us. I guess the bright lights weren't because they didn't like the dark.

"One more for the camps. Did I miss the pickup?" Jeatar said as if he said this every week. He paid no attention to the men with hands on their swords, or the dangerous looks they gave us.

I scanned the jail, trying to act like a scared girl looking for an escape. A long counter ran across the front of the room, with a waist-high gate at one end. A cage sat in the middle, enclosing a heavy door that probably went into the cell area. We'd need keys to get through both doors.

"Identify yourself," one guard said. A sergeant, judging by the rank markings on his collar.

"Geheim, East Quarter. Can I just leave her with you? I'm late meeting friends at the alehouse."

I marveled at Jeatar. I'd never be able to lie that smoothly.

The sergeant frowned and the others snorted. "I don't know how they do it in the East Quarter, but here we finish the work we're given. Do it yourself. Yosel, show him back."

"See if I buy *you* a drink later," Jeatar mumbled as Yosel walked over and unlocked the cell door in the cage. I spotted the pynvium rod hanging on his belt as he passed. The other three guards had them as well.

Yosel stepped aside and let us enter. Then he followed us in and locked the cell behind him. I glanced at Jeatar, and though he didn't look back or even twitch, I was pretty sure he knew what I meant. We'd need that key to get out. And Sergeant Do-It-Yourself might notice if we came out without Yosel.

The heavy inner door swung open and we stepped inside the jail proper. Stink and heat rolled out and my nose wrinkled. We walked into a narrow foyer with brick walls on both sides, with another barred gate at the front.

"Cell five is empty," Yosel said, locking the heavy door again. From what I could see, the entire cell area was T-shaped with the entrance in the middle. "It's to the right." He opened the last gate and started down the aisle. Cells lined both sides, maybe seven or eight feet square. Just enough for two narrow cots.

I counted as we walked. Twelve cells long, six on either side of the door. Most were full. My stomach clenched tighter as we neared the end of the right side. Danello and Aylin *were* there! But . . .

"Oh no!"

Jeatar glanced down, but Yosel didn't. Halima was there as well. So were Barnikoff and a dozen more people from Geveg. They stared at me with sad, lost eyes. Vyand must have captured everyone who'd tried to rescue us.

She must also have Danello's brothers. Enzie, Winvik, all of them! What about Soek and the other Takers from the town house? Did anyone escape?

"Cell five." Yosel stuck the key in the lock.

Jeatar pounced, slamming his elbow against the back of Yosel's neck. He crumpled without a sound. People jumped to their feet.

"Shh!" I said quickly, tugging on the rope around

117

my wrists. The knot came free and I shook the rope away. I went to Aylin and Danello's cell. They stuck their hands through the bars and I grabbed them.

"I'm so happy to see you," Danello whispered. Aylin nodded fast in agreement.

"Me too. We're going to get you out of here."

Jeatar unlocked the cells, even for those I didn't know. I'd bet most of these folks probably hadn't done anything anyway.

"Here," Jeatar said, tossing the keys to Danello. "Lock him up."

Danello dragged Yosel into a cell and relocked it. Jeatar already had Yosel's sword and pynvium. He handed the rod to Danello.

"You know how to use this?"

"Yeah, squeeze the end and snap your wrist, right?"

"Right."

"So what's the plan?" Aylin said.

"There are three more guards out there. We'll have to—"

The heavy door opened. "Yosel? Everything okay in there?"

TEN

Everyone but Jeatar froze. He dashed along the cells fast as fright. Danello followed him a few heartbeats later, the pynvium rod clenched in his hand.

"Yosel?"

The guard hadn't left the foyer yet, but soon as he did, he'd spot the open cell doors and the prisoners outside them. If he even got that far. Yosel was still unconscious and wasn't going to answer him, and only a fool would think that wasn't suspicious.

"What?" snapped one of the prisoners I didn't know. I hadn't heard Yosel speak much, but he did a decent enough impression.

"Everything okay? You've been gone awhile." Keys

119

jangled at the inner gate. Jeatar and Danello were flat against the cells just beyond it, waiting to move.

"Yeah, fine."

I waited for him to say more, but he shrugged and shook his head as if he wasn't sure what to say. Great. *Yeah, fine* wouldn't fool even the lazy League guards.

The gate swung open. Jeatar and Danello tensed. No one came through.

This guard was no fool.

I pictured him standing there, pynvium and sword ready to put down anyone who jumped him. Or ready to sound an alarm. Was the wooden door open? Were there more guards waiting?

We weren't ready to take them all on yet.

I started walking, stamping my feet just a little to sound like someone much bigger than I was, like Yosel.

"We're done here," the prisoner called up, then joined me. We didn't sound quite like two soldiers, but I hoped it would be enough to put the guard at ease.

It was.

He stepped out into the aisle, then jerked, startled. The pynvium rod came up fast, but not before Jeatar launched himself at the guard. Jeatar slammed him

120

against the open door and the rod flew out of his hand.

Danello grabbed the fallen rod and darted into the foyer, his own pynvium rod ready. He didn't flash either, so the wooden door must still be closed. The other guards had to have heard the ruckus.

The fallen guard twisted and threw Jeatar off. He rolled sideways and smacked into the bars. The prisoner lunged at the struggling guard and kicked him in the head. Jeatar got to his feet and helped him carry the guard into a cell and lock it.

I joined Danello in the foyer, and he handed me the second pynvium rod. Jeatar and the prisoner stood behind us.

"Now what?" Danello asked, his face shiny with sweat. "They'll see us soon as we open the door."

"And flash us before we can get the key in the lock for sure," the prisoner said.

I looked at Danello, then Jeatar. "Give me the keys," I said, holding out my hand.

Jeatar dropped them into my palm, much to the prisoner's amazement. He opened his mouth just as a bell started ringing.

"The alarm bell," he said. "They're calling in soldiers from the on-duty house next door."

"Danello, get everyone ready to move when I

signal." I stepped up to the door, keys shaking in my hand.

"Standard reinforcement is four men," Jeatar said before he joined Danello and the others.

Six guards, six pynvium rods. I picked up mine and tucked it behind my back, under my shirt. I'd probably get only one chance.

I unlocked the door and stepped out. The six guards were indeed there, but not positioned around the gate like I'd expected. They stood on the other side of the counter.

"There's nowhere to go, girl," the sergeant said. "Put the keys down and step away from the gate."

I stuck the key into the lock.

"Drop it or I'll flash you."

I turned the key and the bolt slid back.

Whoomp.

Needle pricks washed over me, much stronger than the ones the soldiers in Geveg used. I faked a cry and collapsed, tucking my hand under me as I dropped. My fingers wrapped around the hidden pynvium rod.

"Watch the door. Be ready to flash if you see more."

Footsteps came closer, but it sounded like only one guard. I needed more if I had any hope of getting them all in my flash. I groaned a little, twitched a leg, then a foot.

"Careful, she's waking up."

"Already?"

"Must be tougher than she looks. Took out three men already."

"Or she isn't alone. Anyone in there worth busting out?"

I cracked my eyes open. Three were almost in range. A few more steps and—

I jerked up, yanking the pynvium rod out and swinging it around.

Whoomp.

The three guards hissed and went down, their faces clenched in pain. Two others leaped away, their mouths dropping open. The sergeant lunged forward and thrust the sword through the bars and into my chest.

Cold pain burned and my vision blurred. I fell against the bars, my hand outstretched, searching for flesh. I found none and slumped to the floor. The guard stepped closer and shoved the gate open, pushing me across the floor and out of the way.

I hacked a wet cough. Prayed that Danello wasn't about to race into the cage and get himself hurt. Prayed harder that the sergeant would come closer.

"Is she dead?"

The sergeant shook his head. "Not yet."

"How did she do that? She one of those quirkers?"

"That would explain a lot."

Quirkers. I'd heard unusual Takers called worse, but rarely with so much fear behind it.

The sergeant crouched down, resting his forearms on his knees. The sleeves of his uniform slid up and exposed his wrists.

Just a little closer.

I shivered, cold despite the warm blood pooling beneath me. He wasn't coming closer. I wasn't sure if I had the strength to move fast enough to grab him, but he wasn't giving me much choice.

I darted out and grabbed his wrist, but got mostly sleeve. Only one finger pressed against his skin.

Let it be enough.

I *pushed* my chest wound into him, my breath easing as the pain raced up my arm and out. He screamed in shock and pain, grabbing his chest and falling backward. I jumped to my feet as the other two guards cried out.

Whoomp. Whoomp.

Both pynvium rods flashed and my skin prickled. The sergeant whimpered and lost consciousness.

"Now!" I leaped over his body and went for the pynvium rod next to an unconscious guard. Behind me footsteps echoed as the others ran from the cells.

One of the guards bolted for the door. I flicked my wrist and triggered the pynvium, but he must have gotten out of range. He just gasped as he fled out into the night.

"Nya!" Danello cried.

I turned. The last guard was racing toward me, sword out. Danello was already moving, leaping through the air. I rolled left, Danello and the guard smashed into the wall on the right. Three of the prisoners I didn't know raced past and shoved through the door. Three of the Gevegians pounced on the last guard. In seconds they had him subdued.

"Everyone out," I called, climbing to my feet.

We all hurried out the door and turned left, away from the on-duty house and down the quiet street. Jeatar ran past me, sprinting to the lead. He waved his arm and motioned the group down a side street.

More bells started ringing. The night glowed behind us as men with torches poured out of the on-duty house.

Halima stumbled and fell, her small cry echoing in the night. Danello scooped her up and kept running. We turned corners around buildings that all looked the same, cut through plazas with fountains, climbed low walls, and squeezed down what might have been the only alley in Baseer.

"Everyone in here." Jeatar held open a high wooden gate. A fence surrounded a courtyard with stone benches and a small pond. I hurried inside with the rest and dropped onto one of the benches.

"Are they still chasing us?" Barnikoff asked, chest heaving.

"I think we lost them, but let's make sure." Jeatar shut and locked the gate, then put a finger to his lips.

I no longer heard the bells, but I had no idea if they'd stopped ringing them or if we were too far away to hear. I didn't hear anything but the quick and frightened breathing of those around me.

After a few minutes Jeatar opened the gate and peeked out.

"I think we're clear," he said softly. "We don't have far to go, but we need to be very quiet."

Danello took my hand. Halima had his other. Tears sparkled on her cheeks, but she didn't make a sound. Eight years old and already she knew how to avoid Baseeri soldiers. Tali *still* hadn't figured out how to do that.

Tali.

I closed my eyes for a long moment. She was out there somewhere, hoping I'd come get her. *I'm so sorry, Tali.* I'd be there soon, no matter what I had to do.

Jeatar led us down a street lined with villas just visible behind graceful fences twined with honey-suckle. Soft light burned in the windows. The villas were bigger than the ones Tali and I had grown up in, and some of Geveg's aristocrat terraces could probably fit onto the grounds of one of these.

Much to my surprise, Jeatar stopped at one of the gates and pulled a key from his pocket. The gate swung open without a sound.

"Hurry," he whispered, waving us through.

Inside an aristocrat's villa? What wealthy Baseeri did he think would welcome a dozen escaped prisoners into their home?

I looked at Aylin, whose perplexed expression said she was thinking the same thing.

Perfect rows of flowers bordered stepping-stones carved into interlocking animal shapes. Fish, birds, butterflies. I cringed every time someone stumbled off the path and crushed the plants.

We veered right at the front of the villa, bypassing the inset door of Verlattian teak carved in similar fashion as the stepping-stones. The door we stopped at was not so fine. Simple wood, no carvings. Jeatar unlocked this door and pulled it open.

"Stay in the kitchen," he said.

We filed in one by one. Jeatar caught my arm as I reached the door. "Only a few of us spoke to Neeme earlier," he said softly. "I convinced them to keep your shifting a secret for now. I don't know how long that'll last, though."

I stepped aside and let the rest pass. "Where are we?"

"You'll see."

"Jeatar—"

"Five more minutes. Let me explain it all at once."

"So what will they do if they find out about me?"

"I don't know. Some won't care, but others will."

"Quirkers aren't popular around here, are they?"

His eyes widened. "Not since the Duke started using them to round up his enemies. We can trust these people, but if they refuse to let you stay, I'll put you on a boat and get you home safely."

Without Tali? Not a chance.

Jeatar and I were the last inside. He shut and

locked the door, sliding a heavy bolt across. "I have to speak to a few people, and then we'll get you all settled." He smiled, but I caught the worry in it. "Relax in here—help yourselves to whatever you find in the pantry. I'll be right back."

Several people darted for the glossy doors Jeatar had pointed to, jostling each other to get them open first. Barnikoff stepped forward and yanked them away one by one.

"Everyone will get food," he said. He pulled open the cabinet and started handing out fruit and strips of dried meat.

I spotted three jugs on the far counter and pulled the corks out. Fruit juice. I pulled real glasses from another cabinet and started pouring. Aylin served.

"So what do you think this place is?" she asked when she was finished.

I opened my mouth to answer, but my throat caught, so I just threw my arms around her. "I didn't think I'd ever see you again."

She hugged me back. "Me either. We were so scared. The soldiers said they were going to hang us."

"I'd never let that happen."

Danello walked over and I let go of Aylin. "I'm

so sorry I dragged your family into this," I said.

He pulled me close and rested his head on mine. "It's not your fault. I never should have let them come with us when we tried to rescue you and Tali."

"But we're safe here, right?" Aylin said. "Jeatar wouldn't have brought us here if we weren't."

I reluctantly withdrew from Danello's arms. "I think he thinks it is."

"Should I be worried?"

"Until we're out of this horrible city, I think we all should be worried."

"I was afraid of that."

"Were you with Tali when she was captured?"

They nodded. "When we tried to rescue you," Danello said, "Vyand's men came out from everywhere. It was like they were waiting for us. Da's going to come home and we'll all be gone," he said, voice cracking. "He won't even know what happened to us."

I took his hand and squeezed. If only we'd left when his father had. We could have traded instead of sold the things we'd taken from the town house. We'd never have been at the alley market, the rent collector never would have seen me, and we wouldn't have been on those stupid docks.

If wishes were fishes, we'd eat every night.

"Are your brothers with Tali?" I said.

"I think so. Vyand split us up when we got here, but I don't know where she took them."

Jeatar did though. And if getting Tali out was near impossible, getting *all* of them out was probably beyond impossible.

"Okay, this way," Jeatar said, returning with another man. He didn't look happy.

We followed them out of the kitchen and into a sitting room with a stone fireplace along one wall. Bookcases stretched floor to ceiling on either side. Jeatar went to one and pulled a book off the shelf. He reached behind and something snicked. A quick tug and the bookcase swung out, revealing stairs curving down.

Murmurs ran through the group, but I couldn't tell if they were scared or excited ones.

Jeatar started down, but the big man stayed up, his arms folded across his barrel-like chest. A guard, sure as sugar.

I followed Aylin, the air growing cooler as we descended. Smooth-cut steps, a simple wrought-iron railing, short, wide candles in wall sconces every five feet.

I stepped out into a much brighter—and much

bigger—room filled with Baseeri. The girl I'd helped—Neeme—was there, next to a stack of uniforms. She raised a tentative hand and waved.

Jeatar turned to me and spread his arms wide. "Welcome to the Baseeri Underground."

ELEVEN

Underground?

Danello nodded. "Like the Sorillian resistance, right? My ma used to lecture on that, but the University Elders made her stop."

All emotion vanished from Jeatar's face. "Exactly like that. Some of them are even here."

"I thought everyone in Sorille died?" Danello asked.

"Not everyone." Jeatar turned away and walked toward a woman holding practice weapons.

Had Jeatar survived Sorille?

No one survived Sorille, Papa had whispered, unaware I was hiding under the table. *Not even those who lived.*

I'd seen Jeatar's scars the day I flashed the Slab. Burn scars across his chest and shoulders. Some things never fully healed, even when you took the pain away.

We'd seen Sorille burning. Seen the glow from the flames, a sunrise in the darkest night. We'd smelled the smoke for days as it rolled across the marshes like mist on the lake.

"He couldn't have!" Mama cried. "All those people?"

"We should have known." Papa sounded angry and scared. I'd never seen him scared. "He should have warned us, sent word about this."

"Unless he killed him too."

There were knocks at the door then, and people came in who always made Mama and Papa nervous. Mama wanted to send help, but they refused. Said we'd need those supplies ourselves. Had they been Geveg's Underground? Had Jeatar been part of Sorille's, or had their Underground formed after the Duke killed everyone in his city?

Not everyone.

"So they're fighting the Duke too?" Aylin asked, her nervous gaze on the Baseeri staring at us with their cold blue eyes.

"They're *Baseeri*," I said. "Why would they fight

134

the Duke?" But I pictured the boy who'd helped me, how scared he'd been of the Undying. The pack that ran in terror thinking I was one of "them." A quirker. Even the jail guards had been afraid. What had the Duke done to his own people that he hadn't done to us?

"You never should have brought them here," the woman yelled.

"What was I supposed to do?" Jeatar folded his arms across his chest. His scarred chest. If he was from Sorille, why would he care about Baseer?

"Make them someone else's problem." She spoke lower this time, but we were all listening now.

For a moment they glared at each other; then Jeatar left her and knocked on one of the two doors in the back. A third was on the opposite side of the room next to the practice area. He waited a moment before going inside.

The Baseeri woman now glared at us. So did the others. A sea of black hair and scowls. They didn't want us here, but now we knew their secret and they couldn't just let us go.

"I don't like this."

Barnikoff leaned close over my shoulder. His lip was split and bruises darkened his eye and cheek, all caused by Baseeri soldiers. "We've got your back if you want to teach these reed rats a lesson," he said. Others nodded and murmured agreement.

Aylin didn't look as worried as the rest of us. "Nya, I don't think they want to hurt us."

We stared at the Baseeri. They stared at us. Nobody moved, except Neeme, who got up and carried a stack of uniforms to a cabinet and put them inside. She pulled another stack from a different shelf and carried them to the table. She reached into a sewing basket, pulled out needle and thread, and picked up the first uniform on the stack.

Mending them. Had she stolen old uniforms? But they looked new. Maybe she was tailoring them to fit. Having a few of those would make our lives in Geveg easier.

What was taking Jeatar so long?

The door opened and Jeatar stepped out. Another man followed him. He seemed familiar—tall, wide-shouldered, short dark hair. As he got closer, I caught a scent—metal, fire, and smoke.

An enchanter!

"We're going to have guests, so I expect everyone to show them proper hospitality," he said to the scowling Baseeri.

The woman wasn't any happier with him than she was with Jeatar. "But they—"

136

"Will not be here long." He shot her a look.

"You can stay," Jeatar told us. "We have rooms in the rear, but it'll be crowded. In the morning we'll see what we can do about getting you home, or finding transportation elsewhere if you prefer."

"Told you they weren't planning to hurt us," Aylin muttered.

I glanced at the practice weapons and the uniforms. They were planning something, sure as spit. Something they didn't want us to know about.

"Danello?" Halima said, tugging on his sleeve. "We're not leaving without Jovan and Bahari, are we?"

"No, we're not."

"Good."

The enchanter turned to Neeme. "Could you please show these people to the guest quarters?"

She nodded and jumped up, setting her mending aside.

"Follow me."

Barnikoff and the others followed Neeme through the second door, next to the one the enchanter had come out of. I stayed behind, and Danello stayed with me. The enchanter might not have wanted to talk in front of the others, but I was ready for answers.

"What's going on?"

137

"Let's speak in my office," the enchanter said, pointing to the open door.

So they didn't want to talk out here in front of *their* others either. I looked at Jeatar. He tipped his head at the office.

"That would be nice," I said.

I walked inside. It was warm, with worn books on the walls and carpet on the floor.

"Are you okay?" Danello whispered in my ear. His breath tickled the back of my neck.

"I'm fine." But he did make it hard to concentrate when he did that.

I just didn't like being in a room where the only person I *knew* I could trust was him. Or having thirty Baseeri between me and the exit. Or not knowing where my sister was.

"Who are you?" I asked the enchanter as he sat behind his carved wooden desk.

"Onderaan Analov. Please, sit."

Breath left me. *Analov?* That was *my* name. Nya de'Analov. How could he have my name? How could a Baseeri have an almost Gevegian name?

I sat but didn't stop staring.

"Nya?" Danello touched my arm.

"You're their leader?" I said, finding it hard to speak at all.

"I'm the leader, yes." He folded his hands and placed them on the desk. "You're *their* leader?"

"No."

He smiled gently as if he didn't believe me.

"Um. What are you doing?" I hated the way my voice sounded. Squeaky. Cracked. Not like me at all. "With all these people, I mean . . . and uniforms and things?"

"Trying to get a snake away from the chickens."

He sounded like Grannyma. No . . .

His *voice* sounded like *Grandpapa*. Looked like him too. Same eyes, same nose. *Papa's eyes, Papa's nose.*

My chest tightened. "You're really fighting the Duke? You want him gone?"

"My family has fought the Duke for seven years, since the day he seized power that wasn't his. His father never intended for him to rule. *My* father never wanted it either. When he died, I swore I'd drag that greedy, warmongering fiend off his throne if I had to do it with my bare hands."

I knew that voice. That anger. I'd heard it before.

So much yelling from the first floor. I lay in the shadows at the top of the stairs and listened, like I always did. This time Grandpapa wasn't there. Other

139

men were. They smelled like the heavy black smoke that had been blowing over Geveg all day and night.

"We can go right now and rip that murderer off his throne."

"How? Our forces were in Sorille. We can't launch an attack now."

"He killed them, Peleven, he killed our parents."

Peleven was Papa's name. The other voice had to be—

Onderaan. I trembled. No, it wasn't possible. "Your family is here, too, then? Helping you?" That wasn't what I wanted to ask. I wanted to ask about the uniforms, and what they were doing, and maybe even ask for help saving Tali. But I had to know if his family was alive. If they were, then he couldn't be—

"They're dead. He killed them all."

Not everyone.

I squeezed my eyes shut. It was all a coincidence. This man was Baseeri, with hair dark as night. Papa's hair had been . . . I sucked in a breath. Bald. Burned it all off at the forge, he used to joke. Mama was the blond one. Tali and I got our pale curls from her.

"Jeatar says you lost your family as well," Onderaan said, his voice softening a little. "That your sister was recruited by the Undying. He says you need our help, but I'm not sure what we can do."

I'd been in Baseer long enough to know I'd need help to save Tali. I didn't know the secrets of the city, the patrol routes, which soldiers were lazy and which would run after you. He knew all that—and more. It shouldn't matter who he *might* be. "There has to be something you can do. You have uniforms, weapons, all these people. You know things."

"It's not just her family," Danello added. "They have my brothers too. They have lots of other people's brothers and sisters."

"I understand, but the Duke guards his Takers well. We've been trying to get someone inside, but it's impossible."

I scoffed, my face hot, my hands cold. "All you had to do was send in a Taker."

Onderaan's kind demeanor flickered. "It's not that easy."

"We sent some in and we weren't even trying."

That shut him up. Onderaan stared at me, his mouth slightly open. Jeatar's eyes widened. Even Danello seemed surprised.

"Um, Nya?" he said. He shot me a what-in-Saea's-name-are-you-doing? look.

I had no idea. I was just angry. "You have people and money and resources and all the things you could possibly need to save those Takers."

Jeatar put his hand on my arm. "Nya, you don't understand."

"I *do* understand!" No one in my family would sit back and let innocent people suffer. He was *not* family. He was *not* my father's brother.

I was *not* half Baseeri.

"You think it's too hard," I continued, "or too dangerous for you to risk your fancy villa and save people you know need saving. People who could help you stop the Duke!"

At some point I'd jumped to my feet, though I couldn't say when. I stared down at Onderaan, into brown eyes that were *not* the same shade as my father's. As Tali's. As *mine*.

"You'd rather sit here in your safe chair in your safe cellar while cities burn and lives are ruined and say you *tried* to help, but it was too hard!"

Onderaan stared back, jaw tight, eyes hard. "No, child. We just don't have any Takers."

TWELVE

No Takers anywhere? "I don't believe you. You're just—"

"Maybe we should discuss this in the morning?" Jeatar said while Danello squeezed my shoulder—hard.

"Yeah," Danello said, "she's exhausted—we all are. It's been a rough few days."

"I'm fine!"

"No, you're not," Danello mumbled just loud enough for me to hear.

"I don't think there's anything more to discuss," Onderaan said. "Jeatar, this isn't going to work. I want them all out by end of day tomorrow."

I folded my arms. The sooner I got out of here, the better. "Fine by me."

"She didn't mean it," Jeatar said, shooting me a look of pure disbelief. "She spent the last week in a box."

"Gone by tomorrow."

"Onderaan, they have nowhere to go. They'll just be captured again."

"We don't need the distractions right now. We need everyone focused, and this child"—he waved a hand toward me—"is not conducive to that."

"I'm not a child," I said. What did he know about me anyway? "I've been on my own for years, caring for my sister, my *only* family."

"Get her out of here," Jeatar said to Danello, who grabbed me by the arm and dragged me toward the door. Jeatar turned to Onderaan. "We need to discuss this."

"I'm not jeopardizing everything we've worked for because you feel sorry for this girl."

"It's not that, it's—"

Danello slammed the door shut. The Baseeri stopped and stared, drawn by the yelling in Onderaan's office. I glared back.

"What are you doing?" Danello asked, keeping his voice low. "We need his help to get Tali and the twins out."

"He's not going to help us."

"You don't know that."

"I know you can't trust a Baseeri!"

Danello's eyes widened. Perhaps I'd said that a little loud. Angry murmurs rumbled through the room.

"Come on," he said, dragging me away again toward the guest rooms. "Maybe Aylin can talk some sense into you."

"I don't need sense talked into me." I needed to *make* sense of things that didn't make sense. Maybe Analov was a popular name here. Maybe Papa just had one of those faces that looked like everyone else. Lots of people lost family in the war. It didn't mean *anything*.

Danello shut the door behind us. The hallway was full of Gevegians. They crowded around me, looking for answers I didn't have.

"What's going to happen to us?"

"Can we really stay?"

"Who was that man?"

Gaunt faces, tired eyes. Scared and hungry people who would be turned out tomorrow because Onderaan was too selfish to—

"We can stay the night, but we'll have to leave tomorrow," Danello said, his hand still tight on my arm.

"He's throwing us out?" Aylin said, probably the only one who seemed surprised.

145

Barnikoff spat. "Should have known. Can't trust a Baseeri."

Danello looked at me, his eyes encouraging me to speak yet worried that I might. I looked at the people gathered around us. People who *would* have been safe if not for me.

Saints, what had I done?

I was the one being selfish. I'd made deals I didn't like before. I could have kept my mouth shut and my ears open, learned what I needed here, and convinced Onderaan to help us. I'd have had Jeatar on my side, and he'd already convinced him to let us stay.

I swallowed, my throat dry. "Jeatar is working on it."

"Everyone, go to your rooms and rest while you can," Danello said, sounding like the leader Onderaan thought I was. "Let's show them we won't be any trouble at all."

"*We* won't be trouble?" someone asked. I couldn't tell who.

"I know, but look, these people are fighting the Duke. For all they know we're a bunch of spies. Would you be happy to see us if you were them?" Grumbles all around. "Stay put, stay quiet, do as they say, and let's see what happens tomorrow. At the very least they'll feed us."

A few chuckles.

"Okay, we'll sail it your way for now," Barnikoff said. He glanced at me before he turned and uncertainty washed across his face. The others didn't look at me, but they did return to their rooms.

"We're in here," Aylin said, opening the first door on the right. "Danello, you and Halima are next door, there."

"Can you watch her a bit longer?" Danello nudged me toward the open door. "I need to talk to Nya."

"Do you need me?"

"No, it's okay. Thanks though."

Aylin hesitated, casting me a worried look. "Everything okay?"

"It's fine."

She arched an eyebrow.

"We'll talk after," I said, shaking off Danello's hand and walking into the room. Not as cell-like as I'd expected. A lot like Millie's Boardinghouse, really. Simple beds, one on each side, but the pillows looked soft and the blankets warm. A small table with a lamp sat against the wall between them, a basket underneath for clothes.

It took me a moment to notice Danello hadn't followed.

". . . wrong with her?" Aylin said softly, one hand covering her mouth as if that would hide her words.

"I don't know. She's acting crazy. I've never seen her like this."

I sat on the bed. Folded my hands in my lap. My fingers were cold and I slipped them between my knees. What had I done?

"Do you know what's wrong?"

"No, but it happened right after that Onderaan guy showed up."

Vyand would find us and arrest us. They'd all climb the gallows' steps and hang. I couldn't let that happen. I had to apologize to Onderaan. Explain why I . . .

I sighed and rested my forehead on my knees. Why I overreacted. That's all it was. He couldn't be related to me—it made no sense. I couldn't be half Baseeri. I didn't look like them. Think like them. I wasn't cruel like them.

You hurt people. Killed people. Maybe that was your Baseeri side.

The door clicked shut. The bed squeaked as Danello sat next to me. I sat up.

"What happened?" His arm slipped around my shoulders. Warm. Solid. Safe.

"I got confused."

"Confused? About what?"

"What would you do if you found out your father wasn't who you thought he was?"

He paused. "You mean, like, if he lied to me?"

I hadn't thought about that. *Had* they lied to me? "I don't know." I rested my head on his shoulder. The kind of shoulder you could count on when things got bad.

You could count on Papa.

That's because he was Gevegian. He fought the Baseeri. Baseeri didn't fight Baseeri—except Onderaan and the Underground were doing just that.

Papa had. Grandpapa had. Were they Baseeri?

Danello took my hand, ran his thumb across my knuckles. "Why don't you like Onderaan?"

"He's an enchanter." It just popped out.

"And that's bad?"

"No."

"You're not making any sense."

"I know. I'm not sure what to do." I had to fix this somehow. Convince Onderaan to let them stay, even if he threw me out. I squeezed my eyes shut.

"Well," Danello said, pushing a curl behind my ear, "I think the first thing we should do is get some sleep. Then we can talk to Onderaan and tell him sometimes your mouth gets away from you. He's bound to need help here, and we can offer it. Maybe that's worth something."

"Maybe. No one in the Duke's army knows who we are. They wouldn't connect us with the Underground."

He smiled, but there was worry there too. For his brothers, for his father, for me. "See? Planning already. You'll have it all figured out by morning."

For his sake I had to prove I was worth keeping around by showing Onderaan how we could help him.

"Thanks." I hugged him, feeling better than I had since I got there. "I'm okay, really. You were right before, it's been a long day. A long *week*."

"I'll see you in the morning."

"You don't have to go so soon."

He grinned. "Okay."

I snuggled back into him, warm and safe. It felt good to just *be*.

Much sooner than I'd have liked, someone knocked softly on the door. Danello grumbled but got up and answered it.

"Everything okay in there?"

Aylin. I should have known.

They spoke in whispers for a minute; then Danello left and Aylin slipped inside. He had obviously told her what had happened, which suited me fine. I wasn't in the mood to think about it again.

"I don't know about you," she said, flopping on the other bed, "but I'm exhausted. I don't think I can even think straight anymore. I probably can't even talk without tripping over my own tongue."

Subtle she was not. But it was sweet of her, telling me in her own way it was okay to have lost my mind.

"I'm glad you're safe," I said. "And I'm sorry I got you arrested."

She rolled over and faced me. "It wasn't your fault. I knew we could get caught when I agreed to be sneaky with you."

"Still."

"Pfft." She flicked a hand my way. "What are friends for? I mean, really, if you can't count on your best friend to go to jail with you, what good are they?"

I smiled. "You do have a point."

"I am wise beyond my years."

"This is also true." I slipped off my sandals and crawled into bed. By the time I reached over to turn down the lamp, she was already asleep. I left it on, the pale glow comforting. I'd be able to see anyone who might sneak into the room. I'd noticed the door didn't have a lock. I hadn't checked the main hall door though. We might be locked in even now.

Worry about that in the morning.

I had enough to worry about tonight.

Noises woke me later that night. Thuds, muffled cries, worried words. I was on my feet before my eyes were fully open. Aylin was still asleep. She hadn't even taken off her shoes.

"Aylin, wake up." I pressed my ear against the door. Quiet.

Doors slammed, but it didn't sound like it was in the hall. Aylin mumbled and rolled over. I left the door and stepped onto her bed, then listened against the wall.

"Aylin!"

"Mmmm?"

"Get Danello." I slipped out the door, tiptoeing to the entrance to the main room. I cracked the door.

". . . waiting for us," a man was saying. "I don't know how."

A scoff. "A jailbreak alerted half the city," a woman said.

Our jailbreak? She thought we were responsible for whatever had happened?

"Oh come on, Siekte," said Jeatar. "The jail was nowhere near the League."

"You don't think breaking out political prisoners would have alerted them? Put all the Duke's soldiers on guard?"

"Quiet, both of you," Onderaan said, sounding tired. "How bad is she hurt?"

Hurt? I pulled the door open a little farther and peeked out. Six people stood in the room, three I hadn't seen before, wearing Baseeri uniforms that were probably from Neeme's stash of stolen ones. Another woman lay on the couch, hurt badly from the look of it. A man was on the floor, just as injured.

A door opened and Danello came up behind me. "What's going on?" he asked.

"I think a plan went bad. Something about the Healers' League."

He and Aylin crowded around me and looked out.

Siekte was pressing a folded cloth against the injured woman's stomach. The cloth was already dark with blood. Not good. She ignored the man on the floor. Onderaan didn't, though. He knelt and slapped him across the face.

"How did you know we were coming?"

The man groaned.

"Answer me!"

Aylin pulled away from the door. "Um, I'm thinking his uniform might be real."

If so, then he might be able to tell me where Tali and the others were.

"Traitor," the soldier said.

"You're killing innocents and I'm the traitor?" Onderaan slapped him again. "Did someone tell you we were coming?"

"Why is everyone in the hall?"

We spun around. Neeme stood behind us in a nightdress, rubbing her eyes, her hair a tousled mess.

"Someone got hurt," Aylin said.

Neeme's eyes opened wide. She shoved past us and ran inside, dropping to her knees by the woman. Siekte tried to keep her back but failed.

I stepped forward, but Danello grabbed my arm.

"We should stay in our rooms."

"I have to know what's going on." I ventured out, Danello and Aylin behind me. We stood off to the side, but Jeatar spotted us. He frowned and tipped his head toward the door. I shook mine.

Neeme sobbed, then sucked in a sharp breath.

She looked around wildly, first to the door, then the room. Her gaze fell on me. Jeatar swore.

"Help her, please," she asked me. "Heal her like you did me."

THIRTEEN

All eyes turned toward me. Onderaan's narrowed. "You're a Healer?"

"No," I said, just as Jeatar said, "It's complicated."

Neeme sniffled, dragging her sleeve across her nose. "I'm sorry, Jeatar, I had to," she told him, then turned to Onderaan. "She healed me. A street pack broke my leg and she somehow gave it to one of them."

Onderaan wasn't looking at me anymore. He turned on Jeatar and was inches away from him before I could take a breath.

"You brought the *Shifter* here and didn't tell me?"

"I didn't have time."

"You had time to tell Neeme to keep quiet about it."

Jeatar winced. "Because I knew you'd react this way. I was planning to tell you."

"When?"

"What about Ellis?" Neeme shouted above both of them. "She's dying."

Onderaan gave Jeatar one last angry look and turned away. "What can you do?" he asked me.

"Without a Healer and some pynvium, nothing."

"What about the shifting I've been hearing so much about? Can't you shift into that man?" He pointed at the soldier I needed to tell me where Tali was. The man was unconscious now, his uniform dark with blood.

"It'll kill him."

"He's dying anyway."

My guts said Onderaan didn't plan on letting him live even if he wasn't dying.

"We need to question him," I said.

"He's not waking up."

He would if I healed him. Not fully, but enough so he could talk, tell me where Tali was and how to get inside. I could hold his pain that long.

And then give it back?

It was Tali's voice. She'd hate me for it, but he

was a Baseeri soldier. He was one of the people hurting her. Save Neeme's friend, kill the soldier, save Tali and the others. I'd make that trade. I'd made worse ones for less.

I walked over. "I could—"

Ellis started choking, blood bubbling up on her lips.

"Help her!"

"Shift it now!"

"Nya, you don't have to—"

"Quiet, Jeatar."

I grabbed Ellis's hand and *drew*. Pain poured into me, sharp and hot. My chest burned, my lungs felt filled with sand. I dropped away, gasping.

Danello moved to one side of me. Aylin hurried to the other. They helped me stand and eased me over to the dying soldier.

"Soon as he's awake, ask him . . . about Tali," I said through clenched teeth.

Danello caught on a breath faster than Aylin. He shook his head, but her mouth dropped open. "Nya, you can't," she said. "This is bad enough as it is."

"Ask him."

"You'll hate yourself if you do this."

I'd hate myself more if I let another chance to find Tali pass me by. I reached out a shaking hand

and wrapped it around his arm. Felt my way in. Similar wounds, but lower, piercing the liver, stomach. I stopped the bleeding, eased the shock. Fresh pain cut though me, and I slumped against Danello.

The soldier stirred.

"Where are the Takers being kept?" Danello asked. "The ones deciding whether or not to serve the Duke?"

The soldier looked around, confused and scared. "What?"

"The Takers. Where are they?"

The soldier glared at Onderaan. "Traitor."

I tightened my grip and *pushed* just a little of his pain back. He screamed. I took a deep breath and gathered the pain in the hollow space between my heart and guts, held it there as best I could.

Aylin grabbed my hands. "Nya, stop. There's ugly and then there's just plain wrong." She locked her gaze on mine. "I can live with ugly if we get our people back, but I'm not letting you do wrong. Might as well turn yourself in to the Duke if you start that."

Horror twisted the soldier's features and he rolled away from me. Saints, what was I *doing*? Onderaan put his foot on his chest and shoved him down.

"Answer the girl or she'll put it *all* back."

What? No, I couldn't do that—it would kill him. Aylin stepped away, her arms tightly folded across her chest. She kept shaking her head, a plea in her eyes to stop, like she actually thought I'd do it. But hadn't I already done it? I looked at the soldier. If I didn't shift, I'd die. If I did shift, he'd die.

The soldier spat at Onderaan. Onderaan knelt and grabbed him by the throat.

"How did you know?" he asked, low and threatening. Not the question I needed to know.

The soldier glared, his eyes tearing at the corners. Movement flickered below me. His arm moved up toward Onderaan's heart, a small knife gripped in his hand.

"Ahh!" the soldier cried out as Siekte's blade sank into his chest. The knife fell away. The soldier slumped, dying.

Saints, no!

I grabbed his arm and *pushed* as fast as I could. Pain slid away from me, then—nothing. It crashed against a wall of death and splashed back. I gasped while the pain washed over me.

"Nya, are you okay?" Danello brushed sweaty curls off my forehead.

"No," I whispered. Pain swirled around my chest, making it hard to breathe. I never should have healed him. I was just as bad as the Undying, hurting to get what I wanted.

Danello tucked his arm around me and helped me to the other couch. Neeme and her friend sat across from us, arms around each other, but quiet. An odd mix of gratitude and fear on their faces.

"I'll be okay." A lie. I had a few days before my blood thickened and my body shut down.

"We need to get Nya to a Healer," Danello said.

"Or find her another Baseeri she doesn't like," Siekte muttered. Aylin frowned, but I deserved the barb.

"No one goes anywhere until I understand what happened tonight." No question about Onderaan's feelings. Anger. At me, at Jeatar, at the soldier. "You first," he told the three Baseeri standing by the wall. They looked at Ellis. She started to get to her feet but failed. She sat up straighter instead.

"We hit the League's storage rooms as planned," she began, voice solid even though she was pale. "Got in with no trouble, found the pynvium vault just where our contact said it would be. Kilvet started picking the lock." She paused. "That's when soldiers burst in. Six, seven, I'm not sure. We made it out only because we set the trip lines like you trained us to. The first few soldiers never saw them, went down hard, and caused the rest to stumble. We were almost back to the villa when we were ambushed, about three blocks away, right after we turned onto the street. We killed four, we subdued him"—she indicated the dead man on the floor—"and thought he might know something, so we brought him here."

"There are bodies in the street?"

She winced. "Yes, sir."

Onderaan swore and turned to the three still in uniform. "Go clean it up before someone sees them. And get their gate seals while you're at it."

"Yes, sir." They left as one, darting up the stairs in single file.

"That vault shouldn't have been so well guarded," Onderaan said. "The League has minimum staff, hardly any pynvium at all now. Could we have a spy?"

Siekte looked at me.

"They're not spies," Jeatar said.

"They conveniently show up just when we're stealing the pynvium?" She huffed. "And we have no idea who—or what—they are?"

"I know who and what they are, and they aren't spies," Jeatar said.

Neeme nodded. "She saved me and Ellis. She can't be bad."

"She could have done that to gain our trust," Siekte said. I'd argue it, but nothing I said would change *her* opinion of me. Especially when she was partially right.

"She didn't," Neeme said. "She didn't even know who I was when the pack attacked me."

"Unless she hired them."

Jeatar snorted. "You can't be serious. A raid went bad—it happens. There might not even *be* a spy."

"You." Onderaan pointed to me. "In my office, now. Alone," he added when both Siekte and Jeatar stepped forward.

Siekte gaped at him like he'd asked her to stab him. "Sir, she might shift into you."

He turned to me. "Are you a threat?"

"Not unless you try to kill me."

For a heartbeat I saw his lip twitch into a smile. "Fair enough."

With Danello's help I got to my feet. The pain was better now, trapped where I could manage it, but it wouldn't stay trapped. I walked into Onderaan's office and sank onto one of the chairs. He shut the door and took his place behind the desk, but he didn't sit. For a long minute he just stared at me, his shoulders growing tenser with every breath. I couldn't help but notice he had very broad shoulders.

"How *dare* you accuse me of not caring when you could have infiltrated the camps on your own." He spoke low, but there was fury in his voice. "You judge me and what I'm trying to do, yet you have the nerve to hide that you're a Taker."

My already sore guts squirmed. "I'm a Shifter. There's nothing I can do but get caught by the Duke."

"So could any Taker I sent in there."

"It's not the same."

He scoffed. "Of course not—it's your bait on the hook, not theirs."

"I can't sense pynvium."

His anger faltered. Not a lot, but hopefully enough to fix this mess and convince him to let us stay.

"So you're right," I continued. "I can pass any test they'd give me to prove I was a Taker—but as soon as they asked me to push pain into pynvium, I'd be exposed."

"You could still get in."

This time *I* scoffed. "And do what? Take on an entire army from the inside? Don't you think I'd do it if it would save my sister? Save Danello's brothers? No." I shook my head. "I'm not sacrificing my head to win my heart. There's too much at stake and I

164

need to plan it *right* this time."

Onderaan sat, his gaze locked onto mine. Not as much anger in it; some confusion maybe. I wasn't sure exactly what he was feeling, but it looked like a lot of things all at once.

"So you'd be willing to infiltrate the camps if you could pass as a regular Taker?"

"I'd be there now if I could do that."

Onderaan leaned back in his chair. He studied me, tapping a knuckle against his lips. I knew that look. He had a plan brewing.

"I've been working on something," he said cautiously, as if he still wasn't sure he could trust me. "It was for a more immediate problem, but it might be just what we need to get you inside those camps."

"How?"

He pulled a chain from around his neck. A small key dangled on it. "I don't know how it was in Geveg, but here pynvium has been scarce for over a year," he said, opening one of the drawers in his desk. He pulled out an iron box and unlocked it. "I've been able to smuggle out bits here and there, stockpile it, but those sources dried up months ago. There hasn't been any pynvium available in the whole city since."

How did these people survive without pynvium? "Unless you're the Duke or one of his Undying, right?"

"Exactly. Without it, I wasn't able to finish this." He set a bracelet with three rings attached to it with fine chains on the desk.

My guts quivered and I wanted to run as fast as I could. I couldn't see the carvings, but I knew they were there. "That's glyphed pynvium."

"How did you—" He gaped, then held the thing out to me. "It's on the inside, see?"

I didn't want to see. I pressed into the chair, trying to stay as far away as possible. "Put that away, please."

"What's wrong?"

"That thing! Can't you feel it?"

"No, nothing." He put it back in the box. "I thought you couldn't sense pynvium."

"I can't, but I can sense *that*. Feels like spiders crawling all over me, inside and out."

Just like in Zertanik's. He'd been an enchanter. Had he created a pynvium device as well? Knowing him, it was something he could sell, not something that would help people. Or maybe something he thought he could sell to the Duke. *Like maybe whatever was in that box in the library?*

166

Onderaan frowned. "If you're that sensitive to it, this may not work."

"Why does it feel so wrong?"

"I honestly don't know. I've never met anyone who reacted to it the way you do. Maybe you have a touch of enchanter in you?"

I was tired of being unique. "What is it?"

"A healing device." He shrugged, as if this weren't as big a deal as it sounded. "It's been hard enough getting the pynvium, but finding Healers to use it has been even harder. That's been true for years. I was trying to enchant pynvium to draw pain when triggered, instead of flashing it."

Healing without Healers. It was genius. "Does it work?"

"I think it will."

"You didn't test it?"

"I haven't finished it. The glyphs are correct, but I can't insert the trigger until the piece is complete."

The glyphs. How could something that felt so horrible help people?

"What are the glyphs for? I remember my father writing with them, but I never saw him carve them into anything."

Onderaan didn't answer right away, just stared at me. "They strengthen the enchantment. Most enchantments can be set just by drawing them with water or oil as the pynvium cools."

"The easy ones."

"Yes. Embedded enchantments are difficult to master, but they last longer. Sometimes even permanently."

"Are they dangerous?" They'd have to be if they made me feel this way.

He nodded. "They can be."

"Tell me how it works." I hated the idea of that thing against my skin, but if it got me inside the Taker camp, I could bear it. I'd survived far worse to save Tali before.

He took it back out of its box. I steadied my stomach. "You just wear it," he said, slipping the bracelet over his hand. The rings fit on his fingers. I'd seen similar jewelry in the crowds when I first got to Baseer. "It needs good skin contact, so you press your hand against the patient, squeeze and flick, same as a rod. The pynvium draws away the pain."

"How would it know what to heal?" I asked. Takers needed training to be able to heal properly. No way a simple chunk of pynvium—no matter how carved it was—could do that.

He sighed. "I'm not sure how it works exactly. I have notes and patterns my grandfather gave me. He said they'd been in our family for generations and that they worked. He'd made things himself."

"Healing devices?"

"No. Weapons mostly. The healing device is something I figured out by combining two separate glyph patterns. I *know* it will work."

I wasn't so sure. Who knew what it might do once it was on someone's hand? *Could it do any worse than what you do now?* "So if I wear that thing, it can heal and it'll look like I did it?"

"Yes."

"And what happens if I have to push the pain into pynvium armor?"

He hesitated. "It won't do that. It'll allow for multiple healings, then it'll reach capacity. But," he quickly added as I started to speak, "the Undying don't get their armor for months. There's training and conditioning and tests, so you might be able to fool them long enough to find your sister and the others."

Mights were definitely as bad as maybes. "What do you need to finish it?"

"More pynvium. That's what tonight's raid was for."

"I'm guessing you can't just try again tomorrow night."

"Not now."

169

"And there's no other place to get more pynvium?"

"Not in the outer quarters."

Which meant there *was* more, but getting to it was probably dangerous. If I could help him get more pynvium, he could finish his device and I could get inside the Taker camps and save Tali. "If we agree to help you, can everyone stay? You won't throw them out?"

He hesitated, staring at me just like Papa always did when he was trying to guess if I was serious. "They can stay for now, but there's nothing you can do. The only other place to get pynvium is the Duke's foundry. It's in the Aristocrats' Quarter, which has been locked down for months. Breaking in there will be impossible."

I'd heard that before. "Lucky for us, impossible is what I do best."

FOURTEEN

"You want to raid the foundry?" Jeatar said an hour later in Onderaan's office. He was the only other member of the Underground present. Until Onderaan found the spy—or was certain there *was* no spy—we were the only people he knew for sure he could trust. Which really said something about the bind he was in. "This was Nya's idea, wasn't it?"

"It was a joint decision."

Danello nodded slowly, no doubt weighing the options like he always did. Raiding the foundry was a huge risk, but I needed that pynvium.

"I'm game," said Aylin. She didn't sound as cheery as usual, and I suspected that wasn't because it was late and she was tired. I'd crossed a line and I wasn't sure how to get back. "So what's the plan?"

"We sneak into the foundry, steal some pynvium, and sneak out before they know we're there," I said.

"Basically the same plan as always?"

"Pretty much, yeah."

Jeatar groaned and covered his face with both hands. I guess he was tired too. Onderaan glanced at me. "We haven't finalized the details yet. We haven't even agreed about when."

"We need to go at sunrise, right after the shift change," I said.

"This sunrise?" Jeatar asked. "As in five hours from now?"

Onderaan shook his head. "I think we need to wait a day and go at night."

"No one *ever* expects trouble before breakfast," I said, "and they certainly wouldn't expect us to hit them again so soon after the League break-in." There was another reason for moving quickly, but I didn't want to mention it.

Danello did anyway. "You can't wait a day, can you? The shifted pain, I mean."

"No. By tomorrow it'll slow me down. Make it hard to think. You remember."

"Yeah." He'd held shifted pain to save his father,

172

had suffered almost as much as Tali had. Not being a Taker, it had affected him even faster and almost killed him and his brothers. So far I'd been able to keep the pain coiled between my guts and my heart, but it still hurt. And it would only get worse.

Aylin turned to Onderaan. "Let's hear about this foundry."

"It's behind the inner walls of the Aristocrats' Quarter, near the harbor and the citadel." He unrolled a map of the city. Grids and straight lines, all orderly. I preferred Geveg's curved streets and winding canals. "We're here." He pointed at a section at the bottom of the map. "The foundry is here." His finger moved up, past the thick, dark lines of the inner wall, to a spot near the river. "The gates to this quarter are tightly controlled. Normally it's impossible to get inside without the proper seals, but tonight's fiasco gave us exactly the seals we need."

"From the soldiers killed," Jeatar said.

"Correct. All soldiers have access to the citadel, so we now have four east gate seals. Unfortunately they change them weekly, and I have no way of knowing how long these will work."

"So we might get stopped at the gate?" Danello asked.

"It's possible."

"Getting inside the walls is the easy part," I said. Onderaan had explained the problems with the foundry in great detail, probably hoping I'd agree it was pointless to try. But since it was our only source of pynvium, we *had* to find a way in. "The foundry has its own wall, with guards on the entrance and a patrol on the grounds."

"Will the seals work at the foundry?" Danello asked.

"No."

Aylin frowned. "Then how do we get in?"

"I'm hoping we can figure that out when we get there."

Jeatar groaned and Onderaan nodded slowly. "That's what we've been arguing over for the last hour."

"At least we can go look," I said. "I bet we can think up a good excuse and walk inside."

"I doubt that."

He was probably right, but a little optimism never hurt. "We won't know what our options are until we see it."

"Okay," said Danello, slapping his palms together. "When do we leave?"

"Morning shift change. Just after sunrise." I grinned at Onderaan. "Right?"

He sighed. "If all you're doing is looking, sunrise it is."

"Before we do that," Aylin said, "we have a few things to do first." She looked at Danello. "Hey, Onderaan. You wouldn't happen to have any black hair dye around, would you?"

This time my uniform fit much better. Onderaan had Neeme alter a couple for Aylin and me, swearing her to secrecy about it. Her curious looks said she wondered what we were up to, but she didn't ask any questions. Onderaan was keeping our scouting mission a secret for now, but there was only so much you could hide when fifty people were constantly in and out of the same villa.

"What are they doing?" Siekte asked as we were leaving.

"Reconnaissance," Onderaan said.

"Really? They don't even know the city."

"Jeatar does."

Siekte clearly wasn't happy at all about being left out. Neither were her friends. These folks weren't soldiers, but I suspected at least one or two in the mix had been. They'd set themselves up in some kind of command structure, but I wasn't sure who followed who, though since people deferred to her, Siekte had to be one of the group's leaders. She wasn't quite equal to Jeatar or Onderaan, but she had enough support to be a problem if she wanted to.

"What about my team? They're trained scouts."

"Who have been working day and night for weeks. I assumed you'd be pleased about the rest." Onderaan spoke casually, but his voice had an edge to it. "I've been pushing them too hard, isn't that what you said the other day?"

Her cheek twisted. "Of course, thank you. I'm sure they'll appreciate the time off."

"I'm sure they will."

I belted on my sword, trying not to smile. I really should try to be nice to her, but even Saint Gedu didn't have the patience required for Siekte.

"All set?" Danello asked. He looked good in his uniform, his newly black hair letting him blend in better than his blond hair.

"Let's go."

We left the villa just as the sun's light broke over Baseer. The curfew ended at dawn, but the streets were already crowded. No one gave us a second look as we walked toward the east gate, and a few times Jeatar had to act the part just to get folks to move out of the way so we could pass.

"How do you feel?" Danello asked me.

"I'm fine."

"Nya, I can't help you if you lie to me."

I slowed a step and let Jeatar and Aylin get a pace or two ahead. "My chest hurts and it's a little hard to breathe, but I'll be okay for a while."

"What will you do if we can't get any pynvium?"

"I don't know." Thankfully, it hadn't occurred to him that pynvium wasn't the only problem. Even if I found some, I had no Healer to use it. I needed Tali just as much as she needed me.

And if I couldn't find her or another Healer?

Then I'd have to make a decision I *really* didn't want to make.

"There's the inner wall," Jeatar said. It looked just as solid as the one surrounding the city, only smaller, about twenty feet high. The entrance gate cut through the middle, half as high, with bars thick as my arm.

Soldiers in better-fitting uniforms than ours checked seals at the gate. They didn't look young or bored like so many of the soldiers I'd seen at home. These men and women looked dangerous, like they hoped someone wouldn't have the right seal just so they could start the day off with a fight.

"Next," the soldier called. Two others stood behind her, armed with long spears.

"Everyone relax," I said, pulling my seal out of my pocket. "Real soldiers do this every day."

The seals were wood, about the size of my palm, stamped with the Duke's osprey and some official wording. Along the bottom were more marks of varying depth, some filled with color, others plain.

Please, Saint Saea, let it be for this week.

We reached the front of the line. The soldier inspected Jeatar's seal, turning it over in her hand and running her fingers across the colored marks at the bottom. "You four together?" she asked Jeatar.

"Yes."

Her gaze flicked Danello's way, then stopped on me. "Isn't she a little young for a soldier?"

Heart racing, I harrumphed. "Aren't you a little nosy for a guard?"

Jeatar reached over and smacked me in the head with his palm. "That's another day of pot scrubbing for you," he said, voice hard. "Better learn to keep that mouth of yours shut or you'll spend your whole tour in the kitchens."

The soldier eyed him, lips pursed.

"New recruits," Danello said with a laugh. "They get younger every day, huh?"

The soldier chuckled and reached forward, running her fingers along his chin. "Says the boy with baby fuzz still on his chin."

Danello turned bright red and the soldiers with the spears joined in the laughter.

The soldier checked the rest of our seals and nodded. "Go on in. Try to keep the little one out of the taprooms."

I scowled as expected and they laughed again. The soldier opened the gate and we walked through.

"What were you thinking, mouthing off like that?" Jeatar said when we got out of earshot.

"That someone who looked as young as me would be touchy about it."

He opened his mouth, then closed it. "That's actually smart."

"You don't have to sound so surprised."

Aylin chuckled.

"Which way to the foundry?" I asked.

"This way."

The Aristocrats' Quarter was far nicer than the terraces in Geveg. Elegant villas sat on hills surrounded by lush grass and blossoming trees. Sweetness scented the air and petals drifted by on the wind. No buildings were crammed against each other here. Even the shops and cafés had space between them, usually a small garden or patio.

"Are those soldiers?" Danello whispered as men

in red and gold uniforms approached.

"No, servants," said Jeatar.

"In uniforms?"

"Most of the households have their own colors and seals."

"What for?" Danello looked as baffled about it as I did. But it could be another way to sneak about the city. Servants probably didn't get looked at any closer than soldiers.

"Prominence," said Jeatar. "Shopkeeps know by the colors which house the servant is shopping for, and that determines who gets the best goods."

Danello just shook his head.

The landscaped streets gave way to high hedges, then less fancy shops and simpler town houses. Another few blocks and those gave way to tall warehouses and taprooms, then the military district. The citadel sat like a rock in the distance, formidable even from afar.

"And there it is," Jeatar said. "Anyone thirsty?"

I gaped at him until I noticed the taproom across the street from the foundry. Tables sat under a vine-wrapped trellis, providing a clear view of the street. We could sit and watch and no one would be the wiser. Of course, the tables were mostly occupied by soldiers.

"Are you sure about this?" I asked Jeatar.

"You said you wanted to scout the foundry." He walked up the steps onto the patio and claimed a seat at one of the tables. A few people glanced over, but most ignored him.

"I wonder if they serve breakfast," Aylin said as we all joined him.

The foundry was exactly as Onderaan described. A ten-foot wall ran around the grounds, with two soldiers at the front gate. Heavy wood, not bars, so you couldn't see inside. Tall chimneys and low-peaked roofs stuck above the wall on the left side and a square three-story building sat on the right. Dark smoke poured from the chimneys, but the river wind blew it away from the city instead of into it. Random roars from the furnaces drowned out the rhythmic clanging of the smiths' hammers. A few large trees grew in the yard surrounding it, but they were too far from the wall for us to use them to get inside.

"Ready to give up yet?" Jeatar said.

"Hardly." Though getting inside was going to be tougher than I'd thought. "How long can we sit here without anyone noticing?"

"As long as we keep ordering. Plenty of soldiers spend their off-duty hours here."

"I hope the food is good then. We might be here awhile."

By lunch it was clear simply walking in wasn't an option. The door guards checked every person, and getting those seals—if they even used seals—wouldn't be easy. No supply wagons of any type had arrived, so sneaking in that way wasn't going to work either.

I fidgeted in my chair, the shifted pain eating away at me. It hadn't been too bad this morning, but every hour brought a new ache, a new sting.

"Let's scout the area some more," I said, standing. I tried not to wince, but Danello's face clouded and he stood with me.

"I'll go with you. I could use a break."

Jeatar nodded. "Be careful and don't do anything impulsive, okay?"

"Wouldn't think of it."

Jeatar reached for his drink "Right."

Danello and I headed down. Besides the tap-room, there were ferriers, tanners, glassmakers. In Geveg, day laborers worked wherever there was a job, so odds were someone here worked at the foundry and might know how to get inside. I used to help Papa with his forge, so maybe I could pass myself off as one of the workers.

I'd heard a few folks talking about the League break-in, so we pretended to be investigating any suspicious people who might have been seen around the foundry. No one knew much about the delivery schedule or saw anything unusual, though one of the sand runners at the glassmaker said a carriage came and went most nights.

"What time?"

"Late, after midnight," she said, casting a careful glance into the shop. "I know I'm not supposed to be here that late, but I lost my room a few weeks ago and the foreman said it would be okay if I slept down here 'til I found another."

"It's okay—we're not worried about that."

She looked relived. "Thanks. Hope you catch the thieves."

We kept walking, but every side of the foundry looked as fortified as the front.

"You think he's really making pynvium armor in there?" Danello asked.

I nodded. "Weapons, too, I bet. That might be what the carriage is there for. Picking up weapons to deliver them to the palace. Who'd notice a carriage driving around these fancy streets? Probably everyone has one." We'd seen plenty this morning already, and they were all painted in different colors like the servants' uniforms.

"Wonder what that is." I pointed to a tall stone bridge that ran right over the rear of the foundry, sitting above the city on arched columns. It looked like it started outside the main wall and ran all the way down to the harbor.

"I think it's an aqueduct."

"We need to find out where that goes." If it started in the less-guarded quarters, we might be able to climb up on it and follow it right to the foundry.

"Jeatar might know."

"Let's get back."

Servers were just dropping off lunch plates when we got there.

"Where does the aqueduct start?" I said.

Jeatar's brow wrinkled, as if trying to figure out why I wanted to know. "At Lake—"

"Nya!" Danello said, his gaze darted sideways. "Vyand just walked out of the foundry. She's heading this way."

FIFTEEN

I hunched over my plate, face turned down and away. "Has she seen us?"

"No. She's talking to that big guy she had with her before."

Stewwig.

"Act casual, everyone," Jeatar said, taking a sip from his drink. "Don't give her a reason to look over here."

"What's she doing?" My back was to the street.

"I think she's here for lunch." Danello lowered his head. "She's two tables over," he whispered, so low I barely heard him.

But I could hear Vyand.

". . . care what he thinks—she'll be here."

Stewwig rumbled an answer, but not loud enough for me to catch.

"She went after the jail, didn't she? Trust me, she's not going to leave her—" She stopped as the server arrived at the table.

I glanced at Jeatar. Was she talking about me? *I* went after the jail, and there was no reason for a tracker to be hanging around a foundry. Wasn't like there were any Takers there. Unless . . . *Trust me, she's not going to leave her*— Leave her what? Sister? Friends?

Saints! Tali might be behind those walls, fifty feet away.

"She's tough, and she doesn't run," Vyand said after the server left with their order. "She has to still be in the city, so throw a few crumbs out there and see if she follows them. Tell our contacts to spread the word that we have her sister. That'll bring her right to us."

I gripped my fork tight. Danello and Aylin looked at me, their eyes wide and hopeful. Jeatar watched me, but he seemed worried.

Did she really have Tali, or was it a trap? Did I care? We had to break in no matter what—even if it was all a trick.

⌒⌒

We left after Vyand returned to the foundry. I fought the urge to run, anxious to find the way inside, and prayed Vyand hadn't been lying.

"Do you think Bahari and Jovan are there too?" Danello asked, the same look in his eyes as mine probably had.

"Maybe."

"It's got to be a trap," Jeatar said. "Why hold Takers at a foundry?"

Aylin shrugged. "They're not just Takers, they're bait. And the place *is* hard to get into."

"Which is why it has to be a trap."

We all quieted as we reached the gate and handed over our seals. We kept walking for a few blocks; then Jeatar pulled us to the side of the street.

"Nya, I understand how badly you want to believe this, but think about it. There are other places Vyand could have set up her ambush that would have been a lot easier for you to get into."

"I don't think Nya would have trusted something too easy," said Danello. "I know I wouldn't have."

Jeatar scoffed. "If it involved Tali, yes, she would."

"I don't think it's a lie," I said, annoyed at Jeatar, but there was more than a bit of truth to his comment. "Because it *is* hard to get into, and Vyand has to know even better than we do *how* hard. She wouldn't have chosen the foundry unless there really was something in there I wanted."

"*Unless* she's lying about it."

"No, wait," Aylin said, holding up her hand. "Nya has a point. If she found out where Tali was really being held, she'd just go there. The only reason for Vyand to be at the foundry *is* if she thinks Nya will go there anyway."

Danello nodded. "Nya found us at the jail. Makes sense that Vyand would think she has a way of finding out where Tali and my brothers are too."

Jeatar didn't answer right away, then blew out an exasperated breath. "You might be right. But I still think it's a trap."

"Well, yeah," Aylin said. "That part's obvious."

He frowned at her but looked at me. "I can't talk you out of this, can I?"

"Not a chance."

"She knows you're coming."

"But not that I know she's there." I smiled. "That gives us the advantage." How much of one I didn't know, but it had to count for something.

Aylin grinned. "Soooo, what's the plan?"

I looked up at the aqueduct. "You said that went to a lake?" I asked Jeatar.

"Yes. It starts there and brings fresh water down to the city. There are two cisterns, one by the citadel, the other on the far side of Baseer."

"Can we get up on it?"

"On the aqueduct?" He seemed shocked I'd even asked. "It's a good fifty, sixty feet high out here and can't be more than four feet wide."

I'd walked ledges smaller and higher than that.

"Vyand probably has guards all over the foundry," Danello said.

"We could wait her out," said Aylin. "She'll have to give up and leave eventually, right? Then we'd only have the almost impossible guards to get past, who *aren't* expecting us."

No one said anything. *They* could wait her out, but I didn't have that much time. And neither did Tali and the twins if they were being used as bait. The Duke might let Vyand use them for a little while to get me, but he had plans for them himself.

"That won't work," I said. "They might move them, and I won't be helpful in a day or two even if they didn't."

We walked in quiet for a while until we passed through the gate to Onderaan's villa.

"What if we shared the pain?" Aylin said.

"It'll still kill everyone who carries it."

She shook her head. "I don't mean we all take it at the same time. I take it today, Danello takes it tomorrow, Jeatar the day after, then back to you. Once it's gone you're fine, right? So we can carry it a day at a time."

"Would that work?" Danello asked, looking hopeful again.

"I don't know." Pain overworked the body, but once it was gone, the body had nothing to stress it. "But it would cause some damage every time, and I'd have to heal that each time I shifted. It'll keep getting worse the longer we carry it."

"But it'll work for a while?"

"I think so."

"I'm willing to try," Danello said.

Aylin nodded. "So am I. Let's do it. Set me up with some pillows and a few books, and I'll be good for a day."

Most of me wanted to say no, but Aylin's determined look said she wouldn't let me. Even though it meant hurting my friends, I really didn't want to die. I'd prefer another way to save myself, but the drowning man grabs the closest branch.

"Okay. Thank you."

"What are friends for?"

Jeatar unlocked the villa and we went inside, through the fancy kitchen and down the spiral staircase. The main room was crowded today, thirty, maybe forty people gathered in clumps. Siekte rose as we walked in, followed by three others.

"Back so soon?" she said, crossing her arms. The others mimicked her.

"We found out what we needed to," Jeatar said.

"I'm sure. The Shifter isn't welcome here."

No one was supposed to know about me, and she'd just announced it to the entire Underground. And from their muted reaction, they already knew.

"That's nice," said Jeatar, "but since Onderaan's is the only vote that counts, she stays."

"The Duke is looking for her. That makes us vulnerable."

"The Duke is looking for Onderaan too. Want to kick him out?"

The briefest of smiles flickered across her lips. "Of course not—he's a good leader," she said, though I doubted she meant it. "But he's risking us all by protecting her."

"We're all at risk just being here."

She glared at him. "You know what I mean. Why give the Duke a legal excuse to search all the houses he thinks are part of the Underground?"

How many *were* there? I'd assumed just the one, but if they had villas like this all over the city, there could be hundreds of people, if not thousands. Wasn't that enough to oppose the Duke and drag him off his throne?

"Siekte, you can't—"

"Yes, I can. This isn't a personal vendetta for us. We're not trying to make some point and prove our family was right all along. We want the Duke gone, and there are easier ways to accomplish that."

Jeatar scowled. "We're not assassinating the Duke."

"We have people in place who can do it."

I glanced at Danello. Kill the Duke? Maybe Siekte wasn't so bad after all.

Jeatar shook his head. "We've talked about this, Siekte. Exposing him is the only way to avoid bloodshed."

"Protecting her protects us," Neeme said from the corner of the room. I hadn't noticed her on the couch before. I didn't see her friend Ellis, though. "If we throw her out, then the Duke can find her a lot easier."

"He already knows she's in Baseer! She shifted and flashed and did whatever it is she does, and the whole city is whispering about it. It's only a matter of time until they track down where she went."

"She knows where *we* are," Neeme said simply. "Even a heartless eel like you can see that's a problem if she gets caught. Keeping her here is safer for all of us."

Wait a minute . . . I was all for protecting me, but keeping me here? I had aqueducts to climb and Takers to save. I couldn't be stuck here.

The others started whispering, nervous looks casting about. I guess no one had thought about that part. Even Siekte hesitated.

"Fine, she doesn't leave here."

I stepped forward. "That's not—"

"Demand whatever makes you happy, Siekte," Jeatar said, clamping a hand over my mouth. "It's Onderaan's call in the end."

"Swear you won't leave," Siekte told me, as if I were the one in the wrong here.

I held out my hand. "How 'bout we shake on it?"

She stepped back, her eyes wide. "Just don't go anywhere."

"Just my room." For now. No way was I letting her tell me what to do. And from Jeatar's expression, he wasn't either, even if he had backed down here. Siekte was clearly reaching above herself, and without Onderaan or his own supporters, I guess Jeatar couldn't really take her on.

Jeatar walked with us as far as the door to the guest quarters. "Stay put for now. I'll let Onderaan know what's going on and he'll deal with her. She means well—she's just a bit aggressive in her tactics."

"No kidding," Aylin said.

"How many safe houses *does* the Underground have?" I asked.

"Twenty-three. Some larger, some smaller."

"Can we go to one of those?"

"I'd prefer to keep you here with me." Something in his tone worried me.

"Why?"

"Siekte isn't the only one who's unhappy with what Onderaan is doing. They think he's being too passive."

"They all want to kill the Duke?"

"Not all, but more than I'd like."

"Is Onderaan losing control of the Underground?"

Jeatar nodded. "We lost a lot of support when the Undying appeared. Onderaan was caught off guard. We never even knew the Duke was creating them. It's caused . . . difficulties."

Looked like more than that from what I'd seen. Onderaan had his own civil war to deal with before he could stop one in Baseer. "What about Tali?"

"We'll stick to the plan for now. Keep trying to figure out a way in, and maybe by then Onderaan can calm Siekte down. If we manage to get pynvium and some Healers, it'll go a long way toward proving Onderaan really *can* stop the Duke."

"And if Siekte does something first?" Danello asked.

Jeatar looked grim. "Then Nya might get lots of opportunities to get rid of that pain."

I ran a comb through my hair, my stomach twisted from more than just the pain I was carrying. It had gotten worse overnight, and this morning I felt as if I'd eaten bad food. "I hate this, I really do."

"We had to do it," Aylin said. "Vyand knows what you look like, and you needed another disguise."

"I wasn't talking about my hair." Although I hated that too. Aylin had used the last of the dye to darken my curls. I tried not to notice it was the same black as Onderaan's.

Aylin waved my concerns away. "I can handle a little pain for a day."

"What if something happens to me? You'll have

195

no way to get rid of it."

"I'll live," she said, even though she wouldn't if that happened.

"What if Siekte really doesn't let us out of here?" Danello said.

"Let's hope Nya's new disguise works on her." Aylin started braiding her long hair. "Hand me that cord."

I picked up the leather cord and passed it to her. "At least with the bounty hunters I knew I was a prisoner. I'm not so sure where I stand here."

"Jeatar will figure out something, or move us somewhere safer," Danello said. "He must have a home somewhere in Baseer. Unless you think he lives here all the time?"

"I don't know. I think he travels a lot, so maybe."

"Knife, please," Aylin said.

I gave it to her. "I don't think he'd leave us here if he thought we were in danger. And it's not like Siekte can force us to— Aylin, what are you doing?"

She had the knife blade against the base of her head, just under the top of the braid. She squeezed her eyes shut and sawed through.

"Aylin!" I gasped.

"I told you, you need a new disguise." She brought the braid over to me. "Now hold still while

I tie this into your hair. It's long enough to hold it."

"But you love your hair!"

"It'll grow back." She didn't sound as casual as she probably hoped. I heard the catch in her voice, saw the shine in her eyes as she looked at the braid in her hand. A tiny sacrifice compared to what else she was doing for me.

"You didn't have to do that." I meant so much more than her hair.

"To keep you safe, I'd shave my whole head."

I hugged her, trying not to cry. "Thank you."

"You find Tali and Danello's brothers and we'll call it even."

"Deal."

I sat still while she wove the braid into my hair. A good tug would rip it right off, but it would stay put otherwise. She darkened my eyebrows as well, and lined my eyes with black powder.

"Where did you get all this?"

"From Neeme. She's the only one here who's actually nice." Aylin held up a mirror. "What do you think?"

"Wow." Danello whistled. "Doesn't look like you at all."

I looked older, darker, Baseeri. "Is that good or bad?"

197

"Good for a disguise, but I like how the real you looks."

I blushed.

Aylin stole the pillows off my bed and propped herself up on hers. "Okay, fill me up before you go sneaking for the day." She shoved her sleeve up and held out her bare arm.

I took her hand, placed my other hand on her arm. "Are you—"

"Come on, let's see what Danello's been whining about all this time."

I *pushed* into her, slowly at first, letting her get used to it before I added more. She yelped and gritted her teeth but kept her arm still. I kept *pushing* until it was all gone.

My chest loosened and it was instantly easier to breathe.

"How do you feel?" I asked. Danello poured her a cup of juice from the pitcher he'd brought.

"That maybe all that whining was justified."

"I can take it back."

"No!" She held up a hand, winced, and lay down. "You need to find a way into the foundry, and you need a clear head and strong backs to help you. You're better off with Danello and Jeatar than me anyway. I'll see what I can do here. Maybe Neeme

198

knows something. They tend to ignore her, but I have a feeling she doesn't miss much."

"We'll be back soon," I said. "If it's too much, I'll take it from you, okay?"

"Go already. You're wasting good sneak time."

We left the room and shut the door behind us.

"I asked Halima to check in on her," Danello said.

"Thanks."

"So," he said with a sad smile, "what's the plan?"

I smiled back. It should have been Aylin asking that. "I want to see if we can get up on the aqueduct. It's our best way in past the guards, and if we can climb down into a tree or onto the roof, we might even be able to get in and out without ever touching the ground."

"That pynvium is as good as ours, then."

And with luck, our families too.

SIXTEEN

Siekte and her leeches were waiting for us in the main room. "Nice disguise," she said, blocking my path.

"Whatever I can do to avoid getting caught," I said. "I know how upset you'd be about that."

She scowled at me but didn't threaten to lock me up in my room. Of course, she didn't get out of my way either.

"Excuse me," I said, "but I have a lunch date."

"You swore you wouldn't leave."

"I never agreed to that."

She leaned in close, smelling oddly of cinnamon. "You really don't care that you're putting all these people at risk?"

"I have people at risk too, and they're in a lot

more danger than yours."

A door opened. I didn't turn to look, but from the way Siekte stepped aside and squared her shoulders, it had to be Onderaan.

"Siekte," he said, "let her be."

"She's a security risk."

"No, she's not. Nya, report to me when you return." He spoke again, this time low to someone else. A moment later Jeatar appeared at my side.

"Let's take a tour of the city, shall we?" He grinned at Siekte, but there was nothing friendly about it.

"Lead the way."

We left the villa and moved with the ever-present crowd toward where the aqueduct crossed over the inner wall. Too far above the buildings here to reach it, so we followed it through the city, all the way to the outer wall. Rows of tall boardinghouses butted up against the aqueduct supports. I smiled. It was the first good luck we'd had in days.

"I think that's our way up," I said. The roofs of the boardinghouses were almost even with top of the aqueduct. Getting from the top floor to the roof might be tricky, but we could do it.

"Maybe a three-foot jump from the roof," said Danello.

"Could be more." Jeatar didn't sound as pleased.

"Hard to judge distance from here."

"Worth trying though," Danello said.

Jeatar hesitated, scanning the block and the buildings. "Worth trying. *If* we figure out how to get inside and avoid whatever Vyand has prepared for us."

A man smacked into me, heading the other way. Then another, and a third. I stepped aside, pressing myself against the building. Jeatar and Danello did the same.

"What's going on?" Danello asked.

People were hurrying, scared looks on their faces. They glanced over their shoulders and picked up the pace.

"If we were home, I'd say soldiers were coming."

Jeatar frowned. "Worse."

Three Undying came into view, their pynvium armor shimmering in the sun's light. Folks got out of their way, and those who didn't move fast enough found themselves knocked aside.

"What do we do?" I whispered.

"Don't move," Jeatar said.

The Undying came toward us. My heart thudded in my chest, and I wished I had some of that shifted pain to use.

"You three," the first one said, pointing at us. I

sucked in a slow breath. "Come with us."

"What?" I said, as Jeatar nodded and said, "Yes, sir."

Go with them? Had he lost his mind?

The Undying went to the next building, a boardinghouse with bright yellow and green shutters on the first and second floors. They marched up the front steps and kicked open the door. Faint cries drifted out.

"Do what they say—they think we're soldiers," Jeatar whispered before following them inside.

We went up the stairs, our footsteps light, theirs heavy and foreboding, like they *wanted* to sound as scary as possible. Doors slammed, people yelled. Thumps and thuds of all types echoed off the walls.

The Undying stopped at a door on the second floor. Two stood back while the third kicked it in. He stepped aside, and the other two charged into the room.

"Make sure they don't get past you," the third Undying said to us before following.

Jeatar blocked the door, waving us up to do the same. "We have to," he said softly.

Screams came from inside. Loud crashes, glass breaking.

"Leave him alone!" a woman cried. "He hasn't done anything!"

"Mondri Belaandrian, on the order of Duke Verraad, I hereby arrest you for conspiracy to commit treason."

Jeatar tensed, his hands clenching. He shot me a worried look that spoke volumes.

Saints! He knew him. He might even be part of the Underground.

"Speaking your mind isn't treason," the same woman said. "Get your hands off of— Ah!" A louder crash, like a body slamming hard against furniture. A man cried out, started swearing, then—

"Fenda, no!"

Metal clanged against metal, then a girl screamed in pain.

"She's just a child!" the man sobbed. "How could you?"

Jeatar closed his eyes, looked away. Danello paled.

"This isn't right," I whispered. We had to stop this. Jeatar's eyes flew open and he looked terrified.

"Don't do *anything* but what they say."

"But—"

"Do *nothing*!"

A woman sobbed, a man screamed in anger. I heard nothing from the child. Two Undying dragged a man out between them, his shirt and pants covered in blood. The third had a woman by the arm.

"Please, don't just leave her there," she said, tears on her cheeks. "I need to get her to the Healers' League."

One of the Undying scoffed. "You can't afford the League."

Jeatar caught the captured man's stare. Held it, as much pain in his eyes as I'd ever seen, let alone carried. The man glanced into the room. Jeatar nodded once, so slight I would have missed it had I not been staring.

The Undying shoved the woman into Jeatar. "Deal with her."

"Yes, sir." Jeatar seized her arm, his face blank.

She didn't even look at him, kept crying, struggling, calling for Mondri and her child. The Undying hauled him down the stairs and out the door.

"Thessa, it's me," Jeatar said, his hold loosening but not releasing. I pushed past him and raced into the room, Danello on my heels.

The girl lay in a pool of too much blood. She was thirteen, maybe fourteen. An old sword lay on the floor next to her, its blade clean. She'd never even hurt them.

I pressed my hands against her heart and head, felt my way in. Nothing but silence and death.

"Is she . . . ?" Danello whispered.

"She's gone." Healers knew best how to kill.

How could they do this? Kill a girl just for defending her father? She was never a threat to them.

Men in blue dragged Grannyma away. I ran forward.

"No, Nya, stay back," she cried.

Soldiers turned to me, hands on their swords. I grabbed a book off Grannyma's desk and threw it at one.

"Let her go!"

He drew his sword, stepped toward me. I raised my fists.

"Hey!" the other soldier snapped. "She's a child. Leave her."

Why hadn't I said those same words to the Undying?

"This is wrong," I whispered.

"Yeah." Danello stood there, hands clenched at his sides as if he wanted to punch something.

Jeatar brought Thessa into the room. She collapsed by her daughter, gathering her in her arms and burying her face in her hair. Dark, glossy black. Beautiful hair.

I moved away, walked to the window. "I should have said something."

"You couldn't do anything." Jeatar raised a hand toward my shoulder and I flinched away. His hand dropped.

"I should have tried. I should have spoken out, flashed their armor—something."

"You didn't even know if they had any pain stored."

Leave her. She's just a child.

"I should have tried."

He sighed. "If you had, we'd all be dead. Thessa, Danello, all of us. Except you." He stepped closer, putting himself between me and the window. "You'd be on your way to the Duke. On your way to being something worse than they are."

"I *am* worse than they are. I didn't *do* anything to stop them."

"But you will. We *all* will. Soon."

I looked at the girl. "Not soon enough."

Danello comforted the mother while Jeatar cared for the daughter. He brought the undertaker and helped carry her to the cemetery outside the city. Told Thessa when she'd be wrapped and buried. I followed the three of them to the villa.

Angry voices greeted us, Barnikoff, Siekte, others from both the Underground and Geveg shouting over each other. We stepped into the main room and the shouting stopped.

"Mondri was arrested," Jeatar said, his voice cold. "Fenda's dead."

Siekte gasped, both hands flying up and covering her mouth. She ran to Thessa and threw her arms around her. Fresh tears poured from both. Siekte led her away through the door I hadn't been behind, into the rooms the Underground shared.

No one spoke. We just stood there, useless.

"What was going on here?" Jeatar asked.

Barnikoff stepped forward. "It can wait. Now's not—"

"Just *say* it."

He cleared his throat. "I'm sorry about the family."

"That's not what you were arguing with Siekte about."

"No. I know this is a horrible time to say this, but it's been four days and we want to go home. I truly am sorry, but we have families of our own to think about. Businesses, livelihoods. If we could leave on our own, we would, but you promised you'd get us home to Geveg."

Jeatar closed his eyes, cocked his head to one side as if trying to hold back the screaming I knew he wanted to let out. I felt it too.

"Not now, Barnikoff," I said. Did they not care? An innocent girl just died because her parents wanted a better life for her. The same life we wanted for our families. One without the Duke. We of all people should understand that.

"You're right," Barnikoff said, "this is a bad—"

Jeatar grabbed a chair and flung it across the room. It smashed against the wall and clattered to the floor. "No, you'll leave now."

Danello took a hesitant step toward Jeatar, his hand outstretched. "This can wait, I'm sure."

"I want these people out of my house," Jeatar yelled at Danello.

Barnikoff backed away, looking ashamed. The others wouldn't look up at all.

"Wait upstairs in the kitchen," Jeatar said. "Pack food for three days, no more. I'll be there as soon as I change and wash Fenda's blood off my hands."

Barnikoff ushered them all out, casting a sorrowful look my way.

"They're just Baseeri," he muttered as he passed. "Who cares if they die?"

I looked away. It sounded so horrible, but I'd said similar things before. I shouldn't care—they *were* just Baseeri—but it felt hollow now. Baseeri were trying to stop the Duke, same as we were. He didn't treat them any better than he did Gevegians. They weren't *all* bad. And no child deserved to die for defending her father, no matter who she was.

"I'll be back as soon as I can get them on a boat," Jeatar told me. "Don't do anything impulsive while I'm gone."

I nodded, still numb.

Jeatar headed upstairs. Danello came to me, slipped an arm around my shoulders. Comforting as it was, it didn't make the urge to throw a few chairs myself go away.

"Aylin," I said. "I should shift her pain."

"The plan was to give it to me tomorrow morning."

I slipped out of his arm and headed for the door. "No, I'll take it now."

"Why? What's wrong? Talk to me."

He wouldn't understand. I needed that pain to remind me how terrible it was. How dangerous. How deadly. Because all I wanted to do was find all the Undying and make *them* hurt too.

SEVENTEEN

"Nya, it's been two days," Aylin said, standing over my bed with her arms crossed. Shadows played against the wall of our room. "Give me the pain."

"No."

I kept seeing Fenda, lying there. Like all the other faces of the people who'd died. I couldn't save any of them unless I became worse than the Undying. And Saints save me, right now I wanted to. Carrying the pain hadn't crushed my desire to strike back, destroy the Undying, and take away everything the Duke used to control us.

"This is foolish. You didn't even know her."

"I could have *been* her." I sat up, muscles

screaming as the blanket fell away. "We have to stop him. He can't keep killing people."

"Who? The Duke?"

The door opened and Danello walked in with a tray. Steam floated above a bowl. "Lunchtime."

Was Tali having lunch now too? Was she even still at the foundry? I needed to find a way into that stupid place, but I just couldn't get Fenda's face out of my head. Until I did, the anger would win—and I couldn't let it. Saints knew what I might become if it did.

Danello sat next to me on the bed and dipped the spoon in the soup. "Eat."

"I'm not hungry."

"You're eating this if Aylin has to hold you still while I pour it down your throat." He moved the spoon closer to my mouth. "You're in no condition to fight me, so you'd better do it."

I opened up. He poured the soup into my mouth.

"And another." He filled the spoon again.

After a half dozen spoonfuls I sighed and took the spoon out of his hands. "I feel like I'm five."

Danello grinned and handed me the bowl. "You're acting like you're five."

"Sorry."

"We forgive you."

Aylin snorted. "I don't. Not until she gives one of us her pain."

"She will." Danello grinned again, but he looked worried. "Aylin came up with a plan."

She nodded. "If Vyand won't leave on her own, we trick her into it. We'll go to the docks, act like we're trying to hire a boat home, and wait until she hears about it. She's not the only one who can spread rumors."

"She probably has men watching the docks anyway," Danello added.

Draw Vyand out. If she thought I'd left Baseer, she probably *would* follow. She wanted me more than Tali, and wouldn't care what happened to her if I wasn't here. It wasn't a perfect plan, but I could work with it. "We'd need Baseeri clothes."

"I can get them from Neeme. She's about our size."

"And Danello?"

Aylin rolled her eyes. "Will you let me take care of that?"

We'd need to find a boat captain who would talk, someone disreputable who Vyand would think I'd be desperate enough to hire.

That would get Vyand out of the way, but I

doubted we could we break into the foundry with just two of us. Danello would have to go with me. Jeatar too, maybe Neeme or Ellis if we needed more. We could steal a lot more pynvium with more people. Enough to really help the Underground.

And once we broke into the foundry, I'd do more than just steal pynvium and save our families. I'd destroy whatever it was that was making the armor. Break the molds, burn the enchantment recipes, whatever I had to do to make sure no Undying were ever created again.

I handed Danello the soup bowl. "Get the clothes. Find us maps of the city."

"And after, you'll give me your pain?" Aylin asked.

"I will."

She smiled. "*Now* I forgive you."

Siekte glared as Danello and I left, but with Onderaan there, she didn't try to stop us. Just grumbled to her team and acted sullen. Jeatar was gone again—no surprise there. It hadn't been easy for him to get the Gevegians out of Baseer, and he'd had to spend a lot of favors and money to do it. Ever since, he'd been sullen and withdrawn, coming and going at all hours and avoiding me. Aylin had been keeping tabs on him, but he was a lot sneakier than she was.

The noon heat blasted the crowded streets, and I was actually grateful for the blousy sleeveless top and knee-length pants. I'd be happier if they weren't purple, green, and orange triangles, but at least they kept me cool. We blended in well enough, following the small map Neeme had drawn in a notepad.

A quarter gate loomed ahead, but these gates were just basic ones, and Neeme had given us seals to pass. She swore as long as there was no trouble nearby, the quarter gate guards didn't hassle anyone. I held my breath anyway until the guards waved us through.

River breezes hit me as we reached the docks, cool and fresh after the cloying heat of the city. I followed my nose, past carts filled with goods, coils of heavy rope, and sailors who looked to be loafing.

"Who do we talk to?" Danello said.

"The ones who look like they wouldn't ask questions and might be willing to leave in the middle of the night."

"You can tell all that just by looking at them?"

"Sure, can't you?"

He chuckled. "They all look a little untrustworthy to me."

We reached the docks and stopped. Ships lined a

wharf so long I couldn't see the other end, a mile at least, maybe more. Piers extended deep into the river, longer than even the large ferry docks in Geveg. They curved out on both sides of me, creating a U-shaped harbor guarded by ships with tall masts and wide hulls. I'd never seen ships that size before.

Danello whistled. "That's a lot of ships."

My hope sank. There had to be dozens of entrances onto the docks, and hundreds of boats. The odds of me asking the right captains and it getting back to Vyand required more luck than I'd ever had in my entire life.

"Do you still know who to talk to?" Danello asked. "Vyand couldn't have the entire docks covered."

I squared my shoulders. Tali was counting on me. There *had* to be a way.

"Vyand is a tracker, and she's good. She'd have her men watching the boats she thinks I'm most likely to approach. Gevegian traders, Verlattian cargo ships, small personal skiffs. The more desperate looking the better."

"What if they see us and follow us back to the villa?"

I hadn't thought of that. "You talk to the captains then, and I'll watch to see if you're followed. I doubt there are many folks trying to get to Geveg.

That should be enough to get her attention."

"If she's listening."

I scanned the docks and the ships as we walked. Most flew Baseeri flags, but I spotted three flags I didn't recognize. On big ships too. Maybe they were from cities farther up the river.

"There." I pointed at a small trader, its wide, flat hull good for pulling into the shallows. "That's the same kind of boat Barnikoff used to smuggle our Takers off Geveg."

"I'll go talk to him. You stay out of sight."

"I'll wait right over there."

He headed for the smuggler's boat and I sat on a row of discarded crates between dock vendors. Children laughed ahead and a boy raced out of the crowd, a whole steamed fish in his hands. A lanky man appeared next, and from the way he was yelling, he was not happy about losing a fish. Boy and fish came toward me. It was the same boy who'd helped me my first day in Baseer.

He cut close to me and dived behind the crates. The man elbowed his way through the crowd a heartbeat later, looking around.

"He went that way," I said, pointing in the opposite direction. "Down that dock there."

The man paused, but Neeme's clothes must have

made me look respectable, because he nodded and ran off where I'd pointed.

I waited a few heartbeats. "He's gone."

The boy poked his head out, bits of fish smeared across his mouth. "Thanks." He squinted; then his eyes grew wide. "Stolen girl!"

So much for my disguise. "That's me."

"How'd you grow your hair?"

I wiggled the braid. "It's fake."

He grinned. "Fake on you, but real on somebody."

"My friend."

He nodded and tore off another chunk of fish. "Hungry?"

"No, thank you." I pulled one of the pears I'd saved from breakfast out of my pocket. "I have an extra if you want."

He nodded fast and reached for it, still gnawing on the fish. "The hunt don't find you yet?"

"Not yet. I'm hunting them now."

He giggled and tossed the bones over his shoulder. "They got Iesta."

I winced. The pack leader who'd broken Neeme's leg. If he told them I'd shifted into him, I might have more than Vyand after me.

"Broke his leg and left him hurting. He died."

Died? My chest tightened. It shouldn't have

bothered me—Iesta would have killed Neeme—but I had too many deaths on my conscience already.

"Don't be sad," the boy said, patting me on the shoulder. "Iesta was mean as fire. Nobody liked him none."

"What about your pack?"

He shrugged. "We eat okay. Quenji knows where the open windows are."

"What's your name?"

"Ceun."

"I'm Nya."

His gaze darted sideways and he dropped behind the crates again. I leaned back, covering him, and scanned the docks for whatever had spooked him. The fish seller returned, a frown on his face. He ignored me and vanished into the crowd.

"Ceun, have you seen any trackers around here lately?"

He hugged himself and shuddered hard. "Leave them alone."

"I'm trying to. I just need to know if any have been asking around about me."

Ceun hopped up on a low stone wall overlooking the harbor. A strong breeze blew through, rustling the trees behind us. "Who looking for you?"

"A woman name Vyand. A little taller than me,

219

always neatly dressed, hair perfect. She works with Stewwig, a huge man who never says anything."

His eyes lit up. "Stew-Pot!"

"You know him?"

"He eats what he hunts. That's how he grew so big. You not want to be caught by him."

I laughed. "Have you seen them here lately?"

"No, but the pack might. Can I join your hunt?" His blue eyes sparkled.

If anyone else had asked, I'd have said no, but Ceun could probably take care of himself better than I could. Besides, street packs had eyes everywhere. If anyone could find out who Vyand was talking to in this chaos, they could. And if Vyand heard someone else was asking about me or her down here, it might help lure her out. "You can."

He smiled big as the moon.

"She should have sent men by now," I said four days later. We'd spoken to a dozen boats, played the role of scared travelers trying to get out of the city but not being able to afford it. Ceun's pack hadn't seen any of Vyand's men, and no one was asking about me.

We hadn't found any other way into the foundry, so if Vyand *did* leave, we'd have to try the aqueduct and hope we could improvise when we got there.

After so long, I wasn't sure Tali was even there any-more. Getting pynvium for Onderaan's device might be the only chance I had left to save her.

I tried to ignore the nagging voice in my head that said I should have gone after her first. Every time I heard it, I couldn't look Aylin or Danello in the eye for a while.

"Maybe my plan wasn't so good," Aylin said.

Danello sat up, but it was a struggle. I helped him, and his skin felt feverish. "Maybe you should book passage and see what happens," he said.

"Worth a shot."

We had to do something soon. Danello didn't look well. He'd carried the pain only a few hours, but already his face was pale and sweaty, and he trembled even under heavy blankets. Halima sat with him, trying to get him to eat. Aylin looked glad to be rid of the pain but guilty that it was Danello's turn. I knew exactly how she felt.

Jeatar had left yesterday saying he'd be back in a few days. Siekte still wanted me gone and argued with Onderaan constantly. Onderaan didn't seem as enthusiastic about our plan as he once had been, and I feared Siekte was starting to convince him to get rid of us.

"We'll let you rest," I told Danello, wanting to

hug him. He couldn't take it, though.

"See . . . ya soon."

"We don't have much longer, do we?" Aylin asked the moment our door was shut.

"I'd guess one more shift for each of us."

She paled but nodded. "What are we going to do?"

I had no idea. "Maybe Onderaan can get his healing device to work."

"Okay." She looked as hopeful as I felt.

I left our room and went to Onderaan's door. Neeme and Ellis were sitting in the main room again, playing cards this time. Onderaan had stopped all missions after Mondri and Fenda. Except for whatever Jeatar was doing. That was part of the reason Siekte was so mad.

I knocked.

"Come."

Onderaan was behind his desk, maps and papers spread out in front of him. He looked up. "Nya. What can I do for you?"

"We can't keep shifting the pain. I was hoping you could try your healing device on Danello."

He sighed and rubbed his eyes. "It's not ready yet."

"He's dying. We're out of time."

"I know. I've been studying maps and reports of the foundry. There's no way inside without a full attack."

"The aqueduct will work."

"It's too risky. If you're discovered, escape is unlikely."

I'd find a way. "Will you try the device? Or let me try it? Maybe having a Taker use it would help." My skin twitched at the thought of it on my hands. Better than Danello dying, though.

"I'll try." He pulled the device from his drawer. "No guarantees."

"There never are."

We went to Danello's room. Neeme watched us pass with enough curiosity to fill six cats. I knocked and entered.

"We have an idea," I said. Aylin slipped in behind me, a forced smile on her face.

Danello looked up. "Almost . . . as scary as . . . 'I have a plan.'"

I grinned and blinked back tears. "I'm going to try the healing device on you."

He nodded.

Onderaan handed me the device. My skin started itching the moment it touched me, but I slipped it over my wrist and fingers.

"Just squeeze and flick," Onderaan said.

I took Danello's hand and squeezed, then flicked my wrist.

Nothing.

I flicked and then squeezed.

Still nothing.

I concentrated on the pynvium, pleading with it to draw the pain away. My hand tingled, but it was probably just me, not the device. I pulled it off and rubbed my wrist.

"I'm sorry, it didn't work."

"It's okay. I can hold it."

I took his hand again and felt my way in. Thick blood, but no spots on his organs yet. He wouldn't be comfortable, but he could indeed hold it until tonight. I just needed to have a plan to get rid of it by then.

"I'm sorry," Onderaan said.

"We need to break into the foundry tonight."

He shook his head. "It's too dangerous. You'll wait until Jeatar returns, like we planned."

"Danello can't wait that long."

He sighed, compassion in his eyes, but no sign of giving in. "Wait for Jeatar." He left the room, closing the door softly behind him.

Aylin looked at me, tears in her eyes. Danello was pain sick now, but it would be me in that bed tomorrow. And I wouldn't be getting out of it.

"We'll fix this," she said, her voice catching. "You'll think of something."

The only thing that came to me was taking the pain, knocking on the foundry door, and giving it all to Vyand.

"You rest," I said, brushing the hair from Danello's eyes. "I'll be back later."

We left Danello's room. Neeme and Ellis were standing in the hall, arms folded, faces stern.

"What's going on?" Neeme asked.

"What do you mean?" I said.

"Something is going on. Onderaan has been preoccupied and more secretive than usual. Jeatar is doing Saints-know-what. Siekte is furious and grumbling. You've stopped borrowing the uniforms, but you borrowed other things instead. You changed your looks. You go out all the time, but you three are never actually three anymore. Only two of you are seen each day, and it's always a different two."

I looked at Aylin. She shrugged.

"We've been sharing pain," I said.

"You've been what?"

"I wasn't able to shift all of Ellis's pain into the soldier before he died. We need pynvium and

225

a Healer to get rid of what's left, but there's none available. We've been trying to figure out a way to get some. Until then, one of us holds it every day."

They both looked confused. "Why do you share it?"

"Because shifted pain kills whoever carries it after a few days. By moving it around, we extend the amount of time we can carry it before it kills someone, but it gets worse every time I shift it. It's really bad now."

Now they both looked horrified. "That's awful."

"I know. And we need to go out again and find some pynvium somehow by tonight, so if you . . ."

They were ignoring me, whispering with their heads close together. Neeme frowned, but Ellis nodded. Finally she sighed, and they turned back to us.

"I'll take it," Ellis said. "That'll give you another day, yes?"

I just gaped.

"It will," said Aylin. "Thanks."

"Are you sure?" I said.

"You saved me. Let me help you."

"Me too," Neeme added. "That'll give you even more time."

"Could you split it," Ellis asked. "Give each of us

half so it isn't as bad? Would that spread it out even longer?"

"It might. It would certainly make it easier on you."

"What do we do?"

I took them into Danello's room. He seemed surprised to see them, but he didn't have the energy to do more than glance up. Neeme and Ellis looked less sure once they got a look at him. I picked up Danello's hand and held my other out.

"Just give me your hand. Who wants to go first?" I should have given them one last chance to say no, but we needed them too badly.

Ellis put her hand in mine. "This is going to hurt, isn't it?"

"It'll feel a lot like when you got stabbed. Some of it's the same pain."

She grimaced, but nodded. "Do it."

I *drew* from Danello and *pushed* into Ellis. She cried out and pulled away, but I kept hold of her. Neeme caught her shoulders and held her steady.

"Saints, that's bad," Ellis said, wrapping her arms around her middle.

Neeme licked her lips. "Um—"

"Oh no," Ellis said, pushing her forward. "You're not getting out of this."

I held out my hand. Neeme grabbed it and closed her eyes. I *drew*, I *pushed*, she shrieked, then laughed uneasily.

"That pack leader really got what was coming to him if this is what he felt," she said.

More deaths, more guilt, but I held my tongue. "Do you have rooms you can rest in?"

"Yes, in the other wing." Ellis turned and headed slowly for the door. "We'll be fine. You two—no, make that you *three*—go find pynvium and Healers so we don't have to do this again."

I looked at Danello, sitting up now, even if he did look tired.

"That's sounds good to me," he said.

"Except Aylin and I will go out. You stay here and rest. We'll be back in a few hours with some kind of plan." We were going into the foundry tonight, no matter what. If Vyand was still there, we'd figure out how to get past her when we had to.

Danello looked dubious.

"Don't worry."

"Can I worry?" Aylin asked.

"No."

We left Danello and headed out to the street. I caught Aylin's arm as we left the villa.

"We're breaking in tonight," I said.

228

"I had a feeling you were going to say that."

"We'll need help, though."

"Ceun's pack?"

"That's what I was thinking." There was enough in the foundry to tempt even the most cautious thieves, and if I could show them a way in and a workable plan, they might be willing to help for whatever they could carry out.

We hurried to the docks, no longer needing the map. With its gridlike streets, Baseer wasn't that hard to get around in, really. Hardest part was getting through the crowds.

Several large ships were being unloaded as we got there. I wove between unloaders and the stuff they were unloading, holding my breath more than once from the smell. We reached the stone wall with the good view we'd been meeting Ceun at every day and jumped up on it. It was almost noon.

"What about Vyand?" Aylin asked.

"We'll try Danello's idea. Book passage tonight and hope she hears about it."

"Pretty risky."

"What choice do we have?"

"Stolen girl!"

We both jumped. Ceun was on the wall beside me. The boy was quiet as sunshine.

"You scared me."

He grinned. "Saw Stew-Pot."

My heart flipped. "Where? At the docks?"

"He and his pretty lady got on a boat yesterday afternoon."

"They left *yesterday*?" Saints! We missed an entire night.

He nodded. "Tried to see you too, but you weren't here."

I was such a fool. It had never occurred to me to watch the foundry and see if Vyand left. Not that that would have helped much, since our seals didn't work anymore. But it didn't matter—she was gone! I hugged Ceun and he laughed.

"Ceun, I need your help tonight. Can you get your pack leader to meet me right away? I have an idea that will make you all rich."

His eyes widened. "For that I bring you the whole pack."

"I'll need your help with something else." I pulled out the small bag of coins Jeatar had given me. "Can you find me four or five iron boxes like the fishermen use to keep their flares dry?"

He grinned at the coins. "I can even get those without buying."

"I'll need them by tonight."

"For the rich plan?"

"Exactly."

"I'll fetch Quenji and go shop. Wait here."

I sat back as he raced off into the crowd.

"What are the boxes for?" Aylin asked, settling onto the wall next to me.

"Justice."

I couldn't wait to tell Danello. We had a foundry to break into.

EIGHTEEN

The neighborhood with the boardinghouses was quiet and dark, with only about half the streetlamps lit. A few more would have been nice, since it would have made it that much harder to spot us in the dark above. A half-moon cast enough light to help us see, but it didn't make it easy.

We'd sneaked out of the villa one at a time, and though the guards in the main house saw us, they must have been used to us leaving by now, because no one tried to stop us. Whether or not they told Onderaan we'd left was something I'd deal with when we got back.

If we got back.

Ceun arrived with Quenji, the new pack leader,

and another boy, Zee. Others in the pack had wanted to help, but we figured the more we had, the more likely we'd be caught. All of us carried empty sacks on our belts and backpacks with supplies.

We stood on the top landing in one of the boardinghouses closest to the aqueduct. The window was already open and just big enough for us to crawl through and climb up the outside of the building to the roof.

"Last chance to change your mind," I said.

Ceun smiled. "We all go."

Quenji ruffled his hair. "There's lots of good stuff to steal in there. We'll eat for a year." He laughed. "We could eat for months just from the stories. People talk about you, Shifter, but we'll have truth to tell, not gossip."

I gaped. "You know who I am?"

He laughed again. "You're a legend in the packs. You hurt the Undying. Stole prisoners from soldiers. Braved the inner gates just to spy on Stew-Pot. We help you, we become legends, too."

Ceun and Zee grinned wide at that.

Aylin hid a laugh behind her hand, while Danello beamed. Me? A Baseeri legend? Saints, how sad must their lives be if *I* was the best thing they had to talk about.

"Okay. Time to climb."

Quenji went out the window first, coils of rope slung diagonally across his chest. He crawled up the brick like a lizard, and a rope dropped down a minute later. Danello tugged on it a few times, then tied it around his chest up under his arms. He crawled up without too much effort.

The rope dropped back down.

"You next," I told Aylin. She adjusted her backpack and reached for the rope.

"Maybe you should just try flying to the roof," she teased. "Being a legend and all."

"I could try pushing you out the window."

She giggled and crawled out and up.

"We know you can't fly," said Ceun, so serious, for a moment I thought he meant it. "But we do think you can stop the Undying."

My joyful mood vanished. "I hope so."

The rope dropped again and I tied it under my arms. The windowsill was wide enough to stand on, and the too-colorful shutters nailed to the brick on both sides made easy handholds. It also helped that the boardinghouse hadn't been built with much care. Brick corners stuck out, mortar had chipped away between bricks, both just enough for toes and fingers to wedge into.

Not that I had to climb far. I'd gone only a few feet when the rope tightened and Danello and Quenji hauled me up. Ceun was on the roof with us before they got the rope off me.

"How close are we to the aqueduct?" I asked, making my way to the edge of the roof. It hadn't looked far from the street, but as Jeatar had said, it was hard to judge distance from down there.

"A good jump," Danello said.

Quenji shook his head. "A bad jump."

Bad indeed. The aqueduct was more even to the roof than it had looked, but not as close as we'd thought. We'd have to jump across three feet of space and land on four feet of aqueduct. In the dark.

Aylin leaned in close. "It might be easier to steal some more gate passes."

"That won't get us into the foundry, though. We have to go in from above." I looked around the roof. We'd brought iron spikes to anchor into the aqueduct, but they'd pull right out of the wooden roof. The only other place to tie the rope was around the crenellations along the front and sides of the building. They looked more decorative than solid though.

Danello followed my gaze. "They'll have to do."

"They look like they'd break if we kicked them hard."

"We'll have people holding the ropes as well."

No one volunteered to go first this time. I sighed and stepped forward. "I'll go."

"No, I'll do it," Danello said, then grinned. "I was just hoping I wouldn't have to."

Quenji tied the rope around one of the crenellations while Danello tied the other end around himself. The rest of us lined up along the rope and took hold.

"Here goes." Danello backed up a few paces, then darted forward, leaping into the night. He landed on the aqueduct, stumbled, and dropped flat.

We all gasped, but Danello stood a moment later.

"I'm okay. I'm here." He untied the rope and tossed it back.

Aylin went, landing lightly on her feet. She was the one who seemed to fly. I grabbed the rope.

Saint Saea, I could use a little of Aylin's grace.

I jumped. Darkness swirled around me as I crested the empty space between the structures, then my toes found solid ground again. Strong arms caught me, halted my forward momentum.

"Thanks," I mumbled into Danello's chest, not wanting to let go just yet.

"Don't worry, I won't let you fall."

Ceun climbed up and stood at the edge of the roof, working his arms and shoulders, rubbing under his arms. We waited on the aqueduct, hands ready to grab. Ceun took a running start, then jumped.

His feet hit the stone and hands shot out of everywhere to grab him. He steadied and plopped down.

"That scared me good," he said.

"Scared us too."

He grinned.

"How is Quenji going to get across?" Aylin asked. "There's no one on that side to pull him up if he falls."

"He said to anchor the rope to the aqueduct and he'll climb across," said Ceun, already waving to Quenji.

We pulled one of the spikes out of the pack and hammered it into the brick. Quenji tossed us the end of the rope, and Danello tied it around the spike. Quenji checked the other end, still tied to the roof, and tightened it until the rope was taut. He dropped his weight on it, testing it. It drooped, but not too badly.

He slipped out onto the rope, hands and knees wrapped around, and inched his way over.

Snap!

The rope broke free of the boardinghouse roof.

Quenji grabbed tight, falling down and under the aqueduct. He swung, clinging to the rope.

A door slid open on the balcony and a man stepped out, silhouetted in the light coming from inside. He looked around, then peered over the railing.

"What's going on down there?"

A pause, then the man turned and went inside. The door slid shut.

We tugged at the rope, bringing Quenji closer to us inches at a time. Finally, he reached the top and we dragged him onto the aqueduct. He lay there, gasping.

"Are you okay?" I asked.

He grinned. "What a story this will make. So what's next, Shifter?"

"A long, scary walk."

We followed the aqueduct, Danello in the lead, Quenji bringing up the rear. I think the pack wanted to move faster than the pace Danello set, but it was too dark and too breezy to risk hurrying. A good gust could blow us right off.

Clock tower bells rang when we were about half-way there, two deep, sorrowful tones that floated across the city. The occasional lamp bobbed below, most likely patrols making their rounds. The closer we got to the inner walls, the more lights we saw, both moving and in straight lines along the street.

We crossed the inner wall. Danello stopped and crouched down. One by one, the rest of us did the same.

"There it is," I said. The L-shaped foundry was below. It sat on a hill, and one taller brick section looked like it might be living quarters or offices. The foundries Papa had worked in had the smelting room at the top of the hill, the forge area at the bottom, and this foundry looked the same. Long and wide, with double doors at both ends to allow air flow, open now, even though it was late. Dark orange light lit the grass, and blue light flickered on the walls. Rhythmic clangs sounded unnaturally loud in the quiet night.

"They're working at this hour?" Aylin said, crouched just behind me.

"I guess the Duke doesn't want any delays in his weapons."

"That'll make it harder, won't it?"

I nodded, my guts already churning. I'd assumed the enchanters would be gone at night, but if they were smelting the pynvium all the time, then who knew how many might be inside. It would be well-nigh impossible to get to the forges now. I adjusted my pack, and the boxes Ceun had found for me clanked softly. They were heavy, would probably slow me down and make it harder to climb, but if I left them behind, we'd have no chance at all of destroying the pynvium forges.

"There's the patrol," Danello said. Two soldiers were walking the grounds. More soldiers had to be inside.

I had to risk it. Vyand wouldn't have left unless she thought I was gone or leaving, so odds were the guards wouldn't be expecting trouble.

Unless, of course, it was all part of the trap.

I hadn't mentioned that to anyone, but it was a possibility. Vyand could have made a show of leaving just to see if she could lure me out, same as I was doing to her.

"Quenji," I said, "you and Zee wait here."

He nodded. "We'll haul you up, don't worry. Ceun is our best thief, so he'll go with you."

Ceun smiled. He had a lot of empty sacks looped in his belt.

"Let's anchor the ropes."

We picked a spot right above the big tree centered almost perfectly under the aqueduct. Unfortunately the open foundry doors looked right at it, so anyone coming outside might see us. We'd have to stay in the tree and not get too low. Danello pulled out the iron spikes and Aylin had the hammer. She handed it to Danello.

"Time it with the hammer strikes," I said. I'd been worried about the noise pounding the spikes in would make, but with the doors open, no one would hear us. The only good thing about them working late.

Clang!

Danello swung the hammer.

Clang!

He swung again. He kept it up, hard strikes in unison with the smiths, until both spikes were deep in the stone. Quenji and Aylin tied the ropes around them and gently lowered the ends into the tree below.

Awfully far below.

"Don't look down," Danello said, putting his hand over mine.

"Too late."

"I'll go first this time," he said, looping the rope around his arm. We'd all put on heavy gloves for the climb. "I'll tie the ends to the trunk so it'll be easier to climb down. You should be able to hook your legs around like Quenji did before."

"Be careful."

He chuckled. "If I was doing that, I wouldn't be here."

I smiled back, but my heart was lodged in my throat, making it hard to speak. But I could pray.

Saint Saea, Sister of Compassion, hear my prayer. Let Danello reach the tree safely. Let us all find what we seek and make it out without dying.

He climbed, hand over hand, down the rope that looked so thin. I alternated between watching him and scanning the yard and windows, but no one walked outside or looked out. The clock tower chimed again, three bells.

Leaves swallowed him just before the darkness, then the rope went slack. I heard no crunch or thud or sounds of falling, so he must have made it to the tree. The rope wiggled, then grew taut. Seconds later the other rope started wiggling. Both stopped, looking solidly attached and at a faint angle to the aqueduct.

"I'll take the left one," I said, and Aylin went to the right.

Quenji and Zee helped us slide off the aqueduct and get a firm grip on the rope. My arms strained, but I held on, moving hand over hand same as Danello had, my legs and feet wrapped in the rope under me. Ten feet down and my arms burned, shaking with every inch. Judging by the grunts next to me, Aylin was having similar trouble.

242

"Ah!" she cried.

I couldn't see her, but a ripping sound echoed up—the sound of someone sliding down a rope way too fast.

NINETEEN

"Aylin!"

She didn't scream, even though she had to be terrified. Branches cracked and snapped, but the sounds quickly stopped.

So did the hammering at the forge.

I climbed, willing my arms to keep moving, stop shaking, and anyone who might come outside to *not* look up at the tree. I didn't look down, but my ears strained for the shouts of alarm that would get us all arrested—or worse.

None came. The hammer strikes resumed.

Branches and leaves scratched my feet, then calves, and I was in the canopy. Danello grabbed my legs and guided me to a heavy branch near the trunk. I collapsed into him.

"How's Aylin?"

"About ready to throw up," she answered, "and my hands sting, but otherwise okay."

"Rope burn," Danello said. "Would have been a lot worse without the gloves."

Aylin snorted. "Would have been a lot worse if I'd let go."

Danello climbed over and shook one of the ropes, then the other. "Rest a bit while you can," he said. "We might have more climbing to do."

"Oh, joy," Aylin muttered.

Ceun made it to the tree easier than we had, but small boys were always good at climbing.

"Patrol," Danello said softly, and we all froze.

Peering through the leaves, we watched the soldiers walk by in the well-lit foundry yard. Both wore chain armor and heavy swords on their belts. Not pynvium though. They rounded the corner.

"Let's go."

We started climbing again, heading toward the rear of the building. With luck one of the branches would get us close to a third-story window. Quenji swore no one ever locked windows that high, so we'd probably be able to crawl right inside.

We reached the end of the limb. The thick one

we were on didn't reach the building, though a few smaller ones did.

"Stay here and keep an eye out for the patrol." I stepped carefully onto the limb that reached nearest a window, inching along, testing my weight. The closer to the end I got, the more the limb dipped. I climbed back. "It won't hold me."

"How 'bout me?" Ceun asked. "I'm small."

"See if you can get to the window and tie the rope across."

Aylin peered through the shadows. "Is that room empty?"

"Looks dark, but— Patrol!"

We froze again and the soldiers passed below. And stopped.

Aylin squeezed my hand. I held my breath. One of the soldiers knelt and picked up a broken branch. He glanced up into the tree.

Don't see us, don't see us, don't see us.

He rose, tossing the branch away, and they continued walking.

I exhaled. Too close.

"Ceun, go for the window."

He nodded and scampered across the branch. It dipped, but not deep enough to drop him. He reached the window and stepped off. The branch

246

snapped up and bobbed, but no new branches fell.

Ceun clung to the window like a frog on a tree. He scooted down and pressed his palms against the frame, then lifted. The window opened and Ceun slipped inside. We waited, seconds ticking away, then he popped out. "Toss the rope," he called softly.

Danello tossed an end, Ceun caught it. Both vanished back into tree and room. The rope stretched flat.

Danello didn't waste time. He hung from his knees on a branch and scooted onto the rope. It held. He crawled across a lot faster than I'd be able to.

Aylin went across, not so graceful, but not slow either. Then it was my turn. I sat on the branch and slid back, hanging from my knees. Reached forward and grabbed the rope. My arms shook already and I hadn't even done anything.

Just cross already.

I let go with my legs, tried to swing them up and onto the rope. And missed. I dangled, my arms screaming.

Move it, move it, get those legs up!

I pulled with all my strength and my legs caught the rope, then wrapped around. I said a quick prayer and climbed across, forcing my hands forward, sliding my legs closer.

Almost there.

Footsteps below. The patrol!

I hung thirty feet in the air, out in the open. I had no idea if I'd dislodged any branches. I couldn't move without making noise, and even the small scrape of cloth and leather against rope might alert them.

They passed below.

I exhaled and started moving again, counting the inches until—

"Got you," Danello whispered, scooping me up and pulling me inside. I sank to the floor, muscles demanding a week off, at least.

"Thanks. Where are we?"

"Storage room, I think," he said. "Lots of boxes."

And barrels, and crates.

"Nothing worth stealing," Ceun said, closing the lid on one. "Tools and forge stuff mostly. One box of swords."

"I guess it was too much to hope for to find pynvium in the first room," I said.

"With our luck?" said Aylin. "Way too much."

"Ceun," Danello said, "grab us three of those swords."

"Sure."

I stood, knees shaking only a little, and went to the door. I pressed my ear against the wood. No footsteps, no voices. That didn't mean no guards though.

I tapped Danello on the shoulder and pointed to the door. He nodded and got ready to open it. I waited to the side with Aylin, both of us with sheathed swords raised like clubs.

Danello turned the latch and paused. Still no sounds outside. He opened the door and peeked out. "Clear."

We went to the next room. Tried the door. Locked.

Danello watched the hall while Ceun stepped forward, pulling thin metal sticks out of a pocket. He got on one knee and stuck them into the lock. The lock clicked and he opened the door. We followed and shut it behind us. The room was dark, but gentle sounds of breathing floated about. Impossible to tell how many though.

Soldiers or Takers? I pointed to the door and held up my hand, thumb and index finger about an inch apart. Ceun nodded and cracked the door.

Hall light sliced inside, illuminating the foot of a bed. Good boots sat on the floor, with a sword belt hanging on the foot post. Soldier bunks.

We slipped out of the room in a hurry.

Danello went a few doors down and stopped at one across the hall. Another locked door. Ceun picked it and we went inside again, leaving the door open enough to see inside this time.

Dim, but not dark. More breathing, but also whimpers and moans. Six people lay chained to six beds. My heart soared. There *were* Takers here!

"Jovan! Bahari!" Danello said, darting over to his brothers.

Aylin ran to Enzie, surprise and joy on both their faces. I scanned the beds, saw Winvik and two I didn't know, but no Tali. Why wasn't she here too?

Guilt dampened my joy. I was glad we'd found them, but it wasn't fair. Everyone else was here, even people we didn't even know had been captured, so why not her? My stomach twisted. Had Vyand taken Tali with her?

"What's hurting them?" Ceun said, his eyes wide.

"They're being forced to take more pain than they can handle. The Duke's trying to make unusual Taker abilities surface so he can use them."

"He's making quirkers?"

"Trying to."

"Nya, how are we going to get them out of here?" Aylin asked.

"Ceun, can you pick these cuffs?"

"Already picking."

"Enzie, have you seen Tali?"

"Not since the jail."

"Are there more Takers here?" I asked. Tali had to be too young to be an Undying, so where was she?

"Yes. With the weird slab."

"Slab? Like the one the Healers' League used?"

She shook her head. "It's different. It holds us. Hurts us." She started coughing.

"Do you know where they keep the pynvium?"

"No."

There'd be some in the smelting room for sure, but I'd hoped there would be some stored that was easier to get to.

I put one hand on Enzie's head and felt my way in, checking for slowed blood and spots on her organs. So much pain, almost as much as Neeme and Ellis were carrying, but it hadn't started to kill her yet. But it felt *off* somehow.

Finding so many pain-filled Takers changed things. We'd have to get the pynvium and heal them before we could get them out of here. Worse, even without their pain, I doubted any would be able to climb up the rope to the aqueduct. Quenji and Zee might be able to haul them up, and Danello could go first and help, then maybe Aylin. She was a lot stronger than she looked.

"I'm going to check on the others. I'll be right back."

Enzie nodded, tears dripping from the corners of her eyes.

The others were about the same. They must have been recently filled with pain, though it felt different from anything I'd ever felt before. It wasn't specific pain like a heal normally caused, but a lot of pain all mixed up into one.

I sucked in a breath.

Like *shifted* pain. Had Vinnot found another like me?

"So where do they keep the pynvium?" Aylin said, her face set.

"Smelting room."

"That big noisy room with the open doors?"

"Right."

She frowned but slid the backpack off her shoulders. "Let's hope they don't pay much attention to who works the night shift." She opened the pack and pulled out three uniforms. We pulled them on over our clothes.

"The cuffs are all picked," Ceun said.

"Some more rooms to search on this floor," Danello said, taking the last uniform from Aylin. "We can try those first."

I hated to just leave Enzie and the others here, but until we found pynvium, we couldn't do anything to help them. "Okay, let's check them."

We slipped into the hall and went to the next door. Locked, which was a good sign. Ceun picked it and peeked inside.

"Dark and quiet," he said, then went in.

We followed. My eyes adjusted enough to make out more boxes and crates, a few barrels. I pried the lid off one. Something dark, like sand.

"Danello, open those curtains, please."

He did, and moonlight lit the room.

"What is this?" I scooped my hand into the barrel. It *was* some kind of sand, but coarser, almost metallic.

"Worth anything?" Ceun asked.

"I don't even know what it is. But there's a lot of it if all these barrels are filled with it."

Ceun nodded and pulled a bag off his belt. "Might be worth good coin, then."

I pulled a small bag out of my pocket and filled it with the sand. Might be nothing, but who knew what the Duke was making here. Better to get a good look at it in the light.

"This trunk is locked," Aylin said from the other side of the room. "It's big."

It was. Maybe four feet long, three feet tall, three feet deep. Thick iron bands wrapped around it like a Winterfest gift. My heart quickened. You didn't lock something up that tight unless it was worth a lot.

"Open it. Maybe it's pynvium."

Ceun went to work on the lock. Took him longer than the doors, another good sign. It clicked open and he lifted the lid.

"Wow." He held up a wrist bracer. The entire trunk was filled with armor.

"Let me see that." I brought it to the window under the moonlight. It looked black, same as the sand. I needed more light. I went to the door, listened for noises outside, then opened it enough for the hall lamps to shine in.

Blue armor.

I shut the door.

"It's pynvium. It's the Undying's armor."

Ceun dropped his piece like it was on fire. Aylin started yanking pieces out and filling her arms.

"Are there more trunks like this?" she said.

"Three more about the same size."

"Get as much of the armor as you can," I said,

grabbing more. "This will heal them."

More than that, there were full sets here. Who needed a healing device if we could look like one of the Undying and walk right into the Taker camp? We filled our bags and slipped back into the room with the Takers.

"Does anyone here know how to heal?" I asked, holding up one of the armor pieces. "Or how to push pain into pynvium?"

A boy I didn't know raised his hand, though it barely got above the bed sheet. I brought the armor to him.

"Is this fillable?"

He took it, closed his eyes, and smiled. My heart soared. Seconds later he sat up, the color returning to his cheeks. "I'll heal the others."

"Can anyone else heal?"

"Me, maybe," Enzie said. "Tali was teaching me."

I brought her a piece as well. She held it and her brow wrinkled. "It doesn't want to go."

"Don't rush it, just feel your way in." At least that's what Tali had told me last summer when she was teaching *me*. It hadn't worked, of course. No matter how hard she'd tried, my ability just didn't work like anyone else's.

Her eyes flew open. "I got some!" She'd gotten

rid of most of her pain by the time the healer boy stopped at her bed.

"I can get it!" She jerked away as he reached for her.

He smiled and gently placed his hand over hers on the armor. "Just kind of sprinkle it over, like this." He closed his eyes. Enzie narrowed hers and nodded slowly.

"I see, okay, let me try." She closed her eyes and pushed the rest of her pain into the armor.

"I knew you could do it," I said. I turned to the healer boy. "Can you heal me, please?"

He took my hands, and my arms felt much better.

"Thanks." I picked up the two bracers full of pain and slipped them under my shirt. Clunky to carry, but we needed all the weapons we could get.

Bells started clanging in the hall. Then shouts and thumps. People moving very quickly. Ceun cracked the door a finger width, listened, then shut it again.

"Bad things. The patrol found the rope."

TWENTY

Panicked faces turned to me.

"Back in bed," I whispered. "Make it look like the cuffs are still on you. Ceun, under the bed, hide."

"What about us?" Danello asked.

"We're soldiers. We're here to guard this room. Aylin, turn the lamps up."

I stashed the pynvium and the backpacks under Enzie's bed and drew my sword.

Danello got beside me. "Are you sure about this?"

"We can jump out the window if you want."

"Three stories is a bit much, even for me."

The door burst open and two soldiers came in,

swords of their own ready to swing. Fighting every instinct I had, I sighed in relief and lowered my sword. After a moment, Danello and Aylin did as well.

"Good, it's just you," I said with a dry chuckle. "We were expecting a lot worse. What's going on out there?"

One of the soldiers looked at me, confusion on her face. The other looked suspicious.

"Well?" I said, adding just a bit of worried irritability.

"Have you seen anyone on this floor?" the woman soldier asked.

"Just you. Been quiet all night."

"You've been here all night?"

I nodded. "Don't know why we need three to guard a bunch of sick people, but I wasn't going to argue with that tracker woman." Vyand had probably made an impression while she was here.

"Oh. Yeah, probably a good idea." She glanced at her partner, who shrugged subtly.

"She thinks someone is going to steal them." I laughed, then stopped. Might be pushing it. "What's going on outside? We heard something about a rope?"

The soldiers sheathed their swords. "Patrol found

a rope tied from the tree to the third-floor storage room. Someone might be inside."

"Think they're after these people?"

She scoffed. "Them? Doubt it. More likely the pynvium."

"Or whatever they're hiding on two," one of the guards muttered.

The woman shot him a look and he quieted. "We'll check it out. Stay alert though."

"We will. They won't get in here."

"You need any help searching?" Danello asked.

The woman hesitated, then looked at her partner and shook her head. "No. If Vyand wants you here, stay here. We don't want Vinnot mad at us. Keep the door locked."

"Will do," I said, forcing my voice to stay steady. Vinnot was *here*. This wasn't just a foundry; it was where he conducted his horrible experiments. No wonder it was so well protected, and why there were Takers here. Was Vyand working for him? Is that why she'd had Undying with her?

They left the room, and I locked the door so it clicked loudly.

"Quenji is gonna be mad he missed that," Ceun said from under the bed. He sounded like he was having fun.

"So they're hiding something on the second floor," Aylin said.

"Sounds like it. I bet it's something Vinnot is working on."

It's different. It holds us. Hurts us . . .

"Enzie, tell me more about the weird slab. Is that what they're hiding? Is that where they take you all to hurt you?"

Enzie nodded. "They carry us downstairs and lock us into it. It hurts. Puts pain into you."

"Like I can?"

"Yes. Only it doesn't take it back out."

Jovan shook his head. "It takes it back out. I saw Vinnot do that to six Takers when he brought us to it. I think he took it out of them so he could put it in us."

"It has cuffs on it," Winvik said. "Like the ones on the bed, but not on chains. They grew out of it."

Saea be merciful. Was it to test Takers, or was it some kind of weapon? Maybe both. But if the Duke already had a weapon that put pain into people, why would he need me?

Because you don't look like a weapon.

Forget the risk. I couldn't leave without destroying the pynvium forges, no matter how many soldiers were down there. Without those forges,

Vinnot couldn't build anything else. And I had to get onto the second floor and destroy his pain-shifting device. But first—

"Nya, you have that look again," Aylin said. "You want to do something we're *not* going to like, don't you?"

"We need to get everyone out so I can destroy this place."

She gaped at me. So did Danello. "It's a *foundry*," he said. "Molten metal, lots of stone and brick. They don't break."

"He's right, and the guards are already on alert," Aylin added. "We were lucky to find Enzie and the twins, so maybe we should just get out of here with them and the pynvium while we can."

"*I* can't. You saw what the Undying did to that family. How long until the Undying are breaking down Gevegian doors and killing Gevegian families? And now the Duke has this pain-shifting weapon? Imagine what else he has in here. No, I have to stop him."

"How?"

I grabbed my backpack from under the bed. "With these." I pulled out one of the four boxes Ceun had gotten for me.

Danello looked dubious. "Boxes?"

"These are watertight," I said, holding one up. It wasn't large, about six inches long, four wide and deep. "Fishermen use them to keep rescue flares and tinderboxes dry out on the boats. When my father was an apprentice enchanter, another apprentice accidentally threw a box like this into the forge. It heated up and exploded. Shattered the bricks to bits. Ruined the entire forge. I figure it'll work on the smelting furnaces as well as the forges."

He still didn't look convinced. "Won't the Duke just use another foundry?"

"Not to smelt pynvium. It takes a *lot* more heat to melt pynvium than iron. You need enchanted bricks to do it, and those aren't so easy to get. It'll stop his whole weapons and armor production. The Underground might be able to do something then to bring him down."

"If you can get down there in the first place." Aylin frowned at the door. Alarm bells still rang.

I tapped my uniform. "I'll blend right in."

"*We'll* blend right in," Danello said. "I'm going with you."

"Good," Aylin said. "Otherwise I'd have to."

"But—"

"No discussion." Danello put one finger against my lips. "We do this together or not at all."

I nodded. "Okay."

"So," Aylin said, "how do we get everyone out?"

"Through the front gates, I guess—it's the only way." I went to the window. The front gates had to be on my right. The tree was useless as an escape route now that they had found the rope.

I looked down into the foundry's yard. No bushes between the building and the wall. Lamps every ten feet, all lit. I didn't see any soldiers, but they were out there.

"Strip the sheets off the beds." I turned away from the window. "Make a rope."

"We're going out the window?" Enzie said. "Like you did at the League?"

"Exactly. When you're all down, run for the main gate. Hopefully you'll be able to open it from the inside, but if not, Ceun can pick the lock." I looked at him and he nodded.

Quenji and Zee must have heard the alarm bells by now, seen the patrol and the rope. If they were smart, they'd be getting out of here fast along the aqueduct before they were spotted.

"What about the guards?" Jovan said as he tied sheets together. "They'll be after us as soon as they see us."

Aylin chuckled. "Not if Nya starts exploding

the forges, they won't."

"That'll make them look the other way," Ceun said with a wide grin.

I grinned back. "Wait here until you hear a lot of noise, then run for it."

Danello and I slipped out the door. The hall lamps were brighter, the shades wide open. He drew his sword.

"You don't search for intruders without a weapon out," he said.

"Right." I drew mine.

We headed toward the stairs at the end of the hall. The sounds of doors opening and closing echoed in the stairwell, and men shouting orders. Danello took the lead, moving quickly as if he had someplace to be. We paused at the second-floor landing.

"Not good," Danello whispered.

Soldiers searched rooms on the second floor, with extra guards posted on a door at the far end. If the room was that well guarded, the pain-shifting weapon had to be inside.

"We won't be able to get in there." I hated saying it, but if we tried to talk our way past the guards, they'd get suspicious.

"Maybe we can come back after we put the boxes in the forges."

I hesitated, but Danello was right. "We don't have any other choice."

Danello pushed open the heavy door to the first floor, and heat washed over us. It was a lot noisier, with hammer strikes, furnace blasts, and men shouting. This was the foundry proper, the lower half filled with the forges and metalsmithies, the upper half for the smelting. Two sets of stone steps connected the levels, with long channels in between to pour the ore from the smelters to the forges.

There were four forges, one in each corner of the lower room. Coals burned bright orange in the firepots, their tips white as the sun. The enchanting glyphs glowed blue in the bricks, burning the coal hotter than regular fire could. Two troughs sat in the middle of the room, both filled with liquid pynvium running down the channels from the smelting room above.

Enchanters worked at each forge, scooping pynvium out and filling molds on one side, pounding out bars and making weapons on the other.

My chest fluttered. I'd spent so many hours helping Papa in the forge. He'd lower the raw pynvium into the smelting cauldron and it burned blue, like flaming moonlight. I'd hand him tongs and pokers, mugs of water. The leather coveralls were hot and heavy, but I didn't care. I loved being there.

A pair of soldiers walked around the room, each armed with a sword and a pynvium rod. They watched the enchanters and the weaponsmiths with hard stares as if they were guarding them, not protecting them. They were probably making sure the enchanters didn't steal any pynvium. Plenty here to tempt even the most loyal follower: racks of finished weapons, healing bricks. Nothing large enough to be a League Slab though. Everything here was crafted for war.

Danello tapped my hand, then looked at a forge and shrugged his shoulders. I shrugged back. I didn't know how we were going to get the boxes in there yet.

I headed toward the smelting-room stairs at the other end. One of the soldiers nodded to us as we passed. I nodded back, keeping my face as grim as his. He had to know about the alarm, so he'd just assume we were searching for the intruder.

It got even hotter at the top of the stairs, the blue-white flames burning in the smelting pits, one on each side. Giant bellows blasted the furnaces heating them. Cauldrons bubbled with liquid pynvium, chunks of impurities floating on top, waiting to be swept away. Thick chains ran from the cauldrons to heavy cranes above. Two men were carefully dragging a cauldron along the crane tracks, moving it over the channels to the forge area. The cauldron tipped, and shimmering blue pynvium poured out.

Danello watched, wide-eyed, until I nudged him and shook my head subtly. If he was used to being posted here, he wouldn't be so awed by the process.

By the right furnace five large ore carts of raw, unrefined pynvium sat open, the rough blue nuggets glinting in the firelight. Five! The Duke must have raided dozens of mining towns to have that much. It was enough to keep Geveg in Healing Slabs for years.

The other furnace had three pallets of smooth pain-filled slabs and bricks waiting to be melted down and forged into weapons. Enough to arm—and armor—more soldiers than the Duke probably had.

An enchanter and two apprentices worked at each smelter, their backs to us except for when the apprentices ran to get more ore and had to swing the cauldrons to the channels.

I leaned in close and put my lips next to Danello's ear. "We need to get rid of that soldier."

He nodded and started toward the pynvium bricks, grabbing one when the soldier wasn't looking.

Danello walked up to the soldier and smacked him in the head with the brick. He crumpled to the floor.

One of the enchanters gaped at him, caught mid-turn by the sight.

"I think the heat got to him," Danello said.

"I think that brick to the head got him," said the enchanter.

I hurried over and slipped my hand to the pynvium bracer hidden under my shirt. "We don't want any trouble here."

He shrugged. "Beat each other to death if you want. Not like I can do anything about it." He shook a foot. A chain ran from the smelter to his ankle. Same with the two apprentices working with him.

I gaped at him. "You're prisoners here?"

"Everyone here but the soldiers." He looked me over. "Something tells me you're not a real soldier."

"We're trying to destroy the foundry."

Now the enchanter and apprentices gaped at me. "Foundries aren't easy to destroy."

"People keeping telling me that." I pulled out one of the boxes.

He looked at it and smiled. "You're a wicked girl."

"Think it will it work?"

"Oh yes. But we'll be hanged for it if we're caught."

"Let's not get caught."

He laughed and nodded. "Deal. I'm Sorg."

"Nya. That's Danello."

I kept an eye on the other soldiers patrolling the forge area below while Danello used the smelting tongs to cut Sorg and the other enchanter and apprentices loose. We'd have to subdue both forge guards and free the others before we could do anything more.

"What now?" Danello said.

I pointed to the unconscious solider. "Grab his pynvium rod. I'll run down, get the others' attention, and lead them up here. Flash them as soon as they're in range."

"Got it."

I waited until he was ready behind the crates of pynvium, then ran down the stairs, waving my arms and yelling.

"They've escaped, they've escaped!"

The soldiers looked at each other, then started running toward me.

"This way, hurry!" I turned on my heel and headed up the stairs, angling right at the top as if about to run out the open doors.

Whoomp!

The soldiers dropped without a sound. Pain

stung my skin hard—no rod in Geveg ever flashed that strong.

"It didn't hurt you?" Sorg asked.

"I was out of range."

"Uh-huh." He pursed his lips and nodded slowly, as if he knew I was lying.

"Let's get the others free."

We grabbed tongs and headed into the forge area. Some of the metalsmiths wanted to run as soon as we freed them, but Sorg calmed them down. They gathered around him as we headed to the smelting room.

"Now," I said, opening my backpack, "we need to take these boxes and throw one into each forge." I didn't have enough for the furnaces, but we'd have to improvise.

"You got it." Sorg took two and handed one to an apprentice. Danello took the third.

"Just toss it in?" he asked.

"Aim for the back corner where they won't see it as easily."

Sorg chuckled. "When they see us gone, they won't be worrying about the pits." He tossed the box into the flames.

"What about the smelters?" Danello asked after throwing his. "And the pynvium?"

So many people needed it, but we couldn't possibly take it all. And we couldn't leave it for the Duke either. "We'll take the raw pynvium and leave the rest. Sorg, what would happen if we pulled those cauldrons"—I pointed to the channels running down to the forge—"and dumped it all down there?"

"You'll make a mess that'll take months to cool and a mining crew to break up again."

"Let's do it."

Apprentices grabbed the thick chains that hooked the smelting cauldrons to the cranes and positioned them over the channels.

"Pull!"

The cauldrons tipped, pouring the blue-hot liquid pynvium. The troughs below started to fill up, then overflowed, the molten metal spilling onto the brick floor. It pooled around the forges and tables and racks.

"Pour the other half in the other channel."

They moved the cauldron over and dumped the raw, unrefined pynvium into the melted pain-filled channel. They mixed, overflowing the trough and spilling out on the other side of the forge.

"Get the next one!"

We had to be running out of time. The patrol was bound to come around and see the pynvium flowing

271

toward the yard. I caught Sorg by the arm.

"Collect the pynvium rods off those other soldiers and any gate seals you can find."

He nodded.

"Switch channels!"

The pynvium coated the forge floor now. The wooden weapons racks burst into flame, and swords and rods fell into the glowing pynvium. A column of liquid metal exploded into the air, slamming against the roof and showering the room with blue-hot drops.

"Saints have mercy," Sorg cried, backing away.

More columns of searing metal burst upward, the molten pynvium bubbling like boiling sauce, spraying higher and higher. The roof beams and door caught fire, as did the bellows and any leftover smocks and gloves.

"We'd better get out of here," Sorg said, waving his apprentices toward the pynvium ore. "Everybody grab a cart."

"Wait, the soldiers," I said. "Grab them, too."

"Leave 'em," someone called.

"No."

Sorg snorted, then looked a bit ashamed and ordered the other enchanters to help us. We carried the soldiers out into the yard and dumped them by the wall, far enough away from the foundry.

"You're too soft-hearted," he told me.

"I've had enough killing."

He looked at me, one eyebrow raised. Then his gaze moved over my shoulder. "Patrol just spotted us."

"Hurry, this way." I headed around the burning foundry toward the front gate. With luck, the patrol would alert the other soldiers and we'd get most of them after us. Would be a whole lot easier to flash them as a group than in ones and twos. Even with the pynvium rods, I wasn't sure how many flashes we had left.

More bells clanged and shouts echoed all over. The smell of smoke filled the air. The patrol was still behind us, three more soldiers ahead of us.

"Fire!" someone screamed just as the sheet rope flew out the window. Ceun crawled out first and slid down like the rope was greased.

"Halt!" yelled one of the soldiers. So far none had seen the rope.

I turned, pulling the pynvium bracer out. Five soldiers raced toward us, swords and pynvium rods in their hands. I started to picture dandelions and—

Whoomp!

—came from beside me. The soldiers went down, plowing into the grass. Sorg waved the pynvium rod and laughed.

"Justice, that's what it is. Felled by the very weapons you forced us to make."

The front gate started to open. We readied ourselves for more soldiers. Quenji appeared, Zee right behind him. I spotted booted feet lying on the street just outside the gate.

"Need some help?" he said.

"I thought you'd left!"

"And leave Ceun behind?" His mouth dropped opened as we started shoving pynvium carts through the gate. "Is that—?"

"Yes, and we need to get it out of here fast." I slipped out the last piece of pynvium armor we'd filled earlier with Enzie's and the twins' pain, then saw Aylin and the others running toward us, five more soldiers right behind them. Closing way too fast.

"Hurry, hurry, hurry!" she called, herding the Takers in front of her. They ran toward us, scared as rabbits. Ceun was in the lead, but they weren't going to outrun the soldiers chasing them.

I ran forward, between them, getting closer.

Whoomp!

I'd miscalculated a bit and hit only the three soldiers in the front. They screamed and dropped, clutching their stomachs, their heads, their legs. Quenji dived past me and jumped one of the remaining soldiers, hitting him in the head with a rock. Danello appeared and went for the other, parrying a blow with his sword.

Quenji yelped and staggered, blood on his leg. I darted forward and grabbed the soldier's arm as he pulled back for another swing. He jerked and the sword swung wide, missing Quenji. I spun, ducking under the soldier's arm and grabbing Quenji's hand. Spun again, coming up under the soldier and getting a grip on his wrist. I *drew* Quenji's wound away, shifting it into the soldier. He staggered. Quenji kicked him in the chest and he fell over.

"Thanks," Quenji said, a look of wonder on his face.

I realized my mistake too late. I'd *shifted*. The Duke would know I was here, that I'd done this to him. What if he took it out on Tali?

Danello had his man down. We turned and ran toward the others.

"Follow Ceun," Quenji said as we reached them. "Stay with him."

A heavy bang shook the ground and blue fire

spilled into the night. It licked out of the foundry doors, slithering up the roof, and black smoke curled into the sky. The ground shimmered as pynvium continued to pour down the hill, lighting the base of the foundry in a pale glow. Another bang, then another, bright drops of brick and metal spraying.

What about the thing on the second floor? Was that burning, too, or did the soldiers posted there get it out?

Please, Saint Saea, let it burn.

"Nya, come on!"

I ran into the dark as the last box exploded.

TWENTY-ONE

More bells broke the quiet as we raced for the inner wall gates, pushing our ore carts ahead of us. Fire bells, alarm bells, I had no idea which. Almost hidden in the noise was the toll of the clock tower striking four.

The lamps beside the gate glowed ahead, plus bobbing torches. The alarm must have alerted the gate guards and made them call for reinforcements.

I was out of pain-filled armor. "Who has a pynvium rod left?"

Two enchanters pulled them out.

"Give me one."

They hesitated.

277

Sorg smacked the closest one in the head. "Give it to her."

He did.

"Hang back some." I ran ahead, the rod ready to flash as soon as I felt pain. Or until I saw them, whichever came first. I assumed they had rods of their own, but maybe not.

I felt it first, the sting of blown sand. Four soldiers stood in a line, swords drawn. A fifth held the rod.

I flicked my wrist and the rod triggered, sending pain flashing over the soldiers. Four dropped; the last staggered but didn't go down. He charged. I dived sideways and the blade grazed my shoulder. I gritted my teeth as I hit the street.

Danello lunged for the soldier, his sword swinging. The soldier parried it, but it knocked him off balance. Danello pressed the advantage. He swung again and the sword went flying.

An apprentice shoved past and slammed his ore cart into the soldier, knocking him against the gate.

"Get the keys!"

Zee grabbed them and the gate flew open. We raced down the dark street, turning often to throw off any pursuit. When we were sure no one was following us, we paused in an alcove and caught our breaths.

"Look at all this pynvium," Quenji said, voice filled with awe. "I can't believe you really did it."

"Didn't go exactly as planned, but it turned out okay. Grab a bag, start filling it. We can't exactly roll these carts along the street. It won't be long before there are soldiers everywhere."

We handed out the sacks and backpacks and filled them with as much ore as they could carry, but there were still three carts left.

"We can hide the rest," Quenji said.

The enchanters shook their heads. "That belongs to us just as much as anyone."

"I don't care who takes it as long as the Duke doesn't get it," I said.

Zee got behind one of the carts. "We'll take this one then."

"We'll take this." The forge enchanters and weaponsmiths got behind another.

Sorg patted the third. "I think I can manage this one."

Quenji checked the street and waved at Zee to move. "Shifter, you need our help again, you know where to find us."

"I do. And thank you."

He hefted the bags of pynvium. "It was worth it. Don't get caught."

"Stay free."

Ceun blew me a kiss and ran off with the rest of his pack. I turned to my own pack. Aylin, Danello, Enzie, Winvik, Jovan, Bahari, the two Takers, and ten enchanters and apprentices.

"Do you have anywhere to go?" Aylin asked them.

"I can take care of myself just fine," said the enchanter who had grabbed the second ore cart. "We'll be on our way—thanks for the rescue." He shoved the cart into the street and headed in the opposite direction from Quenji. The weaponsmiths followed.

Sorg tsked and turned to me. "They'll be caught within the day, mark my words. We'll stay with you."

Danello grinned. "I can't wait to see the look on Siekte's face when we get there."

"You can't just bring strangers here!" Siekte burst out as soon as we entered the main room. No one else looked happy to see us either. Enzie and the others took seats on chairs and plopped on the floor. We'd lost three more people along the way—the last enchanter decided to leave the city, one apprentice left when we got close to his family's boardinghouse, and another left when we reached the villa, scared of more aristocrats.

I emptied a sack of raw pynvium on the table. Danello set out six healing bricks. Aylin dumped the set of pynvium armor. The bag of metal sand I'd taken turned out to be finely ground pynvium.

Siekte stared at me, the pile, then the table. "How did you get so much?" She picked up an armor piece. "Is this?" She gaped at me. "Saints! Is that the Undying's armor?"

"It was."

People started talking behind her, and some didn't look so disapproving anymore.

"Where did you get this?"

"The foundry." I tried not to smile as I said it. "And there's an ore cart full of raw pynvium in the kitchen you might want to have someone bring down," I said.

All the color drained from her face. "What did you do?"

"The Duke won't be making any more weapons for a while."

"Oh no. Oh no, you didn't. How could you *be* so stupid!"

I stepped back. Danello came forward. "She did what you said couldn't be done."

"It *shouldn't* have been done, you idiot." She turned to the others. "Send out an alert to the other houses. Make sure everyone is armed and ready."

Several nodded and headed upstairs. The bookcase slammed and footsteps thumped down. Onderaan came into the room, his face a mix of anger and fear.

"You weren't supposed to do anything until Jeatar returned," he told me.

"Wait," Siekte said. "You knew about this? You held *me* back but you let *her* attack the foundry?"

Onderaan ignored her. "Half the garrison is out right now hunting for you. Do you have any idea what you've done?"

"She saved us," Sorg said. "Crippled the Duke. Poked him right in the eye."

Onderaan looked at them like he'd just noticed they were there. "Who are all these people?"

"The Takers and the enchanters the Duke was holding prisoner at the foundry. He was forcing them to work for him."

Onderaan sighed. "You have no idea what you've done."

No, but obviously destroying the foundry wasn't the victory I thought it was. "I thought the plan was to stop the Duke?"

Siekte snorted. "And you just gave him every reason to hunt us down. Onderaan, what's going on out there?"

"The foundry is in flames. There are reports of molten pynvium all over the ground. The garrison has been called out and they're locking down the gates now, all of them. No one gets in or out of the city."

"Then isn't this the perfect time to attack the Duke?" Danello said. "His men are spread out and he's distracted by the foundry."

"If we were *ready* for it," Siekte said. "But we're not, and no one is in place."

"I thought you had people in place. You were bragging about it the other day."

She stiffened and shot a glance at Onderaan, who seemed less happy about that than he was about me.

"What's he talking about?"

"He's confused."

Danello frowned. "Hardly. She said she had people in place to assassinate the Duke."

Siekte looked ready to explode. Onderaan beat her to it.

"Assassination?" he shouted. "How many times have I told you, no. Kill the Duke and Baseer crumbles under civil war. Exposing him, discrediting him, that's how we'll get rid of him."

"Hardly," she scoffed, with a look at Danello. "Do you really think anyone cares what he's doing? They *know* and they do nothing."

"The people don't know," Onderaan said. "And not all the aristocrats and prominent families know the truth."

"They will when he'd dead."

"Which will spark riots. You'll create a hole every power-hungry aristocrat in Baseer is going to try to fill. There *will* be war and the people *will* suffer. That's not the way to win. The Duke stole the throne, so we have to get the High Court to convict him for treason—"

"The Duke owns the High Court—"

"—and the legitimate heir will—"

"Oh, this again? Who cares about legitimate heirs? Have they done anything to help us? You're just trying to prove your family was right, that they supported the true Duke and those who ignored their counsel were wrong."

"They *were* wrong!"

"So what? There's no one from that side of the family left."

"Yes, there is!"

"Rumors, nothing more. Myths told to bolster

spirits. You've never been able to produce them or any proof they exist, so why should we believe you?"

"Because it's the truth."

"If you need proof of what the Duke is doing," I said in the angry lull, "we have proof right here."

They stared at me.

"This is how I proved the Luminary was stealing Geveg's pynvium, that the Duke was doing experiments on Takers. I rescued them and let them tell their stories. These enchanters and Takers can tell you more about what he's done than anyone else. They're your proof. Let them speak to the High Court."

Siekte folded her arms. "They'd never make it there alive, and even if they did, no one would believe them."

"Why not?"

"No one trusts Takers or enchanters anymore, not after what the Duke has done with them."

Onderaan didn't contradict her. Neither did anyone else, not even the enchanters we'd rescued.

"You're fools," I said. "Throwing back the fish 'cause you're hungry for fowl. Who cares if they trust them or not! They can hear the stories, hear what's going on, and maybe then some will start to listen. You can't convince anyone if they don't know what's really going on."

"Exactly what *is* going on?" said Jeatar from the base of the stairs. He looked tired, worn, filthy.

"You're back!" I said, relieved. He'd seen how it had worked in Geveg. He could convince these fools that I was right.

"Nya destroyed the foundry," Siekte said. "And by dawn the entire Baseeri army will be after us, if they aren't already."

"They're out there now. I barely got inside the gates before they were sealed. You can see the smoke and flames from the wharf." He walked over to me, glancing at the worried enchanters and Takers huddled in one corner of the room.

"He'll hunt us down," Siekte said. "The entire resistance. No one will be safe."

"We weren't safe before."

"So we fight," I said.

"Fight?" Siekte said. "He's not going to send regular soldiers after us. He'll send the Undying. You plan on fighting them?"

I smiled. "I'd actually prefer to fight them. A *lot* easier to defeat."

Everyone stared at me like I'd gone mad, except those who knew me. They just grinned.

"You're insane."

Jeatar sighed. "No, Siekte, she's just a lot smarter, tougher, and harder to kill than you are."

But Tali wasn't so hard to kill. The Duke might have his whole garrison out looking for me, but she was a lot easier to find. "Jeatar, if the Undying are being sent after us, does that mean the Taker camps are undefended? Or loosely guarded?"

He raised his eyebrows and I'd swear he was trying hard not to laugh. "You can't be serious."

"I have family to get out of there."

He chuckled dryly. "No, you can't get in. The camps are outside the walls, and no one is getting past the gates right now." He waved a hand at the uniforms we still wore. "They've seen the uniforms now, so they won't be fooled again and they'll be double-checking every soldier to ensure they really are soldiers."

"She's even ruined *that* for us," Siekte added.

"Let's try to salvage this," Onderaan said. "We can create opportunities to gain support for our side. People are already angry, and when the Duke starts breaking down doors and hauling innocent families away for questioning, those who weren't sure will be convinced and join us."

Siekte shook her head. "Those methods aren't working. The boy was right about attacking. We need to use this mess and kill the Duke while we can."

"It'll cause a war."

"And what she did won't?"

"If there's war," I said, "then I need to get Tali. She'll be in more danger than us."

Onderaan snapped around to look at me. "Your sister's name is Tali?"

There was recognition in his eyes, as if he'd finally figured out what I'd been denying for weeks. My hands and fingers went cold. I really didn't want to answer that question. Not to him, not to myself. I didn't want to face the truth. "Yes," I whispered.

"Saints, you're *Peleven's* daughters?"

I nodded.

Onderaan sucked in a breath, then held his hands out to me. "He was my brother," he said softly. "I'm your uncle."

TWENTY-TWO

"No," I said. "My father wasn't Baseeri." *I wasn't Baseeri.*

Onderaan smiled. "His blood was, even if he didn't think so either. He loved Geveg."

"It's not possible."

Aylin grabbed my left hand, Danello took the other. They didn't say a word, just held on tight. Jeatar gaped at me—Saints, they *all* gaped at me.

"You're an Analov?" Jeatar asked.

"I'm a *de*'Analov. It's different."

Onderaan smiled sadly. "No, it isn't. Peleven thought the Gevegian version made them fit in better, but I think he did it for Rhiassa."

Mama.

"You think Tali is with the Undying?" he said.

"Yes. Vyand captured her, but we didn't find her with the other Takers at the foundry. She can't be anywhere else." Unless the Duke had her, torturing her for my recklessness.

"I'm so sorry."

So was I. I tried to ignore the shocked stares of those around me, but they cut into me like a knife, peeling back truths I hadn't wanted to know. Onderaan was family. I had family in Baseer. My blood was Baseeri blood, same as my father's. But I also had Gevegian blood, from my mother. What did that make me?

"Jeatar," Onderaan said, "is there anything we can do?"

Siekte found her voice. "You've refused to act against the Duke, yet now you'll do it for a niece you've never even met?"

"I *have* met them. I just thought they died with my brother. I haven't seen Nya since my father was killed."

"Sorille," I whispered. My grandfather died in Sorille, with so many of the Pynvium Consortium.

Siekte nodded. "Sorille, yes. Look what your family did *there*. Thousands died because they refused to act. You want to duplicate that failure?"

I lifted my head. What did my family do in Sorille?

Jeatar stepped closer to her, inches from her face. "The Analovs were not responsible for what happened in Sorille."

She didn't step away, didn't move at all. "They defied the Duke, forced his hand. All they had to do was turn over—"

"That's enough!" Onderaan yanked them apart. "We're not here to debate history."

"History is *all* this is about for you," Siekte said. "Two brothers fighting over one throne."

"Three," Jeatar said. "There were three brothers."

She scoffed. "Bespaar doesn't count—he never had a chance."

"The Duke still killed him."

"Only because he was hiding in Sorille." Siekte pushed both hands through her hair. "This is crazy. Both of the Duke's brothers are dead and he has the throne, so we're arguing over stuff that doesn't matter anymore."

"Of course it matters," Onderaan said.

"To you maybe, which is the problem. We just want the Duke gone and someone new in his place. You want justice for past wrongs. There *is* no justice here, Onderaan."

"There's just vengeance?" I asked quietly.

Siekte paused, looking at me as if she wasn't sure what to make of me. "It's about doing what's right."

I laughed and sank down on the closest chair, which seem to confuse her more. "Doing what's right is never easy—trust me, I know. You *think* you're right, but you lose track of what you were trying to do all along and then there's blood and screaming and death. Doing a bad thing for a good end just sours the good."

"You'll understand when you're older."

"Unless you cause a war, then I won't get any older."

She bristled. "You've done much more to cause that on your own."

"Siekte, that's enough," Jeatar said. "What's done is done, and like it or not, we have to deal with it. Danello is right about the Duke being distracted, so let's use that. Contact our people, get them in place, reach out to those who haven't been sure. Get to the members of the High Court. Tell them what's happened, what the Duke has done. Saints, take one of those enchanters with you if you need to."

"You can't just use us," Sorg said. "We won't be prisoners anymore."

"Fine, so ask the enchanters nicely if they're

willing to help. If not, tell their story anyway."

"Do as he says, Siekte," Onderaan said quietly. "Gather our people. Prepare for what's coming. Perhaps some good will come of it."

She hesitated, her gaze darting to Jeatar, but she shook her head. "Nothing good will come of this mess. You failed us, Onderaan, same as your legitimate heir. You do what you want, but I'm not following you anymore. If you'd listened to me, we could have used this stupid theft as a diversion and coordinated it with my people to make a real attack. But you botched it, and now we'll be lucky to survive the night. We'll handle this our way." She shoved past Jeatar and headed up the stairs, a dozen people following her, then a second dozen. A handful stayed behind.

"Should we stop them?" Aylin asked.

"Let them go," Jeatar said as Onderaan started to speak. "It doesn't matter anymore." He sighed and sat down.

"I'm sorry," I said, cold and sick. "I just wanted to help."

"I know," said Onderaan when Jeatar didn't answer. "It would have happened anyway. Siekte was getting impatient, challenging me almost every day now. She had the others ready for a fight. You just gave it to them first."

"I'm tired of fighting," Jeatar said. The anger and fire in his eyes were gone. He looked sad, tired, as he said. Defeated.

Onderaan's eyes widened and he went to him. "Don't give up. It's almost over."

"But not how we'd hoped. Baseer in flames, Geveg on the verge of rebellion, Verlatta starving under the Duke's siege." He waved a hand toward the stairs. "And if she does manage to kill him, then all three cities will suffer even more. Constant invasions, one fight after another to gain control. It'll be worse than when . . ." He sighed again and shook his head. "I'm tired of it. I'm done."

"Jeatar, don't say that."

"We'll leave as soon as we can. Bribe the gate guards, fight our way out, I don't care. We'll go to the farm. Anyone who wants to come is welcome," he called to the rest. Then he turned to me. "Your people as well, Nya. None of us ever has to go to Geveg again."

Leave without Tali? I couldn't do that. We had the Undying's armor now, and the best distraction I could ever hope for. If we could get to the docks, we could also get to the camp outside.

Danello stepped forward before I could speak.

"My father's still in Geveg. I have to go back for him."

"That won't be easy. I spoke to one of my contacts there. Geveg's rioting again. The Governor-General declared martial law, closed the docks. He barely made it out."

My guts churned. "How bad is it?"

"Not as bad as here. But with the Duke distracted, he probably won't send troops to deal with it." He sighed. "You might have saved them. They could win their fight."

But if everything Jeatar said was true, then how long would it be until the Duke or someone just as bad showed up, looking for power? Geveg didn't have an army anymore. It had no one to defend it except those willing to fight.

And if the Duke *did* send troops, Tali might be part of them.

"I can't leave just yet. I—"

"It's over, Nya—there's nothing more we can do." Jeatar stood but wouldn't look at me. "I'm going to bed. I posted lookouts upstairs to warn us when the soldiers reach this street. We should be safe down here, but arm yourselves just in case. We'll try to leave in the morning when things have calmed down some."

"But—"

Jeatar didn't turn around, didn't stop. He just walked through the door to the back rooms, closing it with an all-too-final thud.

"Are we going to go with him?" Danello asked. I couldn't tell if he wanted to or not.

"I . . ." I didn't know. Leaving Tali was unthinkable, but without Jeatar's help and the villa to hide in, how would I ever find her?

"We'll go with him," I said softly. "He'll be able to get us outside the city, and that's where the Taker camps are."

Danello nodded, looking relieved. He probably wouldn't be when I told him I was going after Tali alone. He had his own family to worry about, and as much as I wanted him with me, family had to come first.

"Nya," said Onderaan, "can I talk—"

"I need to take a Healer to Neeme and Ellis," I said, walking away. He'd want to talk about Papa, about Tali and me. I couldn't do that, not until I brought her home.

No way were we sleeping, no matter how tired we were. After the healer boy cared for Neeme and Ellis, he and the enchanters and apprentices had been given rooms and gone to bed. The rest of us sat in mine, crammed in like fish in a trap. Me, Enzie, Winvik, Jovan, Bahari, Aylin, Danello, and Halima. Tali should have been there.

"I'm not leaving without Tali," I said.

Aylin nodded. "We knew that."

"You all should leave though."

She sat up straighter. "Not a chance."

"You can't keep risking your lives. Danello almost lost his family because of me." I looked at him, but he didn't argue. "I've asked enough of you. This is my fight, my sister. I'll get her."

Danello hugged Halima tighter. "Nya, maybe you should listen to Jeatar and leave. We only won this time because we caught the foundry by surprise *and* we had help. They're on alert now. The pynvium armor won't be enough to get you inside."

"I have to try."

I didn't know how though. I'd ask Jeatar, but he was probably still mad at me, even if he was willing to help us get out of Baseer. I'd ruined everything for him. Angered the Duke, split the Underground. How many would die tonight because of me?

Aylin pulled the blanket off the bed and draped it around my shoulders. "At least you found out you have family left. That's good, right?"

"Is it?"

"Well, sure. You're not alone anymore."

I wasn't before. I had Tali and Aylin and Danello. We'd been a family for months, watching over each other, protecting each other. I could count on them, no matter what. Could I count on Onderaan? I barely knew him.

"As soon as Jeatar and Onderaan are asleep, I'm going to go to try and find Ceun," I said. Tali was the family in trouble, and she was the one I needed to focus on. "If anyone knows a way into those Taker camps, it's Quenji."

"I'm going with you," Aylin said.

"No, stay with Jeatar. We only have one set of armor, so there's no way to disguise you."

"You could pretend I'm a Taker."

"They'd know you were lying as soon as they touched you. It's better if—"

A bang shook the door. We all jumped. Jovan answered it.

"Soldiers are on the street," said the woman at the door. "Jeatar says grab a sword and get ready." She left, going to the next room and giving the same speech.

Halima started to cry. Enzie tried to comfort her, but her tears came next. They were too young for this. Saints, we were *all* too young for this.

"You stay here," Danello said, pointing at the girls. "Hide under the beds. Jovan, Bahari, Winvik, you hide as well, protect them."

"We'll lock the other doors so it looks like someone is hiding in those," Aylin said, jumping up. "Maybe they won't think anyone is in here if it's open."

"And turn off the lamps," I said as I rose to help her.

We blew out the hall lamps as well, then went into the main room. Jeatar was there with Onderaan and the ten others who'd stayed behind after Siekte left. The enchanter and his apprentices stood by the weapon racks, testing swords. Most of the lamps here had also been blown out. Only the ones near the stairs were lit.

"Are they here yet?" I asked softly.

"Not yet. They're going villa by villa, and we're near the end."

"How many?"

He paused. "Maybe thirty soldiers."

Neeme paled and sank to the arm of the couch, her sword falling limp. Ellis patted her shoulder.

I looked for the Taker boy who'd healed them. He sat at the table by the healing bricks, one hand on the stacks as if getting to know them before he'd have to use them. Saints willing, he wouldn't have to.

I walked over. "Are any of those bricks full?" Onderaan had already removed the raw pynvium ore.

"The one with the pain you had me heal holds some, but it's far from full. The rest are empty. They're all good ones though. They'll hold a lot of healing if we need it."

"What about the armor?"

He reached for it, then shook his head. "Empty. But it'll hold a lot."

I gathered up the armor. "Put this on."

"What?"

"It'll help protect you, and you can heal right into it. Stash the rest of the bricks in case we need them."

"Okay." He fumbled with the straps as I helped him get the armor on. Too big for him, but it would be enough for this fight.

Too big for you, too.

Ill-fitting armor wouldn't trick anyone at the Taker camps. I'd be a fool to even try it. But sometimes a fool's luck saves the fool.

"What's your name?" I said. Tali would be

ashamed of me for never thinking to ask him that before.

"Tussen."

"It's going to be okay, don't worry."

He smiled, but I doubted he believed me. Saints, *I* didn't even believe me.

I walked over to Jeatar, who was going over strategies and tactics that made little sense to me. Danello nodded along with the others, so he must have understood it. I studied the stairwell, winding down so you couldn't see the bottom until the last curve. The wall was flat on one side, so anyone standing there would be hidden from those coming down the stairs. Probably built that way for that very reason.

"What if we put a trip wire there?" I asked, pointing at the base of the stairs. "Didn't Ellis say they only got away from the soldiers at the League because they set a trip wire?"

"I should have thought of that," Onderaan muttered, just as Ellis said, "Yeah, we should."

Ellis disappeared and returned with spools of thin twine. The bookcase door opened and we all tensed. One of the watchers came down. "The soldiers are a few villas down. I locked the bookcase and secured the door. I saw fifteen Undying and ten regular soldiers."

"The Undying will come in first, won't they?" I held the twine as Ellis hammered a nail into the wall.

Jeatar nodded, hope brightening his eyes.

"Then I need all of you to stay back," I said. "That wall there should do it." I pointed to the corner, also out of sight of the stairs until someone stepped into the room. Danello and Aylin nodded, but Onderaan shook his head.

"Nya, this isn't something you can hide from. We've been training for this."

"Let her handle it," Jeatar said, waving the others away. "We just got lucky."

"Lucky?"

"Nya's special." He gave me a brief smile. "She's the only person I know who has nothing to fear from the Undying."

Not if they had pain in their armor. If not, then I'd be the first one skewered. Either way, I guess I'd have pain to use.

A thump came from upstairs and we all quieted. Jeatar doused the last lamps and everyone waited in the dark. Another thump, then a crash, like the door being broken down. Cautious footsteps thudded above us—a lot of footsteps. Voices, an order of some kind, though I couldn't make out the words.

Hesitant steps changed, becoming louder. Heavy crashes as if furniture were being knocked over or thrown around. Searching. They were searching the villa.

Sweat trickled down my spine. The dark pressed on me, and even though I knew the darkness would protect me better than anything else, I still wanted the light.

Banging at the top of the stairs. Smaller thuds, books being yanked off a shelf and hitting the floor. A joyous cry.

They'd found the secret door.

TWENTY-THREE

Breaths quickened all around me, echoing in the dark cellar. I flexed my fingers, ready to pounce. Harder cracks on the door, like an axe against wood, and the door splintered. Wood chunks skipped down the stairs, clicking from step to step.

"Looks like a cellar," a man said quietly.

I almost smiled. After all that noise, he really thought he had to keep his voice down?

"Lamps. You two, take point."

The soldiers came down the stairs, their footsteps ahead of the lamplight. When the yellow glow flickered on the wall, I raised my hands, slid closer. I heard faint shuffles behind me as the rest lifted weapons and prepared.

Shadows, more light, louder footsteps. Almost to the trip wire.

"Ah!" The first soldier fell, the lamp flying out of his hand, splashing oil and fire onto the rug. I jumped onto his back and pinned him down, then slapped my hands against the Undying trying hard to keep his balance. *Please have pain in there.*

Whoomp!

I said a silent prayer as pain tingled along my arms and face. The soldiers on the stairs screamed and dropped, then rolled down the steps. Lamps fell with them, oil spilling and catching hair and uniforms. Soldiers outside the range of the flash cried out. Those only dazed beat at the flames and scrambled away.

"They've got pynvium rods!"

"Move back," a voice ordered. "I'm going down."

So far, so good. I stepped around the edge of the wall. Neeme darted forward and grabbed the fallen lamp, stamping out the flames with her foot. In seconds, the room was dark again, with only a soft glow lighting the base of the stairs.

And the shadow of someone *big* moving down those stairs. He stopped just before the trip wire. Stood there.

My hands twitched. Why wasn't he moving?

If we really had had pynvium rods, we could have flashed him five times by now. Unless . . .

"They're out of pain," he said, and stepped over the trip wire and into the room.

I moved forward, away from the protection of the wall. Light cut through the dark, right at my eyes. I jerked back and covered my face. Saints, he must have opened a lamp right in front of me!

Whoomp!

Pain washed over me, but it was the light that hurt. I blinked away tears and lunged forward. My hands slapped against—chain armor.

Uh-oh.

He grabbed me, lifted, and threw me across the room like I was one of the lamps. I crashed into the table, pain flaring along my ribs, then hit the floor. Soldiers poured down the stairs. Some carried lamps; the rest, swords.

I didn't hear Jeatar order an attack, but he must have. He ran to meet the soldiers, Ellis and Onderaan right behind him, the others a few steps behind them. They looked like spirits, pale and eerie in the bobbing lamplight.

Back on my feet, I searched the wave of soldiers for blue metal. Found a few, but it was too risky to flash them in the room with the others. I headed for the stairwell, staying low, moving fast, trying to avoid the swinging swords and darting blades.

A soldier caught me in the side, his sword cutting easily through shirt and skin. I grabbed him, forcing my fingers under his collar, and *pushed*. He yanked away. I kept moving, was pierced by another blade, this time in my shoulder. I swallowed my cry and grabbed the woman's face with both hands. *Pushed* again. She screamed and staggered.

"Shifter," she yelled, sounding scared. "The Shifter's down here!"

I reached the stairs and found two Undying. One cut me across the chest, the other sliced my thigh. I got one hand on each before I fell.

Whoomp-whoomp!

Soldiers dropped in the stairwell. I grabbed the closest skin and *pushed* away the burning cuts, the stinging wounds. My churning stomach didn't fade so easily—these soldiers definitely had access to Healers and pynvium. They'd be up and fighting again soon.

"Nya!"

Jeatar. I turned and ran down, crawling over the semiconscious soldiers. Jeatar fought against two, one Undying, one regular. Blood stained Jeatar's shirt, and from the way he was staggering, it had to be his. The Undying feinted and plunged the sword into his chest a breath before I reached him.

I grabbed the Undying's armor and pictured dandelions blowing in the wind. Pain flashed, brought down the soldier next to him as well as Jeatar. I shoved the dazed Undying against the wall and he collapsed. The floor was slick with Jeatar's blood, pooling too fast beneath him. I picked up his hand and the arm of the unconscious soldier who had tried to kill him. *Drew* and *pushed*.

Jeatar groaned and sat up. He smiled weakly at me, blood smeared across his face but no longer bleeding. "Thank you."

"Anytime."

We helped each other to our feet. There was so much fighting now. Aylin and Tussen worked in the rear, Aylin dragging the injured away and Tussen healing them to fight some more. Sorg and the other enchanters swung their swords like forge hammers, but they hit hard enough to make people cautious.

Jeatar rejoined the fray, moving like a cat through the dark, his sword flashing, his targets dropping. Ellis and Onderaan guarded and flanked him, cutting through their own share of soldiers.

The Undying alternated, some fighting while others healed the injured, same as we were doing.

Except they did it faster. They could heal themselves and fight at the same time.

We were going to lose if we kept fighting like this—hurt and heal, hurt and heal. They could do it better, and we wouldn't be able to keep up. They'd outnumber us before long. I had to flash faster. Crumble their armor, turn it to fine sand, and even the odds.

"They need more pain," I told Danello as I ducked past him, going for the Undying by the stairs again. I had no idea if he understood, but he nodded and kept fighting.

I dived, rolled, bled, flashed. Tried to focus on the same soldiers, but in the weird light it was impossible to tell them apart. It felt like we'd been fighting for hours, but I knew it was a lie my muscles were telling me. I wasn't the only one tired. Jeatar didn't move so catlike anymore, and the enchanters fell faster.

An Undying's blade sank into my belly. I yelped and flattened my hands against her armor.

Whoomp.

Less pain flashed, barely enough to force her back a step. Fine sand ran down my fingers as she pulled away. Her chest plate crumbled, turning to dust, flashed one too many times.

I gritted my teeth and reached for her, missed, fell to my knees. She was still moving, panic in her voice now, though I had to focus to make out the words through the roar in my ears.

"She destroyed my armor!"

My stomach burned, but it was a cold fire, creeping out and numbing me. My knees buckled, refusing to carry me to her exposed skin. Soldiers moved toward me, fear and excitement on their faces. Not the Undying, though. They were staying away.

I struggled to stay awake, stand up, find flesh.

Swords caught the light. Two of them, coming at me out of the dark. I didn't see who held them, just dim blurs of blue and gray.

Clang!

Another blade stopped one, my shoulder stopped the other. I screamed and fell over. Booted feet passed above my head and another sword clanged. Hands grabbed me, dragged me.

"I got you, hang on."

Pressure and warmth on my skin. Then tingling fire. My head cleared, my vision snapped back. The cold and fire vanished.

"That was close," Tussen said, my blood still on his hands.

Too close. "Thank you."

"We're in trouble, aren't we?"

"Just keep healing."

I scrambled back out. Flashed another Undying and a piece of his armor turned to sand—a bracer this time.

"You can't win this," I said as they paused in their onslaught. They weren't so invincible anymore. Of course, we weren't doing so well either. "You'll be defenseless soon. Might as well give up now."

The big man who'd tossed me across the room squared his shoulders. "Aim for her head. Kill her before she can shift."

My chest tightened. They hadn't been trying to kill me all along?

"Sergeant, orders are to take her alive."

I didn't see who said it, but he sounded nervous about speaking out.

"Accidents happen." He lunged, faster than I thought anyone fighting this long could. I dived sideways. Jeatar and Danello charged forward. Steel met steel as I hit the floor.

The soldiers pressed forward. I crawled away. Onderaan parried a blade meant for me, Sorg took one meant for him. The Underground and the enchanters closed around me, protecting me.

Click—click—click . . .

A noise, metal on stone, barely reaching me over the grunts and groans and clashes. Something falling, dropping . . . rolling?

WHOOMP!

My skin prickled. Screams on both sides echoed in the cellar. Bodies fell, swords clattering to the floor. Footsteps on the stairs. A disapproving *tsk tsk tsk.*

"I don't like people who ignore orders, Sergeant," Vyand said, stepping over him on her way into the room. Stewwig and more men followed behind her, in full chain armor, with almost no exposed skin at all. Not an Undying in the bunch.

I got to my feet, my arms still stinging a bit. A grapefruit-size pynvium ball lay on the floor. After that flash, I doubted it had pain, but it would hurt something awful if I hit somebody with it. I moved half a step toward it. Three soldiers moved a step toward me. I stopped.

"Nice weapon," I said to Vyand. I couldn't get past her. I had nothing to flash. I wasn't close enough to any of the unconscious Undying to flash *them.*

"Handy, isn't it?"

It was better than handy. "Why didn't you use that first and save us all this fighting?"

"Had I been here, I would have." She chuckled and flicked a hand at some soldiers. They started lighting the lamps. "Do you really think I'd send Undying after *you*?"

"I don't understand."

"And how dangerous you would be if you did."

"What?"

She sighed and smoothed her perfect hair. "After I lost you *yet again*, the Duke refused to lend me any more soldiers. I did plant a spy in the foundry before I left, just in case you weren't really gone. Lucky for me I did. I'd have been here sooner, but the idiot apprentice got lost after he left you, and it took him a while to find me. I made it here in time, though." She looked around the much brighter room. So much blood. "Barely, from the looks of this."

I clenched my hands. The apprentice! The one who'd reached the villa's gates and had been "too scared" to come inside. That liar.

Vyand flicked a hand again and four more men came forward, one carrying rope and the rest holding swords at my throat and heart. Stewwig never left her side. His gaze never left me.

"Hold out your hands, wrists together, fingers in fists, please," she said.

I glared at her. She sighed.

"Don't make me kill someone just to get your attention."

I held out my hands. One man looped a rope around them, binding my wrists tight.

"Lower them."

I did. Another rope was tied around me, pinning my arms down. Vyand's men knotted the ropes extra tight with double knots. Next they tied my feet. They'd have to carry me out, but that seemed to be the plan.

"Get her hands."

Another man stepped forward and wrapped my hands with a long narrow cloth. Sweat dotted his brow while he did it, as if he was afraid I'd suddenly be able to bend my hands backward and touch him.

Vyand finally stepped forward, a smile on her face. "Now, let's try this again, shall we? I hereby bind you for, well, more crimes than I have time to list. And this time, you are *not* getting away from me."

TWENTY-FOUR

"What about the others?" one of her men asked.

"Leave them. If I capture her friends again, she'll just work that much harder to escape." She stepped closer and lifted my fake braid. "Interesting. Black suits you."

"Same color as your heart."

She chuckled and dropped the braid. "Bring the horses around," she told one of the men, who nodded and darted up the stairs. Vyand flicked fingers at two other men, and they picked me up. They followed her, leaving everyone else behind. Stewwig stayed between me and her.

"You're really leaving them here?"

She ignored me.

Did she mean it, or would she come back for them after I was gone?

We walked out of the ruined bookcase door and into the library. Through the hall and into the main foyer, light shining through the latticework in the teardrop inset above the door. Horses whinnied. Vyand opened the door, and cool air and rain gusted in, dampening the floor. So did the smell of smoke.

They carried me outside. Rain misted, the air hazy in the pale morning light. Hard to tell without the sun, but it looked like it was a few hours after dawn, midmorning at the latest. It felt like days had passed since we'd destroyed the foundry instead of just hours.

A horse-drawn carriage waited in the drive. A young boy opened the door and Vyand climbed in, then Stewwig. The men hauled me up and propped me on the seat across from her like a doll, then took seats on either side.

"Where are you taking me?"

"If I tell you, will you shut up?"

I considered it. "Probably not."

She chuckled and smoothed her hair into place again. Not that anything more than a hair had been *out* of place. "You've got iron in you, girl. In another life, we could have been friends."

"Probably not."

She laughed, and her men joined her. "I'm taking you to the Duke. Once I hand you over, you'll be *his* problem." She learned toward the window. Smoke still rose into the air where the foundry was. "And from the looks of things, not his only one."

The Duke. I had to escape, but Vyand wasn't like the others. She didn't look at me and see a weak girl. The number of guards and amount of rope proved that.

We rode through the streets, which grew more crowded the closer we got to the inner wall. Soldiers, rioters, people running from both. The foundry wasn't the only building on fire.

"What happened?" Had Siekte tried to assassinate the Duke after all? Did she get the rest of the Underground to attack?

"People tend to get very unhappy when soldiers break down their doors and rifle through their things."

"They're rebelling?"

She shook her head. "That would require forethought. No, these people are just angry. Though I suspect some are taking advantage of the chaos. I suppose there might be a full rebellion by sunset."

The carriage slowed and a man swung down to the window. "It's too crowded to get through here. We'll have to go another way."

"Try going in through the stable. And kill anyone who even *looks* like they're going to rush this carriage." She grinned at me. "That trick won't work again."

That particular trick hadn't been mine. Not that I *had* any tricks, old or new, in mind, anyway.

"What will happen to the others if the Undying wake up before they do?" They'd be helpless.

She shrugged. "Whatever Vinnot's ghouls decide."

Not good. He'd lock up Sorg and the other enchanters again. Force Tussen and Enzie and the others . . .

Enzie!

She was still hiding in the room with Jovan, Bahari, Halima, and Winvik. They had to have been listening to the fight. They must have heard Vyand, known that I was gone. No way Jovan wouldn't do something after that. Enzie might even be able to heal Tussen and get the rest on their feet before the Undying ever woke up.

Please, Saint Saea, let them save the others.

Vyand cocked her head and watched me with

questioning eyes. "You're hopeful again," she said. "What did you just figure out?"

"You really think I'm stupid enough to tell you?"

"Not at all." She grinned and leaned back. "But you've piqued my curiosity."

"You know what they say about curiosity."

"Lucky for me, I'm not a cat."

The carriage kept turning corners, tacking across the growing mob. Eventually we rolled into a stable with more soldiers than horses. Too many guards for one stable. Maybe the riot was getting worse.

Vyand climbed out first and ducked under the cover of a bright green awning, vanishing into the stable with a few quick strides. Her men dragged me out like a sack of coffee, standing in the courtyard with me hanging between them. After a minute Vyand came out of the stall area and waved us over.

Horses nickered, lifting their heads and staring as I was carried by. The stable looked well kept, but it didn't look fancy enough to house the Duke's horses.

We reached the rear and a young soldier opened a stall door. We went inside and Vyand drew a dark blue hood from a box on the wall.

"Before you ask, this"—she dangled the hood—"is so you don't see anything."

See what? A stable with too many soldiers?

She pulled the hood over my head, but not before I saw the young solider pull on a wall sconce and heard the rear of the stall click open. Dank air blew out past me from the dark. Probably a secret way into—and out of—the palace. I could imagine the Duke sneaking off in the middle of the night, maybe even meeting Vinnot at the foundry to check up on his experiments and weapons.

Vyand tightened the hood around my neck, as if seeing the light flicker below me could give me enough clues to help me trace my way back should I escape. That she thought I might cheered me up a little.

Her men carried me into the passageway. It sounded like hard stone under their booted feet, then quiet splashing, as if walking through puddles. They walked for a long time, and though I tried to keep track of turns, it was impossible without having my feet on the ground. Eventually we stopped and metal jangled. A scratch and a snick, like a lock in a door, then we were moving again.

Splashes on stone turned to thumps on stone, then padded steps that likely meant soft carpet, then stone again. We followed stairs up and down. Doors opened and closed, and still no one said a word. We had to be in the palace by now. It smelled clean, not at all like the dank plant smell from the passage. I wondered if they were walking me in circles to confuse me.

A soft knock, then murmured voices.

"Sir, I have the Shifter," Vyand said, and my hood was yanked off.

"About time," a man muttered.

I blinked in the light of a plain, round room with a few benches and a small writing table. A room you passed through or waited in, not a place you spent any time in. Unless you were a soldier. A half dozen men in chain armor stood along the walls, watching me and everything that moved.

Vyand's satisfied smirk vanished. "She was exceedingly difficult to capture."

"So you kept telling me," said the man in front of me. Mid-fifties. Thinning black hair, combed straight back. Gray-blue eyes. Fine clothes. An ocean-blue pynvium circlet with a sapphire stone circled his head.

The Duke.

Anger burned me. *This* was the man who'd hurt us, who'd killed so many, stolen so much? His body was too thin to bear armor, his shoulders not broad enough for a sword. His cheeks were drawn, eyes shadowed from lack of sleep. No wonder he'd had to steal everything he had. He couldn't possibly win it in a fair fight.

I lifted my chin. "You're a murdering thief who's ruined lives and destroyed cities, and you should hang yourself on your own gallows while people cheer."

Vyand shot me an amused look. She'd probably root for me when I tried to escape this time.

The Duke glared, his eyes narrowing. "No doubts that it's her?" he said to Vyand. I bristled. This was my enemy and he wouldn't even acknowledge me.

"None, sir. As you can see, she's . . . unmistakable . . . once you get to know her."

"Fine. Leave her." He indicated a wooden bench by the wall. "Your fee is on the table there."

"Thank you, sir."

The soldiers took me from Vyand and propped me up on the bench. "How can you work for him?" I asked them. "He burned an entire city to the ground just so he could steal the throne."

They ignored me, but the Duke's face reddened. Good.

"Which of your brothers was supposed to rule? Did it matter, or did killing them both just make you feel safer?"

"Get those ropes off her," he said, words clipped. "I'm not wasting good men to cart her around and listen to her nonsense."

Vyand raised an eyebrow. "That's not advis—"

"Do it."

"Very well, sir."

One of her soldiers cut the ropes holding my feet and arms. He left the one around my wrists. Vyand stepped forward and pulled the cloths off my hands, then looked at me and winked.

"Dismissed," the Duke said.

Vyand dipped her head and left the room. I could swear I heard her snicker as she closed the door.

The Duke walked over to me, his eyes bright with excitement.

"So—you're the Shifter."

He clearly didn't want an answer. "And you're something a reed rat coughed up."

He slapped me. I grinned, my cheek stinging.

"That didn't even hurt."

"Bold, isn't she?" said another well-dressed man standing by the window. Older than the Duke, but not by much. Gray hair, same eyes though. A family member? He studied me like I'd seen farmers judge livestock.

"Too bold," the Duke agreed. I stuck out my tongue and his hands clenched.

"Hit me again, I dare you." Stabbing would be better. More pain to shift. I bet I could reach him before the guards stopped me.

The well-dressed man put a hand on the Duke's shoulder. "She's baiting you."

"I know that!"

"A lot of hope to put on one small girl, even if she is bold."

"See that blood on her? Those cuts and tears on her clothes? Vyand's men did that, but they're the ones hurting now."

Vyand's men? He must not know about the Undying's attack on the Underground. Then he hadn't known where I was! Maybe Aylin and the others could still escape and get to Jeatar's farm.

And Tali?

Maybe I didn't need to sneak into the Taker camps after all. Just like me, the Duke was a better prize. I might be able to end this war right here. I'd learned a lot about kidnapping folks, and if I could capture the Duke, I could give him to Jeatar and we could force the Taker camps to let everyone go—including Tali.

"Trust me, there's not a mark on her anymore."

Except my new scars. I'd gladly earn some more if it gave me enough pain to shift into the Duke.

"The Undying can also heal themselves," the man said.

"They can't do this." The Duke pulled something out of his pocket. Pynvium.

Whoomp.

I glared at him as pain prickled my skin. A lot for such a small rod of pynvium, but it was ocean blue, probably pure.

"That tickled," I said, scowling. He lifted the rod again. I winced and threw my hands up, putting the rope in front of the flash. It probably wouldn't do much, but it might weaken the ropes a little.

Whoomp.

"Still tickled," I said.

The Duke turned red again and put the rod away. "Have you ever seen anything like that, Erken?"

"No, such immunity is quite remarkable."

"No one will dare threaten me anymore."

I scoffed. "Don't count on it."

Erken didn't look convinced, even if he did look impressed with me. "If it works."

"It'll work." The Duke folded his arms across his chest, his hands still clenched. "Tell Vinnot to

325

get ready. I want a test as soon as possible."

"Yes, sir." One of the aides nodded and vanished through another door.

If *what* worked? The device that had hurt Enzie and the others? Couldn't be—that was destroyed in the foundry fire. Wasn't it?

"Nothing you do will matter, you know," I said. "Everyone hates you. Every day, fewer fear you. You can't hide what you are for much longer."

The Duke smirked. Not the reaction I was poking for. "Now that I have you, I won't have to hide at all."

A woman in a blue and silver uniform approached the Duke. "Sir? Vinnot's ready."

"Excellent. Sergeant, bring the Shifter."

The soldier on my left yanked me toward a door on the other side of the room. Only then did I notice the faint vibrations under my feet and the hum in the air.

"Where are you taking me?"

"Not so bold now, is she?" the Duke said. "Careful with her—she's not replaceable like the others."

"What are you going to do with me?" I struggled against the soldier, but it was like wrestling with a tree. He dragged me through the door and into the other room. "Tell me!"

"You're happier not knowing," a man said. It took me a moment to place the face. The last time I'd seen him, he'd been lying on the floor outside the spire room at the Healers' League.

"Vinnot," I said. I glared at the man who'd filled Tali so full of pain she couldn't move, who'd experimented on Takers. Who'd created the Undying and sent them out to kill.

"I see my reputation precedes me." He grinned, then continued making notes on a pad. Behind him was . . .

Something.

Pynvium for sure, but a misshapen mix of it, from pure ocean blue to an almost useless blue-gray, and a strange silvery blue metal I'd never seen before. The whole thing was big, a disk maybe six feet in diameter and a foot thick, resting on some kind of stone pedestal waist high off the floor. A spire grew from the center like wax melted from a candle, made from both the silvery blue metal and pynvium in varying purity. Halfway up the spire was a hole about the size of my arm, perfectly round and smooth. Evenly spaced along the disk were curved channels, about arm size, with thinner bands that curved above them, almost like cuffs. Lots of them.

It holds us, hurts us. . . .

I counted. Twelve channels. There'd been six Takers in the foundry. Saints, they *were* cuffs. I pictured six Takers with their arms in those channels, locked down to that disk. Holding them, hurting them.

And the Duke called *me* an abomination? That thing shouldn't exist. I didn't even know what it was, but I knew *that*. It was wrong, same as the glyphed pynvium in Zertanik's office.

I sucked in a slow breath. My stomach quivered, same as it had there, even worse than when Onderaan showed me his healing device. I didn't see the glyphs, but they *had* to be there under all that horribly fused metal.

"How soon will it be operational?" the Duke asked Vinnot.

"Depends on the Shifter, really. We found no others like her to test, so I suspect it'll take a while to reach pliability with her. Strong talents always take longer."

I jerked my gaze away. Pliability sure as spit didn't sound like something I wanted a part of.

"What is that thing?" I asked.

"A life's work," Vinnot said, sighing.

Not a life worth having.

"Insert them now," said the Duke.

Vinnot actually smiled and rubbed his hands together eagerly. "This should be interesting."

Soldiers brought out four Takers from a back room, young like Enzie and the others, the oldest not more than twelve or thirteen. *Too young to fight.* My throat tightened, fearing I'd see Tali, hoping I'd see her. Wishing she was as far from this place as possible, because I had a sudden feeling capturing the Duke wouldn't be enough anymore.

"Let me go!" the first Taker said, struggling. A dark-haired boy with darker circles under his eyes. He wore a long, sleeveless tunic and baggy pants.

Maybe not too young to fight, just too young for the Undying. He fought now, kicking, biting, writhing around like a grabbed cat. It took two soldiers and one aide to shove his arms into the channels and snap the cuffs on his wrists.

"Submit," the aide said.

The boy cried out and slumped, his eyes open and glassy. Then he started moaning softly. Rhythmically.

I had the urge to start struggling too. And screaming. What was the pynvium glyphed to do? Did they know? Did they have any idea what was under all that smashed-together metal?

"Impressive," Erken said. "It really does subdue them."

"I told you it did," the Duke said, more than a touch of pride in his tone. "It's the most remarkable blend. Haven't found a use for the kragstun on its own, but combined with the right pynvium mixture, it makes the mind extremely open to suggestions."

"It affects the mind?"

"The entire nervous system. A few words and they'll do whatever I say."

This was horrific. Hurting people was bad enough, but twisting their minds? Jeatar's words echoed in my ears. *They twist minds and bend wills and create the weapons the Duke wants. How long do you think Tali can last in there?* Was that how he got the Undying to follow him? Would he use something like this on Tali to make her fight?

They inserted the next Taker, and the next. The last one came out of the room, older than the others. Someone I knew, but not Tali.

Lanelle.

A satisfied thrill ran trough me, followed by guilt. Even after what she'd done to Tali and the others— helping Vinnot with his experiments, recording their symptoms, betraying us to the Luminary—no one deserved this.

She slipped into the channels without a sound. They all moaned, one right after the other in a line, their fingers twitching against the disk, as though they were pushing pain into it. Like Jovan had said, the weird slab pushed pain into them.

Saints, was it . . . ? The room wobbled a little. Was it *cycling* pain through them? Was it to test them for abilities? Had Vinnot found a way to keep them alive and still keep them filled with pain? Did the glyphed pynvium draw those abilities out if you *did* have them?

It made no sense. If so, then why insert me? I already had abilities.

I shivered. The Duke *knew* I did. Worse, he knew what kinds.

He didn't want me for my shifting at all. If he had something here that shifted pain into people, he probably *never* cared about that. He wanted me for my immunity, just as he'd shown Erken when he'd flashed me.

He wanted me to *flash* that thing.

If he put me into those channels, forced me to submit like the others, I probably would, too. How much pain was in there? If it could shift pain into people, would it flash with *real* pain? Not just surface pain that knocked you out, like pynvium weapons did now, but pain that would kill?

I thought about Geveg, Verlatta, all the other towns and cities along the river. About Sorille, which had already been destroyed by the Duke's hand. About all the Takers who were hiding, praying a tracker wouldn't find them. Remembered how hard Grannyma had fought, how many she'd healed so they could fight some more. Of all those who had died trying to keep the Duke out of our home, away from our people.

Like Mama and Papa. And Grandpapa.

The weapon was full of pain, probably more than even the League's Slab had been. Once I was cuffed to it, I'd likely flash it however and wherever the Duke told me to. I'd be a walking pynvium trigger. But if I flashed it now, before he locked me in there . . .

Siekte was right. Killing the Duke was the only way to free us all.

I lunged for the pynvium.

TWENTY-FIVE

The soldier holding me lost his grip and staggered forward. The other man hesitated, reacting too late to grab my arm, but he did grab my long braid. It yanked painfully on my head, but tore free.

"Stop her!" the Duke ordered, real fear in his voice. He knew what I'd done to the Luminary. What I'd do to him when I reached that weapon.

The unexpected yank threw off my balance, but I ran as fast as I could. I made it halfway to the disk before the soldiers seized my arms and hauled me back, dangling me off the floor.

The Duke stomped over to me and grabbed my jaw, forcing my face toward him. My jaw tingled under his fingertips.

Saints! He was a Taker!

The Duke squeezed tighter. "Stop it. I won't have—"

I pulled my legs up and kicked him in the chest. The soldiers' grip on me slipped and I fell, landing on the floor right after the Duke did. I scrambled toward the disk but arms grabbed me again.

"Be ready if she shifts," he told the soldiers as Vinnot helped him to his feet. The moment he was stable, he slapped his hand away.

Shifting a bruised butt was hardly going to get me out of this.

"I spent a lot of money to find you, Shifter," he said, glaring at me. "So be a good little girl and do what I say."

"I never do what anyone says." I tried to sound tough, but inside I churned. A Taker. And he was doing these terrible things to other Takers. Not that that should surprise me—I'd seen what he'd done to his own people.

His lip curled. Not quite a grin, but it clearly wanted to be. "Yes, you will." He turned to Vinnot. "Insert her *now*."

"Yes, sir."

"People are tired of listening to you," I yelled at the Duke as his soldiers dragged me toward the weapon. "We're tired of suffering so you can steal everything we own."

The Duke stared at me like I was something he'd found squished under his boot. "You're the ones stealing from me. That was *our* land, *our* mines before my great-grandfather gave it all away. The Three Territories were *Baseeri* territories, and they will be again."

"Never!"

A soldier cut the ropes on my hands. Two more soldiers had tight grips on my arms. One even had his boot pressed over my feet so I couldn't kick anymore. The soldiers holding me forced my arms into the channels, just like the other Takers who were cuffed there. I struggled to pull away, getting one foot free, but it slid uselessly on the stone floor. My skin itched as the cuffs snapped around my wrists.

"Submit," Vinnot said with a small sigh. "And now we wait."

My whole body started tingling, like the feeling I had when I readied myself to heal. It wasn't just in my hands but all over, surging like waves on the shore. The surges kept changing direction, sliding to my stomach, then flowing down each arm. My fingers throbbed with the need to push, though I had little pain to shed.

335

"What's happening to me?" I asked. More questions lingered in my mind, but the urge to ask them was fading. I knew I *needed* to ask them, hard as the words were to form.

Pain prickled my skin like a flash. The disk, trying to shift into me. I fought it, pushed back, but I couldn't sense the pynvium under my hands. I could feel the glyphs though, lurking there, trying to get out.

The Duke's smug grin faded. "Why isn't she submitting?"

"I told you it might take a while. She's older and stronger than the others." Vinnot picked up his pad. "Can you describe what you're feeling?" he asked me.

"A lot of anger." I spat at him, hitting him on the cheek. He wiped it off like it happened every day. It made me angrier, and some of the fog around my brain lifted. The pain grew hotter, clawing its way into me, but I fought it off. Every sting made me want to give in to Vinnot, do as he said. The pain was what made us pliable.

"Amazing," Erken said. "How much pain does it hold?"

"We've no idea really," Vinnot said, watching me carefully. "The records we found with it claimed it

336

would keep absorbing pain as long as pynvium was added, as you can see from the various welds there. During the course of my research, I started looking for a way to empty it, or at least spill off some of the pain and weaponize it, but it kept eluding me. We had someone working on a control device, but then I heard about the Shifter's flashing ability and her amazing immunity. The idea just came to me—focus those skills and turn the disk into a massive flashing device."

"I knew I was good for something." I struggled to hold on to my anger, my hatred, my sense of self. Keep the pain at bay and keep my mind and will mine.

Vinnot chuckled as if surprised I could speak at all. "Oh yes. You're the trigger that makes the entire thing work. Without you we couldn't flash it." He laughed again. "At least not more than once."

"I'll . . . flash it." Soon as I touched it. I pressed my fingers against the silvery blue metal and tried to picture dandelions, but my mind wouldn't focus. I could do this. I *had* to do this. All I had to do was flash the pynvium. Just concentrate. Just—

—*somuchpain—somuchpain—somuchpain—*

TWENTY-SIX

Pain shifted to fire, fire shifted to ice, ice shifted back to pain. Under the pain and heat and cold I could feel something squirming, something screaming.

Eventually I figured out it was me.

I wailed in my mind, but the others were silent. I could feel them though. Despair, agony, fear. Submission. I cried with them as the pain rushed through us over and over and over, making us give up, give in.

A voice came through the pain.

"You are my trigger."

A voice I hated. I shook my head but didn't feel my body move. I screamed *no*, but no sound emerged.

"Sir, perhaps you should let the device work on her a while longer. We don't want her flashing it until we're sure we have control."

"I *have* control. Just look at her."

"At least stay behind the protective wall."

Anger rose up higher than the pain, and as before, my thoughts cleared. I no longer had my body, but I did have my mind, even as it struggled against the order to submit, to do what the Duke wanted. I gathered myself in the small space between my heart and guts, where I always carried the pain I shifted. It wasn't much, but it was all the me I had left.

I hoarded it.

The voice came back.

"You are my trigger."

I said nothing, revealed nothing. Wanted to say yes and reveal all. The need to agree, to serve, tugged at me as if it could pull my acceptance through my fingertips as easily as it pulled the pain flowing through me.

I let the pain wash over me. I would not bend. They could not make me pliable. My mind was strong.

My mind was *mine*.

"You are my trigger."

I ached to say yes, but the anger the voice woke

within me kept me silent.

"Why is she still resisting?"

"Sir, I warned you this could take time."

"Not this much time. The riots are getting worse. This is a perfect opportunity for a full test."

"We really shouldn't press her so hard until we know we have—"

"You are my trigger! You're mine, do you hear me? Mine!"

I rode the pain and smiled.

The pain was constant, the tingle along my hands and feet always with me, but the low throbbing was new. It wasn't like the lulls that came with firm jostling, moving me around like a doll, or the moments of quiet before the pain began again. The throbbing came and went, as did screams.

The disk, trying to swallow me. Banging against my mind and soul, demanding to be let in.

No.

I strained against the thudding pain, willed my fingers to let go and flash, to stop those who kept asking me to do things I didn't want to do. For a moment, I felt myself move.

No, not move. Pressure on my shoulders. Back and forth. Shaking.

"You are my trigger! Say it! You are my trigger! You. Are. My. Trigger."

Pain surged. I struggled, but it got inside, swelled around the me I had hidden away. The need to obey overwhelmed the anger that had kept me safe. *It'll take longer to reach pliability with her. . . .* Not that much longer. My will was fading, stripped away with every surge of pain until— "I . . . am . . . your . . . trigger."

"Finally!"

"We might want to let her simmer a bit longer, so to speak. Make sure she's as pliable as possible."

Vinnot. The *Duke*.

Images burst in my mind, faces and places. Tali sweaty and pale in a room in a tower. Aylin staring at me from between bars. Takers chained to metal. A frail Duke screaming at me to be something I didn't want to be.

"Don't be silly—we did it, we finally have full control. I want to test it now."

. . . you're a better prize than she . . .

I was no one's prize.

I struggled to form the words but they wouldn't rise above my thoughts. They slipped away as a fresh wave of pain rolled over me, through me, blasting away what little defense I had begun to rebuild. I held my breath. Over and over and over, bit by bit, pain within me even as it passed through me.

I ached to flash it. To destroy it. To destroy *him*.

"I—"

My throat caught.

A startled gasp. "Did she speak?"

"Impossible, Vinnot. She has no will to do anything but what I tell her."

I had will, I just couldn't reach it. It lay buried in muck at the bottom of the river of pain. I had to swim down and grab it . . . I held my breath and dived deep.

"Not—trigger."

"She *did* speak!"

"It doesn't matter. She'll do what she's told. They all do."

I never do what I'm told.

"I'm. Not. Trigger."

Frantic whispers. Frightened words. They were scared of me and what I might find at the bottom of the river, lost in the muck.

"Perhaps we should get behind the wall."

"Afraid, Erken?"

I sucked in a long breath, then another, and dived deep into the river again. Down to the cold darkness swirling beneath the fierce heat. I scraped my fingers through the sludge.

A bright spark, like sunlight on water.

I dug deeper, wrapped my fingers around it and brought it with me to the surface.

A purple lake violet.

Tali. Home.

I had to fight the Duke, like they were all fighting the Duke. Fighting like . . . I forced my gaze to Lanelle, across from me. She'd fought me—resisted me when I'd tried to shift into her at the League. Refused the pain I'd wanted to put into her. Could I resist it, too?

I closed my eyes and pictured the pain, cycling from Taker to Taker. I narrowed it, forcing it to thin and trickle as it passed through me. I gathered it between my heart and guts, and though it screamed and snarled to break free, it coiled there, trapped.

It was *mine.*

"Let's test it. Bring him in."

I opened my eyes. A man was dragged into the room, chains on his wrists and feet. The soldiers with him shoved him into a chair and locked his chains to the wall.

"You are my trigger," the Duke said to me. "Count to ten, then flash that man."

No.

My voice didn't listen to my mind. "One, two, three . . ."

Footsteps hurried away and a heavy door slammed shut. The need to obey, to flash, swelled within me, riding the flow of pain like a leaf on the water.

". . . eight, nine, ten." The coil in my guts sprang forward and the pain rushed to fill the void.

Whoomp!

Needles stung my skin, burned my eyelids. The Takers around me cried out, a sharp note above the low moans. The man tied to the chair screamed and slumped, his skin red.

The need to flash rose again, cresting the wave of pain as it rolled into me again.

The door opened.

"Very impressive. Is he still alive?"

A pause. "Yes, sir."

"Hmmm. Can she control the amount flashed?"

Control . . .

I pictured a pynvium circlet and dandelions drowned beneath a river of pain. It crashed over me, angry as a spring flood, bursting out around me.

WHOOMP!

The man on the chair screamed and vanished in a bright mist like a dandelion slammed against a rock. Other voices screamed, some near, some far, too many for me to count. Metal clattered to stone.

"Stop!" A raspy voice filled with pain. "Stop flashing!"

The pynvium under my hand burned. Pain slammed into me, over and over and over.

It's all about control, Nya-Pie, Papa had said, molding the blue-hot pynvium with his tongs and hammer. *You force it too hard, your trigger will flash before it's ready. Too soft, it might never flash at all. You have to find the balance between force and begging. Just ask it to do what you want it to do. Enchanting's about working with the pynvium rather than against it.*

"No."

"You are the trigger. Do as I say and stop flashing!"

The need to flash was so overwhelming, I feared it might tear me apart. So much worse than the need to obey. I reached into the disk and *drew* in the pain so there was nothing *left* to flash. The pynvium whined, like a scream in my mind. It wanted the pain that was mine. Wanted to control *me*.

Help me, you giant chunk of blue metal. Help me and we both win.

The need to obey *couldn't* win. The need to flash I'd meet halfway, compromise so the disk and the pain would get what it wanted and leave me alone.

I pictured tiny dandelions growing around silvery blue metal cuffs. Blew softly, so only a few seeds drifted away.

whoomp.

The Takers cried out. The pynvium's whining grew louder, the vibrations under my feet stronger.

"Sir, hang on, we'll get you out of here!"

Booted feet slapped against stone. Bodies dragged. Doors slammed.

I pressed my hands against the pynvium. The Takers were awake and aware now, their eyes wide and frightened. They pulled against the cuffs. The need to flash swelled again. I focused it on the metal locking us to the disk.

whoomp.

Takers screamed and jerked in their binds. Some fell to the ground as the cuffs broke away.

"Run," I said through clenched teeth, fighting the need to flash again. It crushed the need to obey—the Duke, Vinnot, even myself. The Takers stumbled about, looking lost. Some headed toward the door, the others staggered and fell.

I pressed my palms into the pynvium, the disk glowing deep blue under the metal welded to it, like the glyphs in the forge. The air shimmered above it, the ground rumbled below it. The metal looked too hot to come near, but the pynvium was no hotter than a stone in summer. Warm, but it didn't burn.

At least, it didn't burn me.

Pain poured off the disk and swirled around me, trying to regain control, make me submit. I ached with the need to flash more than a tiny burst, but the Takers weren't all out of the room yet. My skin prickled like needle stings across my whole body. The whine grew as if begging me to release it. The pain still cycled, but now it had nowhere to go but into me.

I had to let the pain out, *needed* to let it out, though my mind screamed at me to stop.

WHOOMP!

My torn and bloody clothes vanished. Screams echoed and fell silent.

WHOOMP!

The walls cracked. The stone under my knees turned to grit. The silvery blue metal crumbled and blew away. Pynvium sand poured off the weapon as the impure metal disintegrated. A sound in my head—rock against rock—then something within me . . . changed. No, not just me, the disk, too. A wave of . . . *something* . . . rolled between me and the disk, grinding, moving, turning.

I fell to my knees amid the pynvium sand raining

down upon me. I crawled away, the broken floor biting into palms and knees. Crawled past dropped swords and red mist.

My stomach quivered, flipping and twisting worse than anything I'd ever felt before. I rolled over, forced myself to my knees. Looked back to what I knew I'd find.

Glyphed pynvium.

And nothing else. The silvery blue metal, the welded pynvium—all of it was gone, melted away, but this *thing* beneath remained. I could hear it, feel it. The glyphs glowed blue now, carved deep, pulsing like a heartbeat.

Like *my* heartbeat.

The glyphs pulsed. My skin split.

Pain. It was pulsing pain, but—

The glyphs pulsed again. Air left my lungs as if sucked away.

I gasped, felt weak.

The glyphs pulsed. My heart fluttered as if my *life* were being sucked away.

Saints' mercy, what have I done?

TWENTY-SEVEN

I staggered toward the open door, dented and broken but still on its hinges. The disk continued to pulse, slower now, no longer matching my heart, but stronger, each wave rolling out a little farther. I collapsed in the other room between two bodies. Lanelle and a boy. Their skin was red, scoured as if rubbed with sand, but they were alive. The Duke and his men were gone.

I shook Lanelle. "Wake up—we have to get out of here."

Lanelle stirred, the boy moaned. I shook them harder. The disk pulsed and pain sucked at my feet. I yanked them away from the door. The wall protected us, but it wouldn't for much longer. Already cracks split the stone, and chunks rolled out and fell to the floor with each pulse.

"Come on!"

Lanelle's eyes opened. She jerked and whimpered.

"Wake up!" I shook the boy as hard as I could. He woke up, eyes pained and scared.

"You!" Lanelle said, backing away from me.

I helped the boy to his feet and put an arm around him to keep him standing. I offered her my other hand. "Come with us or die here, I don't care which, but choose *now*."

She grabbed my hand and we clung to each other, stumbling out of the small waiting room and into the palace. A long hallway stretched in both directions. I picked the side where the blue rug was the most worn.

I found stairs leading down and followed them. A plaster wall shattered as we passed, and the life-stealing pain brushed against my back.

We staggered forward as one, almost tripping and rolling down the steps.

"Where is everyone?" Lanelle asked when we reached the next floor. A grand room, dark woods, rich paintings. No people.

"Running like us?" the boy said.

I nodded. "If they have any sense."

I spotted double doors in the far corner and headed toward them. Plaster dust drifted down, turning the wood white and rugs a bluish gray. The room beyond looked like some kind of reception hall, so we kept moving, hunting for a door or a window that led to the outside.

"Did you get him?" Lanelle said as we paused at an intersection.

"Get who?"

"The Duke. Is he dead?"

"I don't think so." I didn't see nearly enough red mist in the room to have killed him.

She huffed. "Too bad."

I turned left, mostly because pain pulsed from the right. Glass cracked, racing along the panes like lightning across the night sky.

"Hurry."

We found a door heavy enough to lead to the outside. The boy stopped.

"Hold on." He pulled off his tunic and handed it to me, clearly trying hard not to look down. "You can't go outside like that."

I didn't look down either. My clothes had disintegrated along with the silvery blue metal, the chained man, and who knew who else. My cheeks warmed and I pulled the tunic over my head. It didn't fit well, but it covered everything it needed to.

"Thanks."

"You saved my life. Least I could do."

I pulled open the door and sunlight blinded me. The rain had stopped and the sun hovered high in the sky. We'd been connected to that thing for hours.

"Come on."

People were fleeing the palace. Some ran with nothing, others carried bags or artwork or food. Windows shattered and stone crumbled from the room with the disk, the damage rippling out like a stone dropped in a lake.

A pulse, and glass fell. Another pulse, and walls crumbled. People dropped, gasping, caught by the wave. We ran down the wide steps of the palace entrance, over the ruined marble walkways. Even more people were in the street, running away from the palace.

We slipped into the crowd, holding hands to keep from being yanked apart. Scared faces surrounded us, many with red skin and blisters. Soldiers ran alongside, some even stopping to help others when they fell.

"Where can we go?" the boy asked, holding tight to me.

The villa was all I knew, but by now Jeatar and the others would be gone. Either arrested or running, but they wouldn't be there. *Please let them have escaped and gone to Jeatar's farm.*

"The docks." Ceun might still be watching the low stone wall. With so much chaos, the Taker camps had to be less guarded now, and I could still find Tali. I looked around, unsure how to get there from here.

"This way," Lanelle said, leading us.

I wondered if she'd been living here and then captured, or working for Vinnot until he'd needed one more for his life-stealing weapon. A small part wondered if she was leading us into a trap, but even Lanelle couldn't be that stupid.

Either the pulsing had stopped by the time we made it to the wharf gates or we'd outrun its range. Thousands of people crammed the street, fighting their way to the front. Soldiers yelled, but no one paid any attention to them. For every step, more people shoved their way ahead of us and knocked us back.

A sharp whistle blew, followed by hooves on stone. Heads around us turned.

"Soldiers?" Lanelle asked, frowning.

"I hope not." All these people crammed in like crabs in a trap—it would be a slaughter.

A carriage drove up. Armed men on horseback ordered the mob aside. Very few moved, though more probably would have if there'd been anyplace to go.

"Make way," a man yelled, cracking a whip over their heads, and when still no one moved, across their backs.

Nervous mumbles ran through the crowd.

I tugged at Lanelle and the boy. "We'd better move."

"Yeah."

We tried to walk against the crowd, get out and away from the wall and carriage, but the mob cried out and slammed us sideways. More men leaned down from the carriage and beat at those in the way, swinging long reed poles.

Another surge and the crowd broke. We stumbled into the clear spot and smacked up against the door of the carriage. I grabbed the open window to keep from falling.

A woman laughed.

I looked up. Vyand.

"You're as wily as a mongoose, girl."

I couldn't breathe, and not just because Lanelle and the boy were pressed against me on either side. I had nowhere to run, no pain to shift, nothing to use to—

354

Vyand wore pale silk. Her hair was loose, and glossy black curls flowed around her shoulders. She hadn't moved either, looking quite relaxed, a cup in her hand.

She flicked the other hand and the door opened. "Need a ride?"

"I'm not going anywhere with you."

She shrugged. "Suit yourself, but getting through the gates won't be easy."

"But you'll capture me again."

"There's no warrant for it. My contract with the Duke is fulfilled."

Did she mean it? Did she really not care that she'd found me again?

"Please," Lanelle whispered in my ear. "I don't want to stay here."

Don't blame your feet if you turn away the horse, Grannyma always said.

"Fine, we accept." I helped Lanelle into the carriage and climbed up after her.

Vyand slid over, making room for us all. After a breath, I sat next to Lanelle, across from Vyand and up against the door in case I needed to jump out.

When we were all settled, she reached a hand out the window and banged on the carriage. "To the wharf."

"Yes, ma'am."

The shouts got louder and more threatening as the carriage started moving. Every bump made some part of me hurt. One lunge and it could all be Vyand's.

I had no idea what to say or do. Getting help from Vyand was like riding a crocodile across the river.

I glanced at Lanelle and the boy. Among us we could hurt both Stewwig and Vyand, fancy tracker or not. I knew there wasn't much pynvium in Baseer right now. It could be enough to kill them both.

Haven't you killed enough?

"You really don't want to capture me?"

"I really don't. I was paid for that already, and there's no Duke around at the moment to order your recapture. " She sipped from her cup. "It was always just a job, you know. Never personal."

"It was to me."

For a moment, she actually looked ashamed. It wasn't enough to let me forgive her, or trust her, but if she could feel the tiniest bit guilty, maybe there was hope for her. *And hope for me.* I'd done things I wished I hadn't, too. Still, after everything she'd done, I couldn't understand how she could just walk away and act like it wasn't horrible.

"Where *is* the Duke?" I said, both hoping and

dreading I'd killed him.

"Healers' League, last I heard. Something about getting caught in a terrible pain flash." She smiled and toasted me with her cup. "Nicely done, by the way."

So I hadn't killed him. I wasn't sure how I felt about that.

"You did get the ghoul, though."

"Vinnot? He's dead?"

"Almost sure of it."

I smiled. It was wrong, and Tali would box my ears for it, but my heart felt lighter knowing he was gone.

The carriage reached the gates and was waved through by harried soldiers struggling with terrified people.

"Where should I drop you off?"

"Here's fine," I said. Vyand didn't need to know where I wanted to go from here. She probably assumed we wanted to hire a boat. Or maybe steal one.

A boat!

Jeatar had said he had a boat waiting. If they got out of the villa, they would have headed there. Danello and Aylin wouldn't have let him leave without me, but he wouldn't risk everyone's safety for

357

long. I had to get Tali out and get to them before Jeatar convinced them I wasn't coming.

I opened the door and jumped out.

Part of me wanted to say thank you, but thanking Vyand seemed wrong. Another part wanted to fill her with pain 'til she screamed. "I appreciate the ride."

"You're an interesting girl, Nya. Maybe next time we'll be on the same side."

"Probably not."

She laughed again as Lanelle and the boy stepped out of the carriage. Vyand waved and continued down the wharf. I'd guess she had her own boat docked somewhere.

"This way," I said, heading for the wall.

"Stolen girl!" Ceun waved at me. Quenji sat beside him, a large sack between them. Aylin sat on the other side. She squealed and ran at me the moment she saw me.

"You're alive!"

"So are you." I hugged her as tight as she hugged me, but part of me wished she'd already left. She'd never let me go after Tali.

"Barely, but we made it. I think Jovan has a future as an army commander one day. You should have heard him ordering us all around." She noticed

358

Lanelle and her grin vanished. "What is *she* doing here?"

"She's going with you."

"Oh no she isn't. You can't trust her!"

Lanelle winced and looked away.

"Vinnot was experimenting on her. I think she's learned who she can trust now."

Aylin snorted.

Lanelle huffed back and looked at me. "I'm pretty sure I can trust *you*, but that's as far as it goes."

"Good enough?" I asked Aylin.

"No, but I can see you're not changing your mind, and we don't have time to argue."

"Then it's settled."

Aylin's eyes narrowed. "Wait a minute, what do you mean, 'she's going with *you*'? You mean us, right?"

"No. I'm going after Tali."

She sighed, and for a heartbeat, guilt washed across her face. "I was afraid you'd say that." She whistled, and arms grabbed me from behind.

"Hey!"

"We had a feeling you were going to try to stay," Danello said, holding me tight enough that I couldn't touch his skin. And Saints help me, right now I really wanted to.

"Quenji, grab her legs." Aylin picked up the sack

while he reached for me. I kicked, struggling in Danello's arms.

"Let me go!" No one helped, and I wasn't sure what I'd do if someone did.

"I'm sorry, Nya, but we're not letting you get yourself killed." Aylin looked at me, tears in her eyes. "Jeatar scouted the Taker camps. The Duke has all his men there now that the palace is gone. Not even you can get in."

"Yes I can!"

Quenji finally got my legs, and he and Danello started carrying me down the dock.

"Don't do this, please. I need to find Tali." Tears ran down my cheeks. How could they do this to me? They were my friends, my family. Tali was their family, too. They couldn't *do* this!

"We'll find her—just not today," Danello said, his voice breaking. "We'll have to come back."

"No!"

Lanelle and the boy followed us, but neither did anything to help me either. I'm pretty sure I saw Lanelle smile.

"This is kidnapping."

Aylin shook her head. "This is love. We love you too much to let you die, and you *will* die if you go anywhere near that camp."

Halfway down the dock I stopped fighting, too

tired to struggle anymore. Smoke darkened the sky, fear and pain filled the air. Who knew how many lives had been lost since last night? How many more might be lost if this really did spark a civil war? I couldn't leave Tali here. I just couldn't.

"But she's still out there." My throat didn't want to let the words out. I'd failed her, lost her. Left her to the Undying and whoever seized control of them now that Vinnot was dead. Jeatar had said the Undying were twisted, bent to the will of their commander.

Even if I found her again, would she still *be* my Tali?

Aylin put a hand on my shoulder. "I know, and we'll find her."

"How? We're running away."

"We'll come back for her. But we can't stay, you have to know that."

Tali.

I stared at the smoky skyline one last time as they carried me belowdecks.

TWENTY-EIGHT

I'd never forgive them for this.

"Open this door right now!" I pounded on the cabin door, but they'd locked me in. In with my guilt, my anger, my anguish. They were supposed to be my friends. Not even Onderaan would have done this to me.

"Let me out!"

They didn't. I wasn't sure if they were even out there. It was too hard to hear anyone in the hall over the creaks as the boat left the dock and bobbed on the waves. For a long while, voices shouted on deck and canvas flapped in the wind.

And still, no one opened the door.

I dropped onto the bunk when my hands were

too bruised to bang on the door any longer. After a minute, a soft knock rapped from the other side.

"Have you calmed down?" Danello said.

"No."

"Will you hurt me if I come in?"

"Yes."

A pause. "Okay. We'll be waiting out here, so tell me when you're ready to talk."

Never. Not after what they'd done. I grabbed a footstool and flung it at the door.

"You made me abandon my sister!"

"I know, and we're really sorry about that. It hurts us, too."

I threw something else. I didn't bother to see what it was. "Not enough if you left her there."

"If we'd thought for a minute we could have saved her, we would have stayed in Baseer with you."

I wanted to call him a liar. Scream it at the top of my lungs, but Danello didn't lie. Aylin did, but not to me.

I dropped onto the bunk. Why did they do this? I had to know. I needed to see their faces, look into their eyes, and ask why they left Tali behind.

"I won't hurt you," I said, and was almost certain I actually meant it.

Danello must have had doubts, too, because he

waited a minute before opening the door. He stuck his head in, cautious and ready to jump back.

"I can come in?"

"Yes."

He did, shutting the door behind him. Someone else locked it again.

My anger flared, but only for a heartbeat. It hurt too much to fight anymore. "Aylin's not coming in?"

"No. She's more afraid of you than I am." He smiled warily. "But not by much."

"Kidnapping me was her idea?"

He nodded.

"And you agreed?"

"I knew she was right. You'd never leave unless we forced you." He took a tentative step closer, hands clasped in front of him. "I didn't want to lose you."

So we lost Tali instead.

"How could you do this to me?"

He winced, glanced away, but met my gaze again. There was sadness there. "We didn't know what else to do."

"So you chose leaving?" I felt the urge to throw things again.

"We had to make a choice. You or Tali. We knew we couldn't save you both, and we knew we couldn't save Tali. We did what *you* would have done."

Breath left me.

Danello nodded slowly. "It was hard, but we made a choice for someone who couldn't. You."

I closed my eyes, fighting back tears. It wasn't a choice I would have made. *But you did when you chose saving Aylin and Danello first.*

Soft footsteps crossed the cabin. I opened my eyes.

"What if she dies?" It would be my fault.

Danello sat next to me, still wary. "She won't. She's tougher than you think. You taught her how to survive, just like you taught me."

"What if it's not enough?"

"It will be."

I stared at him, wanting to pound my fists against him almost as badly as I wanted to curl up in his arms.

"I am so, so sorry, Nya."

I buried my face in his neck and sobbed. He held me, stroking my hair and telling me everything was going to be okay.

But it wasn't. It might never be okay again.

The boat pulled up to a weather-beaten dock that looked like no one had stopped there in years, but the wood was solid and reinforced if you looked closely. Someone had gone to a lot of trouble to make it look old and unused.

Six wagons were waiting for us, all with drivers and armed guards. They greeted Jeatar respectfully, the rest of us politely. We had more gear and supplies than I'd have expected, and they stowed it as we found seats. I wondered how they'd known to be there until a small cage of messenger birds was unloaded. Jeatar must have told them we were coming.

He always had an escape route planned. Probably why he was still alive.

I didn't speak on the ride in. Aylin tried to talk to me, but I just stared at the marshes, then the fields and rolling hills. Miles of them as we rode deeper inland. After an hour, we reached a stone wall with a heavy gate, and one of Jeatar's men let us through. The wall didn't look old at all, but strong and fortified. It stretched as far as I could see on either side of the dirt road. Jeatar's farm must be huge if this was the boundary to it.

"Wow," Aylin said as we approached the farm itself. "This is amazing."

I had to agree. The farmhouse was even bigger than the villa, two stories tall, with huge trees in a vast courtyard. Vines of flowers wrapped around a wooden fence that enclosed the main grounds. Well-tended fields spread out for miles, with silos and barns and other buildings I didn't recognize. I'd been to the marsh farms a few times with Mama, but not enough to know much about them.

"You could fit all of Geveg into those fields," Aylin said.

I nodded.

Men and women came out of the farmhouse to meet us and carry the supplies inside. Halima and some of the other children raced ahead, chasing butterflies through the gardens. The Underground members scanned the area as if sizing up its defensibility. I doubted they had to worry about that, though. Jeatar seemed to have more than enough guards out here.

I stepped off the wagon. I had nothing to carry, nothing I owned anymore. Birds sang, cheerful and unaware.

Tali would love it here.

Jeatar pulled open double doors and stepped inside the farmhouse. The rest of us followed. A pretty, plump woman appeared from what smelled like the kitchens and walked to Jeatar's side. Too old to be a wife, though it had never occurred to me before that Jeatar might *have* a wife.

"That's the guest wing there," he said, pointing down one wide hall on the right. Dark wood floors shone under the light from tall windows. They were all open, and a whiff of honeysuckle blew in on the breeze. "Ouea will show you to your rooms and take care of anything you need. There's a bath area at the end of the hall, though there are only rooms for four at a time. You'll have to take turns. Dinner will be in a few hours, but there's food out now if anyone's hungry."

Folks hesitated, torn between food, a bath, and a soft bed.

"It'll be there no matter when you're ready."

Some laughed and followed Ouea down the hall. Others went for the baths and the kitchen. Jeatar caught Aylin, Danello, and me before we could leave.

"Your rooms are upstairs," he said, pointing over his shoulder. "It's safer there, more security."

"Thank you," I said. Danello smiled and hurried after the twins and his sister, already heading for the food. Aylin lingered, but after a moment, she left us and walked upstairs. She stopped halfway.

"Are we sharing a room?" she asked me, voice trembling. I hadn't spoken to her since we'd left—*Tali, you left Tali*—Baseer, but she hadn't stopped trying.

She'd done what I couldn't do. I hated it, but Aylin saw things I didn't. She figured people out better than me. She often just *knew* the right thing to do, no matter how complicated it all seemed.

"Yes, just one room," I said, wanting to smile but unable to. Not yet.

Aylin did it for me, her relief as bright as her smile. "Okay. I'll get a good view, too. Best on the floor, don't you worry." She dashed the rest of the way up, and I heard doors opening and closing.

"She knew you'd be mad, but she did it anyway," Jeatar said, more than a touch of awe in his voice. "I'm glad she did. I don't think anyone else could have stopped you."

"No, probably not." I could have convinced Danello to let me go if it had been just him. Not that he would have attempted it in the first place. Odds were he'd have tried to talk me into leaving, then stayed with me when I didn't. I'd have gotten us both killed. "Aylin's right more times than not."

He nodded, still looking sad. "I wish I could have done more."

"A helping hand is never wasted."

He chuckled wryly. "Saint Nya, Sister of Optimism."

Me? A Saint? Hardly.

The wind blew the curtain, sending a sunbeam across his eyes. He squinted, annoyance wrinkling his face. For a heartbeat he looked like the Duke. He even had the same eyes.

Siekte's voice echoed in my mind. *Who cares about legitimate heirs? There's no one from that side of the family left.*

And Jeatar's quiet whisper. *Three. There were three brothers.*

Maybe I wasn't the only one with a Baseeri uncle.

"You're—" I bit my tongue, silenced my question. It was crazy to even *think* it. Crazier than the idea of me being a Saint.

"I'm what?"

"You're wealthier than I thought," I said instead. "This farm. The villa." That was a guess, but he'd called it *his* house, and even though Onderaan had appeared to be in charge, he'd deferred to Jeatar, protected him, defended him.

They defied the Duke, forced his hand. All they had to do was turn over—

Turn over what? Or more likely, *who*? Jeatar's

370

father? Jeatar had barely escaped Sorille when the Duke burned it. The Duke went after Sorille because his rival was there.

Jeatar had money, power even, though he was obviously hiding it. He cared about what happened to people and tried to make their lives better, when he clearly could hide on this farm forever and ignore it all. But he didn't. He fought for something he believed in, no matter what the cost.

What if that cost is Tali?

I wouldn't let that happen. Onderaan was connected to Jeatar, Grandpapa was connected to Sorille. My family was connected to his family, and though I didn't know how, I knew why. We all wanted to stop the Duke. We were all willing to make sacrifices to do it.

"It's family money," he said, and the sadness was back again. "Not much left."

"Oh." Because he spent it to stop the Duke? Helped fund the Underground, kept them fed and armed and safe as possible?

"Come on, let's get you some food," he said. "I know you're hungry."

"I always am." I followed him into the kitchen, sunny and bright like the rest of the farm.

My brain whirled. No, it had to be a coincidence,

371

a trick of the light. If Jeatar *was* the legitimate heir, Onderaan would have known. He would have told people, used Jeatar to rally both the Underground and those who secretly opposed the Duke. He would have presented him to the High Courts and exposed the Duke's crimes.

Unless Onderaan *didn't* know.

Jeatar might be hiding from all of us. Trying to do in secret what the rest of his family couldn't— stop the Duke, restore independence to the Three Territories, and end the wars. Hiding was smart since the Duke would certainly kill him if he discovered he was still alive.

But hiding wasn't going to work. The Duke wasn't going to stop, and if by a Saint's luck he *had* died in the flash, the wrong people would try for the throne and nothing would change but the owner of the boot against our necks.

None of us would be safe. Not me, not Tali. No one.

Jeatar handed me a plate of sliced fruit. "You have that look again," he said as if that worried him.

Maybe it should. "I was just thinking."

He nodded, compassion in his eyes. "We'll go back and find Tali when it's safe, I promise."

"I know. I was thinking about something else."

His eyebrows rose. "Really?"

I nodded. "Really."

Like a future where we wouldn't have to hide, where we could march right into Baseer, into the camps and free Tali and every Taker the Duke ever kidnapped. Where the Undying would be disbanded, and no one would ever experiment on Takers again. Where the people of Geveg and Verlatta and even Baseer could work and play and live in safety.

A future with Jeatar on the throne.

ACKNOWLEDGMENTS

I can honestly say this book wouldn't be what it is today if not for the help of quite a few folks. It was one of those stories that fought me the whole way through, and the extra hands (and eyes) played a huge role in whipping this sucker into shape. I-can't-believe-you-didn't-divorce-me thanks go to my husband, Tom, who took care of all the things I couldn't while on deadline and losing my mind. Big grateful thanks to Donna, who never made me feel rushed even though I was well past deadline. For her keen eye and wonderful advice when I knew the story wasn't yet there and I needed direction. I-so-needed-that thanks go to Kristin, who kept reminding me that second books are often a disaster and I wasn't alone in my struggle. Much love and hugs to Ann, who dutifully read almost every version, even the really bad ones. And another heap to Juliette, who cut through the bad to point out the good and kept me focused on the heart and soul of the tale. Big thanks to Bonnie and Birgitte, who always see things I don't and make me look at what I've written with their eyes. Three cheers to the Bloodies, Dario, Aliette, Doug, Keyan, Genevieve, and Traci, who did just what I asked and pointed out everything they thought was wrong with it. Extra thanks to Ruta and Julie, for keeping me updated on so many things and making the process go so smoothly. Special technical thanks go to Phil, who helped me understand smelting and how I could do terrible things with it. And last but not least, thanks to all the unnamed folks who worked so diligently to bring my little novel to the shelves who I've never even met.

Every last one of you rocks.